WALKING OUT
OF THE DARK

Bad luck took his sight.
With hope and humor,
My brother didn't let it take more.

Steven R Malikowski

Publisher's Note: This book is based on a true story. The only character that is based on a single real person is the character Mike. All other characters are composite characters that are based on several real people. A similar approach is applied to key events in the story, such as beep baseball, blind skiing, and schools for the blind in 1976. In this book, the key events are based on real events, but key events in this book have been changed to accommodate the composite characters. Other than the characters previously described here, any resemblance to individual people, living or dead, or to businesses, companies, events, institutions, or locales is completely coincidental.

Book Layout ©2013 BookDesignTemplates.com
Cover photo courtesy of:
Tim and Madie Photography LLC timandmadie.com

Ordering Information:
Special discounts are available on quantity purchases. For details, visit the website listed at the URL at the top of this page and contact the publisher.

Dedication & Acknowledgements

There are many people I would like to dedicate this book to. Instead of mentioning all of them, I'll dedicate the book to an emotion they share. It's in the elegant and simple quotes below.

Elegant Quote

For sudden the worst turns the best to the brave.
—Robert Browning

Simple Quote

When you're going through Hell, keep going.
—Often Attributed to Winston Churchill

In those quotes, Browning and Churchill help us with inspiration. I want to acknowledge the people who helped me with many hours of careful work.

I'll start with people who have helped from the start to finish. Carrie Almaer and Barb Franz saw the earliest drafts, told me which parts of the story worked, and most important, they told me which parts did not. Other reviewers have helped for fewer years but have given wonderful suggestions. They include Sue Paradeis, Brad Bussy, and especially, Gabriella Zepf. Other friends who gave me insightful suggestions include Luke Woodham, Gary Hickey, and Kathleen Keller.

Most recently, people involved with blind sports reviewed sections related to their sport. They include Blake Boudreaux, Judy Byrd, Judy Dixon, Jonathan Fleming, Stephen Guerra, James Michaels, and Jon Walker. Even though they pointed out mistakes, I take responsibility for any that remain.

I am an independent author, but as you can tell, this is far from a solitary experience. In addition to family and friends who have helped, there are professional organizations and services that gave back far more then they received. The Association of Independent Authors (ALLi) offers important guidance, particularly their advice on making independent publications at least as good as mainstream publications.

Based on advice from ALLi, I hired some talented editors. One is Eliza Dee, and the other is Tia Bach. Both are a part of Indie Books Gone Wild. The artists that created the cover also gave more than I expected. Timothy Galdunick took the picture for the cover and generously gave me permission to use it. Erika Gizelle Santiao used the picture to create a cover that shows the story.

A final group I want to acknowledge are the people that helped my brother when he attended a school for blind adults. They include teachers, administrators, and other students. They are part of this novel, but since there were so many, I could not include all of them. Instead, this story uses a few composite characters, where each character represents a few real people. Composite characters also protect the privacy of real people. In a further effort to protect their privacy, I used fictitious names for the school, town, and other key locations.

I hope you enjoy this story as much as I enjoyed working with people who helped me write it.

Contents

CHAPTER ONE

Back to School

The sun hadn't set, but shadows couldn't get much longer. That concerned Mike a little. In sunlight, he could see more than most who were *legally blind*, and in darkness, bright storefronts and streetlights could guide him, at least keep him on the sidewalk. But this was dusk, when the light was lowest. Sunlight was fading. Streetlights weren't lit, and beyond the sidewalk, many lights were moving. Those lights were being pushed by a ton of metal, on four wheels or more. Mike kept walking.

The temperature was going down with the sun, so Mike shoved his hands deeper into his parka. He noticed the blurry image of two blinking neon signs. They reminded him of something his counselor had said last week. "This road connects Bridgman School for the Blind to Mariner's Motel, which'll be your home for a while. Mariner's is *two* blocks from those *two* blinking signs. Like I've been saying, you need to use your memory for things your eyes used to do, like making sense out of a disorganized world. Fortunately, there's a lot of room for improvement."

Mike stopped thinking about his counselor and focused on the two signs. Even though they looked like a blinking haze, Mike could tell that one was orange. He knew this color, especially in neon. It was a familiar sight. After all, he enjoyed going to bars as much as any other guy in his twenties. The color of the other sign was less familiar, less clear. Mike thought it might be blue, maybe purple. He hadn't seen a blue or purple one before, so he wondered what it looked like. The only way to find out would be to get within a few inches of the sign, stop walking, and move his head around it, to slowly examine the sign. Unfortunately, that would draw more attention to himself than he wanted, especially in this neighborhood. He kept walking.

Still thinking about old orange neon signs and new neon signs, his head snapped toward the street. A horn blared, and a man shouted, "Idiot!" Mike didn't know what had happened. The horn and shouting had probably come from a careless driver who'd crossed paths with an obnoxious driver.

Of course, he didn't drive anymore, but Mike had spent almost a decade behind the wheel. It wasn't long ago that he'd been a teenager laughing with his friends while driving. Sometimes, they would laugh at the friend who was driving when he tried some creative driving stunt. That usually involved speed, weaving, or something else that had seemed funny at the time. At the moment, on this sidewalk, those stunts concerned him. He thought about the drivers passing him right now. Some of them had their own version of creative driving stunts. Many were in a hurry. Some drove too close to the car in front, and some were driving too close to the sidewalk; at least, it felt that way to Mike.

His thoughts shifted to something his dad had said a few years ago: "There are a lot of things you can do in a bad situation; try to choose something that doesn't make it worse."

Mike focused on what he could do. He could see a little. He could hear the cars and trucks, smell them in some cases. Mike could also remain calm and focus on what mattered most. Besides, his vision was supposed to fade in the next few months and years. He had to find ways to live with other people's mobility or restrict his own. He kept walking.

He started feeling a strange satisfaction. Even when his limited sight was at its lowest, he could be in an uncomfortable situation and stay rational. This was a part of blindness he hadn't expected, an odd opportunity to be a little brave, maybe even proud. Then he felt something else, something falling out of a back pocket from his blue jeans. His folded white cane had started coming out. He thought about unfolding the long, white cane and using it. At the least, it would show others that he was blind. Mike smiled, tucked it back in, and decided that even proud people were entitled to an unwise decision or two. Besides, he was almost home and was still learning how to use the long cane without hitting people.

It was odd to think about this place as home. Until a week ago, home had been a small house in farm country without sidewalks, buildings, or traffic. Now, he lived in the city of Portage Bay. He had always enjoyed cities, but that was for visiting family or sightseeing. Walking next to a busy road every day didn't provide the same pleasure.

He slowed down because some shadows were collected in front of him. Each had a familiar shape—five or six feet high, about two feet wide, two narrow pillars on the bottom half, one wide pillar on the top half, and a ball on top. Put together, this was the blurry shape of a person, a group of people in this case. Traffic sounds and smells also increased. The new unleaded gas was the worst, smelling like rotten eggs.

The combination of a group of people and increased traffic usually meant a crosswalk. Being with people at a crosswalk comforted Mike. He was still getting used to living with less sight, and crosswalks concerned him, especially at dusk. Crossing alone could put him on the receiving end of a careless driver.

The group started to move, and he moved with it. As he walked down the next block, there were fewer lights and sounds, which was fine since this long day had started to wear him down. The sun had set a bit more. That made it easier to see city lights but harder to stay warm.

He started thinking about his first week in this new city and the first day of school tomorrow, but he chose to save the thoughts for later. He wanted to return to his room at Mariner's Motel, get off his feet, and watch some TV.

Mike knew he was getting close to Mariner's when the greyness he'd been seeing started cycling to lighter shades of grey. The light came from the big sign above the motel's entrance. His parents had commented on it when they'd brought him here. They thought the sign's flashing lights were too bright and brash. Mike suspected many people felt the same way, including those driving by him now. They had finished regular jobs and were driving to comfortable homes.

People at Mariner's were different. If they noticed the sign at all, it was at night when the flashing lights looked even brighter. They stayed in the motel because it was cheap, and it allowed them to leave town for a while, if their work or play made that a good idea. Their play usually involved booze or other drugs. For those who did work, it usually involved something after dark.

"Hey, new guy, back again?"

Mike slowed, mostly out of the manners he'd learned growing up in small-town Minnesota. The question came from Ruby. He was still getting used to talking with someone in her line of work, but since they lived in the same building, it felt right to answer her question.

"Yeah, home sweet home," he replied, noticing Ruby's shadow come closer.

"Well, we all know this home isn't that sweet, but I know some ways to warm it up."

"You want to loan me your long johns?"

"Honey, you tried that joke last night. Come on now, it's about time you experienced one of the wonders of our fair city."

The shadow came even closer. Mike could feel its heat by his cheek. He smelled cigarette smoke and heard a whisper.

"And, since we're neighbors, I'll give you my Halloween special, what I call my trick *and* treat."

Ruby hadn't tried that before. Mike lifted his eyebrows, cleared his throat, and took a half-step back, partly because she was bigger than he thought.

"Sorry, honey, I didn't mean to scare you."

"That's okay, Ruby, and, ah, thanks. But, I think I'm just going to watch some TV."

"Watch some TV? I thought you were blind."

"I can see a little."

Ruby's voice changed from seducing streetwalker to curious neighbor.

"I can't figure out how someone can see only a little TV and still watch it. It drives me crazy when my TV doesn't come in right."

He sighed. "It's like, let me think." Mike paused and turned his head, toward the street. At first, he thought about Ruby's question, but his mind wandered to the change in her voice. When she wasn't trying to sound sexy, she stretched her vowels. He watched a car slowly pull up and stop. The headlights went dark, but the engine kept running.

"It's kind of like that," Mike finally answered, still looking at the car.

"It's like parking a car?"

Now, he really noticed her vowels, especially the two *a-r* sounds in her question.

"No, it's like driving a car with the lights off."

"In the dark?"

"Unfortunately," Mike said with a tired sigh.

"That sucks."

"Yeah, it does," he replied, hoping the conversation would end soon.

Ruby was quiet for a moment, and he saw her shape get lower, as if she was crouching. She stood up again and said, "I just noticed that a friend of mine is in the car we've been talking about." She changed to her business voice. "I gotta go take care of some things, but you stop by again later if you want. I'll be around."

He suspected she wouldn't be around. Ruby wasn't like the street-walkers he saw on TV, but she seemed to keep busy. Mike just hoped they would drive away this time. A couple of nights ago, it had sounded like she was doing her work in a car near his room.

"Okay, Ruby, have a good night."

He entered Mariner's Motel and heard the TV behind the desk. He walked toward the sound and rotated slightly to the right when the image of the main desk appeared. After a few steps, he could see the dark frame of a doorway. He walked through it and into a hallway.

Hallways at Mariner's contained only slightly more light than the sidewalk he'd just walked on. He could tell that some of the wallpaper was missing, but other images were less clear, probably some kind of stains or dents. Mike told himself he didn't need to waste money on a fancy hotel, so this place was fine. Besides, he'd spent enough time in old cabins to feel comfortable nearly anywhere. Still, he avoided pressing his fingers against the wall for guidance.

His room was on the third floor. The stairs were at the end of the hallway, which he knew was close because he'd passed under two lights in the ceiling. One more light to go. When he'd lost his sight, Mike had worried that climbing stairs was going to be one of those daily challenges that would be frustrating to learn again. Going upstairs turned out to be the easy part. Going down was harder. Sometimes, a foot would roll off the edge of a step, and it was still hard to be sure when he was on the bottom step.

After noticing a third light above him, Mike reached for the handrail, hoped it was cleaner than the walls, and placed a hand on it. He carefully raised a foot to the first step and started climbing the ones after it. When the handrail ended, he walked into the hallway of the second floor.

Mike walked under one light, reached in his left pants pocket for a room key, walked under a second light, and let his right index finger glide along the wall, as lightly as possible. Eventually, Mike felt a doorframe and used it to find the doorknob. Since his right hand was on the doorknob, it was easy to slide his fingers down to the keyhole. He unlocked the door with his left hand, turned the knob, and pushed the door open with his right shoulder.

For years, Mike had relaxed his shoulders after closing his door. Since he'd lost his sight, he relaxed them a little more. In his home, the level of light was consistent. There was no risk of someone running a red light and ruining his day. There were no people who were more interested in his blindness than in him. In his home, he was just Mike again.

After flipping on the light switch, he took off his coat and thought about his previous home. He instinctively stepped to his small fridge, opened it, and took out the stuff for some sandwiches. His previous home was a simple house in the farmlands of Central Minnesota, but it was special. After saving for years, he'd bought the land and helped build the house. Mike made two sandwiches, thick with meat and cheese, on top of the fridge. His home before that was his parents' house, which was also in the country. After opening the fridge, he put the loaf of bread and other sandwich stuff back inside. His parents' place was simple too, but it was large enough for them, his three sisters, and his brother. It was also built before they moved in. He took out the cardboard carton of milk, shut the fridge, and picked up the sandwiches. His room in his parents' house used to seem small and old, but it was larger and newer than the room he was in now.

He walked a few steps to the desk, sat down, bit into a sandwich, and unfolded the spout on top of the milk carton. After drinking out of the carton and taking a few more bites, Mike rotated the desk chair and pushed the plastic power button on his TV. While it warmed up, he finished the first sandwich and drank more out of the carton. A strong voice came from the TV. Mike moved his face close to the screen to see the image more clearly.

"According to a new poll, Gerald Ford continues to close on Jimmy Carter in next week's general election."

"Jerk better not win," Mike said to the television. "Ford's a crook just like Nixon, running the country without being elected. Politics can't get any worse." He bit into the second sandwich, turned the channel selector with a clunk, and heard a milder voice.

"So, visit your Sylvania dealer today to see the next generation of color television."

Mike mumbled at the TV, "The first generation of color TV did wonders to improve the quality of storylines." He took another bite and turned the channel again, with another clunk.

"Repeating our top story, a truck driver was killed yesterday while delivering a load of timber in Portage Bay. According to eyewitness reports, the driver honked repeatedly and yelled 'bad brakes' out his window. Witnesses also reported that he tried to slow his semi by shifting down. Sadly, the truck broke through the barriers to the lake, and the driver drowned. No other injuries were reported."

Mike pushed the TV's power button again to switch the power off. "Tough way to go, bet that water was cold." After thinking about the driver, his appetite faded, and his glance wandered. First, it went toward the window next to his desk, which had a view of an ally. Next, his glance wandered toward a textbook on his desk, which he wanted to read tonight. After finishing the last sandwich, he brushed some crumbs off the desk, turned on a lamp, and placed the textbook where his sandwiches had been a moment ago.

The book came from his counselor, who'd said it would get him off to a good start. Before coming here, he'd finished a few chapters and became accustomed to reading large print. That used to be only for old people. This textbook was about mobility, learning how to get around a city or building with less sight. He opened the book, reached for a magnifying glass, and read. The heading showed that he was in

Chapter 5. He thumbed some pages forward and saw Chapter 7. The pages brushed against his face. He turned some pages back to get to the start of Chapter 6, looked through the glass, and continued reading.

He read a few pages nonstop, but eventually, Mike had to reread some paragraphs. A while later, he read sentences aloud to stay focused. He started to feel warm. The heat in his room was usually too high, and he hadn't found a way to lower it. He'd asked the people at the front desk to lower the heat a few times. They said they would take care of it "right away." Mike realized that when Mariner's staff said "right away," it meant, "Stop asking for stuff, right away. If you want service, you can go to a more expensive hotel, right away. So, you should let me watch my TV, right away."

Mike stood up and opened the window. He felt awkward about letting cold air into a heated room, but it was the best option he had. He sat down again and tried finishing Chapter 6, but his mind began to wander. Tomorrow was his first real day at Bridgman School for the Blind. He'd spent some time there during the last few days—getting to know the walking route to the school, finding his classrooms, and filling out forms. He met some people as well. The receptionist introduced him to a guy named Donald, who ran the place. Donald then introduced him to more people, mostly teachers. They seemed nice enough, but something still felt strange about going to your *first day of school.*

He thought the days of starting school were long over, especially since life had become a familiar routine of work and house projects. A few years ago, he'd taken some classes at a vocational-technical college, but that had been about advancing his skills. This was more like going back to the basics. He started thinking about what would come next, when he was finished with this review of basic skills.

He wanted to return home and pick up with the life he enjoyed in the country, but that was unlikely. Losing his sight meant he couldn't drive, and living in the country meant driving—to work, to get groceries, and to see friends. He'd worked so hard on building that house. Now, it would have to go. He wondered what else would go and what other new problems would come.

Mike sighed and decided that was enough anxiety for one night; funny how worry usually set in around this time. He closed his book and got ready for bed. Tomorrow and the first day of school would come regardless of how much he worried. Better to face them with a good night of sleep.

.   .   . .

Mike paused when he could see the entrance to Bridgman School for the Blind. About a week ago, his counselor had given him a tour of the school and introduced him to some staff, but now, it was real. He checked again that he had his cane, a notebook, and a marker to write with. After thinking about going back to the basics, he shook his head and walked toward the entrance. A comforting thought came to mind: *the sooner I start, the sooner I'll finish.*

The receptionist asked a simple yet already familiar question as he entered the school. "Can I help you?"

Mike thought about her level of sight. She always noticed him quickly and seemed aware of subtle movements. He introduced himself, reminded her they might have already met, and said it was his first day.

"Welcome back. Your classes will start in Room 5. Would you like someone to guide you, or would you like directions?"

Mike was feeling independent, so he responded, "I'll take directions."

"Continue walking down this hallway until you arrive at a dayroom, which has a TV, a few couches, and a skylight. Walk diagonally through the dayroom, forward and to your left, to another hallway. Room 5 is the second door on the left."

Mike thanked her and walked down the hallway. Several people were walking or standing, so he tried to look confident, while wondering if he should have asked for a guide. He hoped the dayroom would become obvious. A sound emerged that he couldn't place. It made him feel concerned, but he still didn't know what it was. The sound faded, and he looked for the dayroom again, trying to recall the exact words the receptionist had given him.

A loud cry suddenly filled the hallway. Wanting to help, he stopped walking, looked around, and tried finding the source of the sound. He waited and expected someone to rush by or call out instructions. Nothing happened. Other people paused and continued what they were doing, so Mike kept walking. The crying also continued, in waves. It became louder and clearer when he saw sunlight coming from the ceiling. Mike vaguely remembered the receptionist mentioning a skylight. The hallway opened up to a room with couches, decorations on the walls, and a TV. He could see a man crying and others offering comfort. Mike tried to politely ignore the man and walked across the dayroom, toward Room 5.

He found the room easily enough, since a big 5 with an arrow was painted on the wall, pointing to the door. He was still thinking about the crying when a woman asked, "Are you here for the start of classes?"

Mike replied that he was and tried focusing on navigating this room, on starting the first class in his first day at school. But he couldn't help asking, "Did you hear that?"

"Yes, I heard," the woman said. She walked into the room with him and added, "That's one of the things we're going to talk about. For now, we need to get ready for class. Are you Mike?" He nodded, and she continued. "We have small classes at Bridgman's, and the other students are already here, at least all the new ones."

Mike looked at the woman for a moment. She was about ten years older than him and wore a simple dress, which was more formal than other teachers. She was also at least a foot shorter than him, but her disposition wasn't small. She stood straight and sounded confident.

The two stopped at a round table, where three other students were sitting. Mike said "Hello" to the student on his right and "Good morning" to some students on the other side. He heard responses back but focused on getting seated. He put his notepad on the table and sat down, realizing that his cane was in his back pocket. He leaned to one side, took the cane out, and set it next to his notepad.

The woman who'd greeted Mike at the door made an announcement from behind him. "Normally, we don't serve coffee in our classes, but we make an exception for these orientation sessions. In a few minutes, we should have some treats from our cooking class. Let me know if you want cream or sugar in your coffee."

She placed a tray on the table and poured coffee for everyone. He guessed she was a teacher. Mike could see and hear students sip their coffee. He didn't like coffee but also didn't want to refuse it and draw attention to himself. He took a small sip and did his best not to cringe at the potent flavor. At least pretending to drink coffee meant that he didn't have to try and make conversation.

The teacher sat down at the round table and spoke to everyone. "Once again, I want to welcome all of you to Bridgman School for the Blind." She took a sip from her coffee, and Mike thought she sounded more like a 1950s' grammar teacher than some of the modern teachers he'd met.

She continued speaking. "We are expecting one more student to arrive, but we're already running a bit late. My name is Margaret Roberts. I teach the course called Independent Living. Normally, our communication instructor leads this orientation session, but he's at a conference. I'll give you an overview of what we're going to do today, but first, I would like each of you to introduce yourself. I'm not an expert on communication issues for people who have recently lost their sight, but I do know that meeting new people can be challenging. Would anyone like to start?"

Nobody replied.

"In that case, I'll ask one of you to begin. Norman, would you mind starting?"

"Yeah, why not. I'm Norman Grant. I used to coach high school football in Duluth before the problem with my eyes got worse."

The words resonated inside a large, fit body. Mike felt them as much as he heard them, since Norman was the student sitting on his right. That voice could easily carry across a football field and instantly correct a wayward player. Apparently, the voice had been used for that purpose for a few years, since it had gravelly tones.

"My blind coach said I should check this place out," Norman added.

"Your blind coach?" Margaret asked.

"Yeah, sorry, that's what I call the counselor that State Services gave me. I don't care for the whole counselor thing, so I call him my blind coach."

"I see," Margaret replied. "You can refer to your counselor in any way you want, but everybody here has one. We refer to counselors fairly often, so blind coach may be a little confusing." Her voice continued to remind Mike of a 1950s' grammar teacher. It was friendly and firm. After hearing it a while, he felt like sitting up straighter in his chair.

"Yeah, all right, maybe I'll change," Norman said.

"It's up to you, but in any case, please continue your introduction."

"My wife and I have lived in Duluth for about ten years. We don't have any kids. I used to think of my players as my kids, but it's hard to keep in touch with them now."

Margaret responded, "It is difficult keeping in touch with people from hobbies and jobs we had before losing our sight, but many blind people still enjoy sports. Some of them are bowling, beepball, and downhill skiing."

"You have blind folks playing ball and skiing?" Norman asked.

"Yes, we do. That's one of the topics you'll learn in our recreation class."

"I enjoy a challenge, but that sounds hazardous." The last word sounded so gravelly that Mike's throat felt sore just hearing it.

"You're right, Norman. It can be hazardous." Margaret paused briefly and continued. "But I imagine you've told your players that sports can be a metaphor for life."

"I don't put it exactly that way, but sure, every coach says stuff like that."

"What do you think of that phrase now, for you and other students?"

Norman thought about the question. When he replied, he flexed some of the muscle in his voice. "Listen, lady, I said that stuff to high school boys, who have more strength and spirit than any group on the planet. I don't want to make this into a big deal, but things are a little different here and now. It's one thing to be young and fit. It's another to be older and blind, especially with fancy ideas like sports being a *metaphor for life.*"

The tone in Norman's voice still showed control and some respect, but Mike was glad he was not on the receiving end of the words.

"You're certain of that?" Margaret asked. "We're really that different than the young men you coached?"

Mike was impressed with Margaret's resolve, or outright courage. He probably wouldn't have questioned Norman's statement.

"No disrespect, but I'm certain enough."

"No disrespect taken," Margaret replied. "You'll learn more about blind sports next week in the recreation class. For now, I'd like to continue with introductions. Albert, could you go next?"

"Hi, I'm Albert Klausin. I used to sell men's suits in Rochester. Before that, I sold cars for a few years and drove a bus if you want to go way back. That was ten, maybe fifteen years ago—since I sold suits, I mean."

Albert's voice was gentle and content, very different from Norman's.

Albert continued. "I don't have a traditional family, but I have a few friends who feel like family. We like to say we've adopted each other. My counselor's been suggesting I come here for a few years. There always seemed to be a reason why I'd put it off. My sight took a turn for the worse a few months ago, so I decided it was time to show up. I've figured out a lot of things about living without sight, but I'm looking forward to learning from the experts here."

"We're glad to have you, Albert. And thanks for your comment about the expertise of our staff, but I like to think that anyone who's earned the title of expert is smart enough to keep learning, especially from experienced students like yourself. Mary, could you go next?"

"Sure, I'm Mary Stenson. I'm from Pipestone. My husband and I have lived there all of our lives."

Margaret interrupted Mary. "I'm sorry, I can barely hear you. Could you speak a little louder?"

Mary cleared her voice and tried speaking up. "Sorry, my husband and I have lived in Pipestone all of our lives. We have two daughters. One is just finishing college and the other is just starting. For the last ten years, I've worked as a checkout clerk at the Red Owl grocery store." Mary's voice was even softer than Albert's.

"Thanks, Mary," Margaret said. "What do you hope to get out of your classes here?"

Mary's voice became quieter and more hesitant. "I'm different from Albert. I never expected to be here. I'm just..." Her words trailed off. "I'm not really sure. I'm just looking forward to working with all of you."

"Thanks, Mary. We hear that a lot, about people not expecting to be here. Schools like ours are different from a college or university. At those places, students spend months or years looking at schools. Then, they apply to a few and attend one. Our students don't do that, but the learning that occurs here is as important as any learning at a university."

Mike expected he would introduce himself next. He was figuring out what to say when a sound came from the door behind him.

"Hey! Good morning, everybody!" a cheerful voice called out. "I know I'm just a little late, but the people in the kitchen wanted me to bring this tray in."

Margaret's voice sounded impatient when she said, "Good morning, George. We were just introducing ourselves. Why don't you go next?"

"I'd be happy to," the man called back. The short phrase sounded cheerful, and based on what Mike could see, the man's movement and chubby shape gave a similar, jolly impression. The man continued speaking. "I'm George Ferguson. I grew up here in Portage Bay, down by the lake. I enjoyed this independent livin' class so much that I decided to take it again. I may even take it a third time."

"It's interesting that you mention decisions," Margaret said. "We were just talking about that. It's very generous that you brought in the tray, but it is a decision with implications. I think we can postpone our introductions while you explain the policy about being on time and the decisions students make about time."

"I'd be happy to. I know a lot about that one. You see, when you can't see so well, time becomes a lot more important. My favorite example comes from riding the bus. If you're not on time to the bus stop, you have to wait, sometimes an entire hour. And, I'll tell ya, that can be a mighty long hour when it's cold out. Even worse, you're out there shivering when you could be in a warm bar enjoying a cold beer. My favorite is The Tacklebox, but I'm happy to say that Portage Bay has a respectable variety of drinking establishments. So, the moral of the story is that you need to always be on time. Here, have some treats."

"George, that was a good answer. Unfortunately, it answered a question I didn't ask. I asked about the school policy regarding timeliness. Mind trying again?"

"I'd be happy to. Timeliness is truly next to godliness. Hang on, let me put it another way. If you don't manage your time well, you start doing things like studying at the last minute, or studying so hard at the last minute that you show up a little late for class. At least, that's what I've heard. You shouldn't really show up late for class because you end up distracting everybody, and the teacher has to repeat stuff. It's just not a good idea. In some cases, students have gone so far as to skip a class entirely to avoid disrupting the entire class. At least, that's what I've heard. There, did I answer the question this time?"

"Not really. I wasn't aware that our school policy showed such respect for people who skipped a class, but I'm glad you enlightened us."

"Happy to."

"I have the more formal and less creative version of this policy. I'm supposed to read some policies, so I'll start with this one. But first, please give me the tray and sit down. There's an open chair next to me." Margaret took the tray, set it on the table, and pulled out the chair. While George sat down, She took out a paper, put her hands on it, and spoke. "Bridgman School for the Blind encourages you to attend all class sessions for a few reasons. First, this is only a three-month program, so each class session is important."

Margaret read more policies, but Mike listened less after noticing her hands. Although individual fingers weren't clear, he could tell her hands were moving over the piece of paper. She was reading aloud from Braille, which he hadn't seen before. He watched for a while, but a moment later, her dress caught his attention. At first, it looked black, but now, he realized it could be blue, maybe dark blue.

Something else caught his attention. She was looking at the students while her hands were moving. Her eyes appeared as dark dots on a fuzzy face, but he could still tell she was looking around while reading with her fingers. That impressed Mike. He could barely find the bumps in Braille text, much less read them while looking around. He started wondering how much Margaret could see. She clearly noticed him when he walked in. Maybe reading Braille was less disruptive than putting a paper close to her face, or maybe she wanted to show students what they would be doing in a few weeks. He shifted his attention back to what she was saying.

"These policies exist because attending class is a simple yet effective way to succeed. Staff at Bridgman School care about your current and future life. We want to spend time with you and help in any way we can. Therefore, if you have more than two unexcused absences, we will ask to meet with you to discuss this issue. The next rule only applies if you are trying to get our Work Skills Certificate. In that case, you will have to repeat a class after four unexcused absences. This consequence illustrates the importance of attending classes. Our staff sincerely hopes not to ask anyone to repeat a class."

"But they will," George said without thinking.

"When we must," Margaret added.

Mike heard Norman quietly comment, "Sounds like hardball."

"I'm afraid this session is starting out with more rules and regulations than on the services we want to provide, even the fun we often have. Let's try returning to the original lesson plan, which means we should finish the introductions. Mike, I think you're next, and last."

"Hi, everybody, I'm Mike. I live in the country outside of St. Cloud. Before I came here, I made tractor parts in a factory. I also went to a technical school for a while. I agree with a lot of the things that other people have said. I didn't expect to be at a school like this, but I'm looking forward to learning as much as I can. I'm not married, but I see my family a lot. I don't know what else I should say."

George commented to Mike, "I've enjoyed a beer or two with guys who've probably used those tractor parts. A couple probably held the same parts you did, since they fix their own machines."

"George, please, we should return to the lesson plan."

"All right, sorry."

Margaret continued. "Next, I'll give a brief overview of the classes you'll be taking. It usually takes three months to finish all the classes. Most new students expect to take classes in Braille, mobility, and independent living, which is the one I teach. There are also some classes you may not expect, about financial management, typing, leisure, and counseling to help you adjust to vision loss. You'll be together for many of your classes, but some classes are individual, such as mobility."

Margaret explained more about each class, but Mike's mind wandered, since the descriptions reminded him of similar first day of school presentations he'd heard in high school and technical college. The class in counseling came to mind. He'd spoken with counselors about his vision loss, regarding personal and work issues, but something felt strange about focusing a class on the subject. Then he remembered the crying he'd heard earlier; maybe the counseling class wasn't so unusual after all. The tone of Margaret's voice changed, in a way that caught Mike's attention.

"Time for the little speech I mentioned. I'm not as good at this as other instructors, but please bear with me. Bridgman School for the Blind is named after Laura Bridgman, who was the inspiration for Helen Keller's education. I'll describe more about Laura in a couple of weeks. We've been helping people like you for over fifty years. In the early days, all we could do was give a few workshops in some borrowed space. These days, we have our own building with more workshops and classes. It still seems like we're always running low on money and can't provide as many services as we'd like. We just try to do a little better every year, whether the State gives us more money or not. Lately, we've been pretty lucky with grants, so that helps."

Margaret sipped her coffee, and Mike thought about her voice. It still had a firmness that showed she was in charge but also a sincerity that showed she wanted to help. She put down her cup and slowly moved her gaze to each person at the table, while speaking again. "We're proud of the students we've helped in the last five decades. They've also taught us a lot. For example, most students come here ready to learn about getting on with their lives, or at least ready enough. That's great, but you can still expect some challenges. People react differently to challenges. Some react with humor. There have been moments here where I laughed so hard that breathing became a problem. Other people react to challenges by becoming quiet. Some people talk." Margaret stood up and started walking around the table.

"Those are pretty easy reactions for us to work with. A few are more dramatic. For good reasons, some students need to cry once in a while. That's not surprising. This may sound odd, but I have a little advice about crying. If you feel the urge, don't make much of an effort to hold it in. Usually, that just makes it burst out later. I recommend you excuse yourself if you can, find a comfortable place, and let it out. We'll talk more about this in the counseling class." She stopped walking around the table, right behind Norman.

"There's one more dramatic response I need to talk about. Some students respond to challenges with anger. Responding with anger makes at least as much sense as other responses. And in many ways, we encourage students to let out their anger just like we encourage students to let out their sadness. But we are more careful with anger. If any student lets out anger in ways that threatens anybody or anything, we *will* calm the situation. This place must feel safe. Having said all this, another pattern we've noticed is that angry outbreaks are rare. Crying is more common. With all these reactions, students usually work through them and carry on very well with their classes. Any questions?"

For a few seconds, nobody responded.

"I'm feeling kind of weepy," George joked. "Can we take a break?"

Everyone laughed, including Margaret, who replied, "We've been going for about an hour, so yes, everyone can have a short break, except for George." Her tone became more serious when she added, "I would like to talk to you for a moment."

Mike stood up and walked out of the classroom. He also thought about the lecture George was going to get and similar lectures he'd personally received years ago.

Mike arrived in the dayroom and looked around. There was a big easy chair next to him, couches along the walls, and a few people sitting. He noticed the television and wondered if it was one of those new color ones. A deep voice interrupted his thoughts. "Hey, Mike, that you?"

"Yeah, it's me, Norman," Mike answered and then asked, "What do you think of this place so far?"

"Not bad. It's a little different being a student again, since being in school has usually meant being a coach. I can't complain, though. Seems like a good school."

Mike agreed and Norman asked, "So what do you do for fun in Central Minnesota? Ever play football?"

"Tried it, but it wasn't a good fit."

"Wrestling?"

"Not really."

"Basketball, track, cheerleading?"

Mike smiled and answered, "Didn't have the legs."

Norman grunted a laugh.

"So, is there any sport you enjoy?"

"Well, there is one winter sport my friends and I try once in a while. It's a form of tag."

"Winter tag?" Norman slowly spoke each word.

"Yeah, with snowmobiles."

"Winter tag with snowmobiles. I don't imagine you had much of a crowd watching the game, or cheerleaders."

"Never did, never figured out why, either," Mike replied, trying to hold back a laugh. "It's a great sport."

Norman sighed and shook his head. "Tag with snowmobiles? Sounds hazardous."

"It wasn't that bad. The snowmobiles didn't actually touch, usually. We used snowballs to tag each other. After all, we didn't want to be reckless."

"Right," Norman said. "It still sounds hazardous."

"We like to think of it as more of an adventure sport than a hazard," Mike said. "It's not too different from football that way."

"Well, maybe," Norman replied, sounding unconvinced.

"I guess I like a little adventure. Haven't you ever thought of sports as a metaphor for life?" Mike asked. The words left his mouth before he realized their risk.

"Don't start with me," Norman grumbled.

Mike thought about apologizing for the joke and how replying too fast with jokes was an old risky habit. Then again, Norman might not even think of his comment as a joke. Mike chose a safe response.

"Fair enough. Truth is, I played some football in high school and an occasional softball game. It's just that, usually, I end up in games like snowmobile tag."

Another voice joined the conversation. "I heard about another creative sport from around St. Cloud, goes back a few years." The voice came from George. Mike was surprised and relieved that his lecture had been short.

George continued. "It's quite an action-packed game, really. You got the big and clean team, the small and scrappy team, and you definitely got crowds cheering. No cheerleaders, though."

Norman sighed. "I'm not sure I want to know what this sport is."

"Aw, c'mon, Coach, give it a guess," George replied.

"Don't call me Coach. That's only for my boys," grumbled Norman.

"How about you, Mikey? Any ideas?"

Mike was intrigued. It was rare that someone described a creative sport from his hometown that he hadn't heard of. "I'm not sure. A lot of sports have different teams and crowds. Could be a demolition derby or dog show. Could you describe some more?"

"I'd be happy to. One thing's for sure, this ain't no dog show. Cars are sometimes demolished in the process, and come to think of it, dogs are involved once in a while. There, that's your hint."

Mike felt an answer coming. "One small question. What makes the crowds cheer?"

"Sorry, you've already had your hint. Give it a guess."

"Just for the fun of it, could I make a partial guess?"

"Not sure. Make your guess and we'll see," George replied, enjoying the game.

"My grandpa had a small farm, and once in a while, he'd head into the woods, trying not to be noticed. If someone asked where he went, he'd smile a little and say he had to 'go cook.' That have something to do with it?"

George laughed a knowing laugh. "Yeah, that has something to do with it."

"What is it?" Norman asked, with surprising interest.

George's laugh faded as he answered, "It's mostly water, some corn, bit of yeast, and some very careful cooking. The sporty part involved guys in the country, most of the time."

"Well, I'm not from the country. Are you going to tell me what this is about?"

A loud voice broke into the conversation. "Anyone here for the orientation class, our break is almost over. Please start returning to Room 5." All three knew it was Margaret.

"It's about cooking," Mike replied to Norman, heading back to the room as the other two men followed.

"Cooking? You guys are not talking about cooking."

"Sure we are," George added.

"Cooking in the woods?"

"*Creative* cooking in the woods," George clarified.

"Creative cooking in the woods with demolished cars and cheering crowds?" Norman asked, sounding impatient.

"And no cheerleaders," Mike added and entered Room 5.

George laughed loud enough that he received a stern comment from Margaret. "George, please."

"Little humor, not too much," Mike said and smiled.

George grunted another laugh.

"You guys are going to drive me nuts," Norman muttered while finding his chair.

The break had been more refreshing than Mike had expected, but he still felt strange sitting in a classroom where he would relearn the basics. The rest of the day reminded him of other first days in other classrooms. A lot of important information was presented about classes, teachers, and the school. But just like other first days at school, Mike retained little of it.

Several hours later, as he walked out of Bridgman's, Mike thought about his first day at school and the people he'd met. The people seemed all right, but he was still looking forward to finishing school and going home to the country. These thoughts continued until he saw the two neon signs and focused on returning safely to Mariner's Motel.

CHAPTER TWO

Exploring

Mike woke up and tried to roll over, but the chair he was in wouldn't allow it. He turned off the TV and moved his face close to the clock on his nightstand. It was a little after 9:00 p.m. He yawned and mumbled, "I gotta start getting to bed on time." During the last few nights, he'd finished reading the book from his counselor, scanned some notes from school, and watched TV until after midnight. On this night, he must have dozed off in the desk chair while watching the news.

He stood up, undressed, and tossed his clothes somewhere toward the chair. After getting under the covers, he enjoyed a long, slow stretch. The muscles in his back relaxed, especially some that had become tense in the chair. He rolled his shoulders and pulled up the covers. Mike started thinking about his house in the country, but soon, he let go of these thoughts, and they wandered forward on their own. He followed them into the wonderful darkness of deep sleep.

Parts of the darkness gradually became lighter, until more of it was grey than black. At a sleepy pace, the grey changed to light grey, and then to white. He felt himself squinting at a bright landscape, a white landscape. A line in the middle stayed dark. It was a straight but jagged line, like an old saw blade, dividing the whiteness into top and bottom halves. Cold air rushed past his face. A buzzing sound started and became louder. Mike looked down and saw his snowmobile, the green Skiroule 340 his dad had bought a couple of years ago. Glancing up, he noticed some details in the jagged line. They were thin triangles, all dark and pointing up. Trees; it was a tree line.

Nothing but snow appeared between him and the distant trees, so it was safe to look at the snowmobile again. He instinctively looked at the carburetor, which stuck out from the center of the engine. Soon after his dad had bought the sled, Mike adjusted the carburetor to get more power. He kept on adjusting it, always hoping for the smallest increase in power. That had led to adjusting other parts, and eventually, to taking parts off, sometimes for repairs and sometimes to see how the parts worked together.

Right now, the parts worked as one wonderful, screaming machine. He gripped the handlebars tighter and pressed harder on the throttle, a lever under his right thumb. The sled responded instantly. He was surrounded by a white field of soft snow, what his friends called perfect powder. The tree line was still far in the distance. He glanced down again at the sled he knew so well. The easiest part to see was the air filter. It stuck out farther than the carburetor, a few inches in front of his waist. Just behind the filter was the small lever that adjusted the choke. A few inches up were the two spark plugs, which he'd fouled and cleaned many times.

He shifted his gaze to the right side of the snowmobile. There was the black rubber handle that fit so well in his hand. It was attached to a wound-up rope for starting the engine. He smiled at the many times he'd pulled that rope and heard the engine fire to life. That sound was even more fulfilling when he thought about all the times he'd pulled the rope and nothing had happened. At best, that had led to an aching right arm. At worst, it could lead to hours of repairing the engine instead of enjoying a ride. Those frustrations made this moment even better.

Instinct told him to look up, since the tree line suddenly became close. There was an opening in the tree line, and a snowmobile path going through it. He eased back on the throttle and made his way to the path. After entering the woods, he continued to slow the sled and let it stop. He enjoyed the screaming sound of the engine at high speed, and he enjoyed the sound when it was idling. Each sound helped Mike understand what the parts were doing. After listening for a while, he reached to the upper right of the small dashboard and rotated the key to stop the engine.

Sounds of a winter woods had their own power, a powerful silence. Snow absorbed much of the sound, but some escaped. A gust of wind blew through dry leaves. Mike could hear almost every step of a squirrel climbing a tree, sharp claws against cold bark. He enjoyed the sounds of the woods until his instincts urged him to explore more, on this machine he knew so well.

He turned the key again and grabbed the black handle on the right side of the engine. He held his left hand firm on the handlebar and pulled the cord with his right. The engine almost started after the first pull, but nothing happened. That was strange. A hot engine should start with half a pull, which could mean it was time to adjust the carburetor again. He pressed the throttle a couple of times and pulled the cord harder. The engine came to life. He drove slowly down the path.

A new sound made its way into his dream. It was almost like a wolf howling. He looked around for the wolf and wondered why it would howl. They usually avoided snowmobiles. The sound became louder and began to cycle, from loud to soft. He stood up while driving, to get a better view. The sound cycled faster. He drove faster and searched more intensely. The sound changed again to a higher pitch. It almost sounded like a woman. He drove on and tried to find her, puzzled about why she would be out here. The trees became blurry. It became louder. He blinked, looked up, and saw the ceiling of his motel room. He recognized the sound. It was the voice of a woman, Ruby's voice. She was repeating one word, "Yes!"

Mike sighed and said, "Another satisfied customer."

He was too annoyed to sleep, so he decided to rest for a while. Mike pushed back the covers a little and heard Ruby repeat the word a few more times. Her room was below his, so he'd heard her before, but the sound was louder this time. When her voice finally faded, he started thinking about school again, until a chill distracted him. That feeling reminded him of opening the window last night to cool the place down, before falling asleep in the desk chair.

The window was only a couple of steps away, so he got out of bed to close it. When his hands were on the window frame, Mike could hear a man groaning. He was tempted to open the window farther and yell at Ruby and her client, but yelling would make it harder to relax and return to sleep. Besides, that kind of groan probably meant they were finished. He shut the window and returned to bed.

He lay in bed and tried returning to sleep. Thoughts of Ruby's work came to mind. It was so strange to him, a sad but persistent part of human history. Mike dismissed these thoughts so he could calm his mind and sleep, maybe return to the dream. He pulled the covers up to his chest; just the feel of them made it easier to relax.

He wondered about the other students in his classes and what they thought about him. Hopefully, they didn't think he was strange for finishing a textbook. He should probably avoid commenting on what he read, or play it down more. He always read ahead in school but didn't like getting noticed for it. Then again, maybe this group was different. George didn't seem like a reader, but Albert did, maybe Mary too. Norman probably read books about sports, as long as there were plenty of pictures.

Mike realized he'd let his thoughts become too active again when he should try harder to sleep. "Try harder to sleep, strange combination," he said and rolled over, pulling the covers closer. The building was now surprisingly quiet. He let out a deep breath and consciously relaxed the muscles in his face. Finally, sleep seemed to return. If only he didn't feel a little warm. "Ignore it," he told himself. He took in some deep breaths and let each out slowly. After a moment, he seemed to be dozing off.

A very slight tug came from an eyebrow. He didn't want to guess what it was, since thinking about it would only wake him more. After trying to ignore it for a few seconds, Mike felt a drip of sweat roll down his face from the same eyebrow. Instinct told him to wipe it off, but that simple act could be enough to prevent the sleep he hoped for. Another drip seemed to form. He tried again to ignore it, but the previous drip and this new one had made his face itch.

"Dammit."

He rubbed the sweat off his face and continued running the hand up to the top of his head. After giving it a good scratch, he sat up in bed, knowing he was awake. Only time would tell if he was awake for the day or just a couple of hours. The first order of business was to open the window. With some practice, he would learn exactly how far to open it for different room temperatures.

Cold, fresh air drifted over him, with a few snowflakes. He looked more carefully out the window. "Nice flurry," he said to himself and looked lower. Outside, a light below his window lit the alley. He hadn't looked at it much, since any alley appears slightly worse than the building next to it. Considering Mariner's, that wouldn't provide much to gaze at. Still, the snow caught his attention, reminding him of days in the country or maybe the dream.

He opened the window more, sat on his desk, put his feet on the chair, and enjoyed the cool, quiet air. "This isn't a snowy woods, but it can still have its moments, especially when Ruby's shift is over." He scanned the alley and buildings. His sight might be better today than it had been yesterday. He'd heard that could happen. Mike scanned higher. The sky on his right was darker than the sky on his left. "Sun must be rising soon, might be a good time to get to know the neighborhood, maybe have a warm breakfast for a change."

He stood up and said, "Are you talking to yourself?"

"Yep, got a problem with that?"

"No, no problem. It's a bit strange, though."

"A lot of people are a bit strange. I'm strange in a good way."

"Okay."

"A good breakfast is more expensive than your normal breakfast."

"I know, I know. I'll keep it cheap."

"Hmm," he grunted, summarizing both sides of the conversation.

He looked at the clock and saw it was just after seven. His first class was at nine, plenty of time to find a place to eat. He grabbed the clothes he'd thrown toward the chair the night before, sniffed a shirt, and decided it could be worn one more day. He dressed quickly, feeling excited about a bit of exploring. On the way out of his room, he grabbed his parka and put it on before reaching the stairwell.

As he walked out of Mariner's, he instinctively turned right, the direction of the neon signs and Bridgman School. He paused and realized that he'd never walked the other way. This morning walk was for exploring, not following a routine. He turned around and started walking in the opposite direction. After a few steps, he stopped again and sighed.

Mike remembered what his counselor had said about using memory to make sense of a disorganized world. The textbook about mobility said the same thing, just not with the colorful tone of his counselor. This could be an exercise in frustration if he didn't find a landmark or two, or three or four. "Just like fixing my snowmobile. Taking it apart was fun, but getting it back together is easier if you start by looking around for a while."

He scanned the area, trying to find a landmark. The blinking sign from Mariner's provided some light. Streetlights provided a little more. The building across the street was larger than he remembered, clearly taller than Mariner's. "Could be a good landmark."

He wandered toward the building to get a better look. His body jolted when he stepped off the sidewalk and onto the street without adjusting for the small step down.

The jolt reminded him of walking down steps, but since he was now standing on the street, he looked for traffic. There had been so few cars that he'd forgotten about them. The few drivers who were out had their lights on and seemed to be careful. *Typical of morning people*, he thought. With this light traffic, Mike could jaywalk with no worry, a welcome return to past comforts.

In the middle of the street, he stopped, partially because he could and partially to get a better look at the building in front of him. He wanted to see how tall it was. With luck, the building might have something unique or lit, hopefully both. The light was also better here, compared to the sidewalk by Mariner's, which was lit by the flashing sign. His eyes no longer adjusted well to flashing lights, so the steady glow from streetlights made it easier to use the sight he had.

The building was about four stories tall, maybe five, but Mike couldn't see anything unique, not even windows. That could be from his low vision, or maybe there were no windows. The top was generally flat, but probably uneven. As far as he knew, this was an older part of town, so maybe the top had some arches or decorations, like many brick buildings of decades past. He wondered if the building was brick. He also thought it might be time to stop standing in the middle of a street. He finished crossing the street, stepped carefully up to the sidewalk, and touched the wall of the building. Sure enough, it was brick. He looked up to see if windows would be visible from this angle; no luck. "Might be a warehouse."

Mike gave up trying to find anything unique about the building and continued walking in the same direction, with Mariner's on his left and Bridgman's far behind. He walked for a while longer and enjoyed the peaceful morning. It was slowly interrupted by the sound of a car, ahead and to his right. The sound meant there was probably a cross street ahead, so he walked slower. As the car passed, its lights created a line in front of him, from right to left. The line wasn't level. It started lower than it finished, showing that the road in front of him was on a hill.

He looked down the hill and wandered down it. After taking a deep breath of cool air, he let out a relaxing sigh. This was the kind of walk he'd been hoping for, although it was steeper than he expected. "If this goes downhill any faster, I could just slide to breakfast, wherever that is." The hill could be one landmark, but like the warehouse, it was too ordinary. He walked farther down the hill, instinctively looking for something that blinked, or some other lit sign.

He was surprised at how ordinary the buildings continued to be. The wall next to him had some large windows and doorways, but it was hard to tell if they were from closed shops, abandoned buildings, or maybe part of the warehouse he thought he'd seen earlier. If they were shops, he expected they would have more character, to attract customers. Maybe this was a part of town where old world brick brought in more people than new world storefronts, or maybe they were for sale. He scanned up the wall, in case something above him could be a landmark. All he noticed was another streetlight. The snowfall had increased, forming a cone as it passed under the lamp.

The walk became as peaceful as the snow that gently floated down. Traffic continued to be light, and the buildings continued to be ordinary. Mike crossed another street and thought he should try more of these morning walks. After enjoying the relaxing walk for a while, he started to look for a landmark again.

Finally, something was different. He heard some cars idling and walked toward the sound, until their lights were clear. Red brake lights appeared before Mike noticed the brighter white headlights. He stopped at a place that was about even with the headlights of the front car.

He waited and continued scanning, still looking for a landmark. He also thought about using the intersection as a landmark. It was permanent and noticeable but not unique. All the cars were waiting at the traffic light, so Mike started walking across the street. A horn blared, and the car it came from quickly stopped a few inches away. Mike guessed it was the front car he'd just stood by. It must have turned right.

"Jesus Christ! You trying to get killed?" yelled the driver, who'd rolled down his window to make sure Mike heard him. It was the new law that allowed right turns on red, good for cars but bad for Mike.

"Sorry, sorry, I didn't see you," Mike said as he stepped back to the sidewalk.

"Well, maybe you should look where you're going! Goddamn idiot."

The car roared off to Mike's right. He clenched his teeth—angry at the driver for being a jerk, angry at the State for passing a law that could kill him, and angry at himself for not seeing the car. He could have missed the car if it had pulled up very slowly or quickly, even if he had normal vision.

As the last car pulled away, he told himself to calm down and enjoy the rest of the walk. It was probably a typical problem between walkers and drivers, but as he stood next to this quiet street, he felt like a schoolkid standing in the corner of a classroom, unable to move without permission. In this case, permission came from the "Do Not Walk" light across the street. He resented the light. The dim blur was controlling his movements; at least, that's how it felt. He continued staring at the sign and became more annoyed. It shouldn't take this long to change. He sighed and asked himself, "Are you getting pissed off at a light?"

"A little."

He waited and thought about doing something useful. Mike tried to find ways to see the damn sign more clearly. He'd been told that parts of his peripheral vision were better than others, sometimes better than his direct vision. He focused his eyes on the area around the sign, testing his vision. Just as he started noticing some differences, the light changed. It was now a bit higher and a dim green instead of a dim orange. "A watched pot ..." he said and started crossing, still looking and listening carefully.

When he was nearly across, Mike paused just before the "Walk" sign and looked closely at it. He didn't expect how important and elusive it would become. While he looked at the sign, it changed to "Do Not Walk." He shook his head and kept walking downhill.

The sidewalk became slightly brighter. Maybe the sun was coming up or maybe a lot of snow had come down. Enough snow on the sidewalk would reflect more light. Something didn't seem right about either option. After walking farther, Mike heard a bell ring twice in a familiar way. It was odd hearing something familiar when he was in a place he'd never walked before. After a few more steps, the double bell rang again. The source of the sound and light became clear. It was a gas station, a well-lit one. Like most stations, there was a rubber cord by the pumps, which rang a bell when cars drove over it.

Finally, this could be a landmark. He was three blocks from Mariner's, down the hill and near a gas station. He remembered something from his classes or maybe from the book he'd read. There were three important steps with a landmark. The first was to find something unique. The second was to get the name of the landmark, and he had no idea what the third was. But he wanted to find the name of this place. He wandered toward the gas station, hoping the name would be lit up somewhere. A car left the pumps, driving away from Mike. He moved forward cautiously, not wanting to repeat his recent close encounter with a car.

"Pardon me, son, can I help you?"

Mike hadn't noticed the gas station attendant.

"Ah, no, sorry. I'm just out for a walk."

"Are you sure you're okay?"

"Yes, yes, I am. Thanks."

"All right, but since you're walking real slow through the entrance to our station, I do recommend that you pick up your pace a bit. Sometimes folks pull in here kind of fast."

"Thanks, I will," Mike said and walked toward the gas station attendant. "Would you mind if I asked you a question?"

"Sure, fire away."

"Could you tell me the name of this gas station?"

"The name? Why, it's right up there in big letters."

Mike saw the shape of an arm rise up.

"I must have missed it."

"Ya can't read big letters under a bright light? That's a new one."

"It's a long story," Mike replied.

"Yeah, I'm sure it is. This place is called Tank's, and surprisingly enough, that also happens to be my name."

"Thanks."

"Sure thing. Anything else I can do for ya?"

"No, but thanks again."

Mike walked away from the gas station and thought about how there really had been something else. He wanted to know the name of the street he'd been walking next to, the one on the hill, but he didn't want Tank to say there was a street sign "right there."

Mike stopped at the street that went downhill. He looked up the hill, toward Mariner's. Going that way would assure a meal in ten or twenty minutes, although it would be a cold sandwich. At least that would be familiar. He looked straight ahead and saw a dark grey haze, probably another street. That was unfamiliar territory, away from Mariner's and the hill he'd become a little familiar with. Going that way didn't feel right. He looked right, down the hill. "One more block.

I'll look for one more block for a warm breakfast. If that doesn't work out, I'll settle for my trusty bologna and cheese sandwich." He walked downhill.

He had to cross one more street to go one more block, and as far as he could tell, there were no crosswalk signs. He stopped and looked for cars. A few drove by, more traffic than he'd seen this morning. He saw someone walk toward him, which meant it was probably safe to cross, so he did the same, quickly.

After reaching the other side, he slowed down and scanned the buildings in front of him. Lights came from them, not as bright as Tank's but brighter than other buildings he'd walked by. The closest building had something lit up behind a window. Mike walked closer to get a better look. Before looking, he paused, glanced left and right, and listened to see if anyone was nearby. He wanted to see what was on display but only if nobody would notice him putting his face close to the window. All he heard was a car and the creaking sound of a sign above the door moving in the breeze. He glanced up but couldn't see the sign. Must not be lit.

He shifted his glance toward the glass and moved his face about half an inch from it. Some things were displayed and lit up. The first shape he noticed was a large X in the back, created by two narrow lines. The lines were about five feet long with a ball at the bottom. "Rod & reels," he mumbled. After he realized that, a green or grey item above the middle of the X became clearer. It was a mounted fish.

He looked left and right again to see if anyone was coming, then returned his gaze to the middle of the X. He bent down a little and looked lower. A box was at the bottom of the display, below everything else. The top of the box was open, and there were several small colors inside. Something was familiar about it, but not enough. Mike wanted to figure out what the colorful box was, but he became self-conscious again. He stood straight and looked left and right.

Nobody was nearby, so he looked up. A few inches above his head, a simple word was written on the glass: Beer. Some other words were written above that, in an arch: The Tacklebox.

"I'll say one thing about this place. They have some fun names. A gas station named Tank's and a bar called The Tacklebox." He looked at the colorful box again and recognized some of the fishing lures, which had puzzled him a moment ago.

He walked toward the next building. It had a larger and brighter window. On the other side of the window, some signs showed the word *Sale* in large, handwritten letters. He couldn't easily read what was on sale, so he glanced down and saw two small pyramids of stacked cans. There was also a familiar and fresh scent in the air. He wanted to figure out what the smell was, but he saw someone inside step near the window, dressed entirely in white. Mike wasn't sure if the person was looking at him or working. Once again, he didn't want to draw attention to himself, so he took a few steps down the hill. The pleasant smell returned. He instinctively took a deep breath. "Fresh bread, cool. I'll have to stop by for groceries sometime."

Another smell made him hungry. "That's probably a grill at a café." He scanned the next building and walked toward it. A bright light over the door lit the sidewalk. The café had two large windows with a door in the middle. The rest of the building was brick. *Stella's* was painted in big letters on the window closest to him. He stepped inside and scanned the room. He could hear a few people talking and the sound of silverware tapping against plates. Since the café had consistent light, he could see more in here than on the sidewalk.

He found an open table, took off his coat, and put it on the back of a chair. Mike sat down and rubbed his hands together. He'd been eating his own cooking for over two weeks, mostly cold sandwiches. He was going to enjoy a warm meal, as long as it wasn't too expensive. Some shapes on the table were blurry but unmistakable. Two were cylinders about six inches high, right next to each other, one red and one yellow. A folded piece of thin cardboard rested between the containers. Some smaller shapes were near the red container, one dark grey and the other white.

"Chilly morning out there. Care for some coffee?" a waitress asked Mike.

"No, thanks, never picked up a taste for it."

"All right, can I get you a glass of water or something?"

She drew out the vowels on the word "water," sort of like Ruby.

"How about a Coke?"

"Sounds good. Do you know what you'd like, or do you need some time to look at the menu?"

Mike didn't feel like explaining that he couldn't read the menu or asking about the specials. For him, asking usually led to a waitress describing a list of options that didn't interest him anyway. Instead, it felt right to ask for a familiar favorite. "I'll just have a burger."

He could see her eyebrows lift, even with limited sight.

"A burger? A Coke and a burger, for breakfast?"

"Breakfast of champions," Mike replied in a playful tone.

"If it works for you, it works for me." She started writing down the order and continued speaking. "Come to think of it, we used to get orders like that early in the morning. Back then, guys were working the night shift and having lunch. That changed when they closed the plants." She looked up again. "Want some fries with that?"

"How much more would they cost?"

"Fifty cents."

"Could I get half an order of fries?"

She smiled and said, "You do remind me of guys from the plant, friendly bunch and a little cheap. I'll see what I can do about a half-order."

The waitress left and returned a moment later with a can of Coke and a glass of ice. Based on her voice and the way she moved, Mike guessed she was about ten years older than he was. He also sensed she didn't mind his unique choice for breakfast.

It was unusually comfortable to relax in a café. Mike opened the can, set the pull-tab near the edge of the table, and poured the cola into the glass. He sipped it and thought about his walk. In all, he'd walked just over three blocks. He tried not to dwell on how much effort it had taken to walk a few blocks. Next time, the walk would go a little faster, and he'd explore a little further. Each place on his walk came to mind, the warehouse across from Mariner's, the hill, the stoplight, and Tank's.

He started craving something else to think about, like the morning news. Reading a newspaper over breakfast probably wouldn't happen again, but on a future walk, maybe he'd try to find a small radio with an earpiece. That would work for later, but right now, he wanted some way to pass the time.

Mike settled for looking more closely at the table. He scanned the surface and rested a hand on it. The table was made of a light-colored wood, probably pine. He moved his hand slowly across it, toward a spot on the corner nearest him. The spot was a dent. He ran a finger along the outside edge and felt more small dents. The dents made him confident the table was made of pine, since that wood was light and soft—cheap, too.

He shifted his gaze and scanned the café. He thought about how it was easier to see when there was consistent light and when there was no risk of being run over. The café looked surprisingly similar to restaurants back home, but with a gritty-city feel. The TV show *All in the Family* came to mind. Mike couldn't remember a time when people on that show ate out, but if they did, the café would look something like this. Based on the size of people nearby and their deep voices, they were mostly men. Mike felt like they were the kind of guys he used to work with at the tractor parts factory.

"Here you go, darl'n, a burger and fries," the waitress said as she placed the meal and silverware in front of him. He thanked her, and the woman told him she would be back later if he needed anything else.

He looked at the plate, especially the fries. Some had already fallen off, clearly not a half-order. He wondered if she'd misunderstood his request for a half-order but didn't feel like asking about it. Maybe he would ask when the bill showed up, probably not though. The extra warm fries would feel good on this cold morning, and they were still cheap.

He put these thoughts aside and bit into the burger. It had been a long time since a warm meal had tasted so good. This walk had its challenges, but at the moment, it was worth it. Mike took the ketchup bottle, ate some of the fries near the plate's edge, and filled that spot with ketchup. After enjoying more of the burger and fries, he wondered how long it had been since he enjoyed a treat like this. No clear answer came to mind, so his thoughts wandered back to the present and how good this meal felt. It occurred to Mike that the reason he was enjoying this meal was that he'd woken up so early, which made him say, "Thank you, Ruby."

"You're welcome, honey, but my name's not Ruby. It's Rocky." It was the waitress again.

"Sorry, I talk to myself once in a while, old habit."

"Yeah, I've seen that before. It's a far cry better than some of the other habits I've seen here, depending on what you say."

"I'll try to keep it clean."

"Thanks. I was just stopping by to see if your breakfast was all right. Looks like it was."

"I guess I've been eating my own cooking for too long."

"I've seen that a lot too."

"Did you say your name was Rocky?"

"I did, but I only tell that story to people who come back."

Mike smiled. "Works for me. Hey, Rocky, could I pay up now? I need to be in class by nine."

"I had a feeling you might be going to the school." She looked at her notepad and said, "One Coke, one burger, and a half-order of fries. That'll be a buck fifty."

He almost thanked her for the extra fries but suspected she'd rather keep that quiet. He took out his wallet, held it close to his face, and tried finding two dollars. Unfortunately, telling the difference between bills was still difficult. The light here was comfortable for eating breakfast, even reading a paper for sighted folks, but it was a little dim for Mike to identify bills in his wallet.

"It's tough for me to see small details sometimes. I'm pretty sure I have two dollars in my wallet. Would you mind getting them for me?" he said as he moved his wallet slightly in her direction.

"Sure thing. You're kind of a trusting soul, aren't ya?"

"How can anyone not trust a lady named Rocky?"

Mike saw the shape of a smile on her face. "Can't argue with that. Okay, I have two dollars." Rocky said, while she placed his wallet on the table with two quarters in change.

"You keep one, and I'll keep one," he said while taking a quarter. He stood up and started putting on his coat.

"Thank you, honey. You have a good day, and if you see George, you tell him to stop by soon. Haven't seen him in a while."

He was surprised. "You mean George from Bridgman's?"

"The one and only," Rocky answered as she wiped the table.

He smiled, realizing that Rocky had figured out more than he expected. "I'll be sure to tell him." He zipped up his coat and added, "George will be in my nine o'clock class."

"If he shows up."

"You know George pretty well."

"Most people do. George is a good guy, but he has a problem with time, always has." Rocky paused. "Sometimes, it's hard to tell what is a bigger problem for him, time or sight."

That comment surprised Mike again.

"You better get going. The snow's picking up, and you don't want to show up after George."

"Will do. It was good meeting you."

Rocky said the same to him and walked over to some other customers.

He walked out of Stella's Café and looked around. The light was better than he'd expected, much better than before breakfast. There was more traffic as well, people and cars. He walked up the hill toward Mariner's. He sighed and thought about one of Rocky's comments. How could anyone think that losing track of time could be worse than losing your sight? Losing your sight changed everything. Nothing could compare.

Mike paused when he saw a couple of people waiting to cross the street. His thoughts continued. He'd learned to solve a lot of problems from blindness and was learning how to solve more. But there always seemed to be another problem to solve, and time was the biggest. Sure, you could do anything with enough time, but when everything took longer, you simply did less. You just couldn't do as much as you did before losing your sight. Rocky couldn't understand how tough and frustrating that was.

Mike heard a double bell off to his left. He told himself to focus on landmarks, but his thoughts returned to Rocky. She didn't seem like someone who'd make cheap shots; just the opposite actually. She seemed like someone who shared her thoughts calmly, clearly, and with a sort of gritty honesty. Then again, Mike had only just met her.

He heard the sound of a shovel scraping against the sidewalk and looked around to make sure he didn't get in the shoveler's way, or get hit with a shovelful of snow. A comment from Margaret entered Mike's mind, when George had been late to class. He couldn't remember what she'd said, but her tone had been clear. She had little patience with George being late, if any. He shook his head. It was just hard to believe that a problem with time came close to the problems with blindness. This topic had become tiring, not what he'd hoped for when he'd started this little exploration.

He looked up at the snow floating down. It really was snowing more than when he'd started this walk. Looking up seemed to cause a long yawn. An early morning siesta sure would feel good right now. Unfortunately, he had to quickly return to his room, pick up his things for school, and try to get to class on time. He paused to join another group of people waiting to cross the street. A while later, he glanced to his left and saw the flashing sign of Mariner's Motel.

The hotel lobby was quiet this early in the morning. Mike noticed that even the TV was off. When he reached the second floor, a phone was ringing. He thought about how Mariner's might be cheap in terms of money, but there was a cost in lost sleep. If Ruby hadn't woken him earlier, this ringing phone would have done it. "If some jerk takes calls this early, the least he could do is answer the phone." As he walked closer to his room, he realized the ringing was coming from inside it. He put aside the irony of calling himself a jerk as he rushed to get inside.

"Hello."

"Michael, you are there," his mom said slowly in one of her playful tones.

Mike smiled and replied, "I suppose. How're you doing, Ag?" He rarely called her Mom, using the nickname Ag instead. It was short for Aggie.

"Pretty good. Still getting used to the colder weather. Sorry about calling so early. I tried calling a couple times this week, but you weren't home. I just wanted to see how you were. Did I wake you up?"

"Oh no, you know me, always an early riser."

"I suppose," she replied with a doubting tone. "How's school going? Are you getting good grades?"

He laughed a little, knowing his mom was intentionally asking the question as if he were in high school. "Oh yeah, top of the class as usual."

"Good, good. Are you getting settled in okay? I still worry about that cheap hotel you're living in."

"It's actually all right. I've gotten to know some of the people here. They're okay."

"You sure?" she asked, with a more serious tone. "I thought I saw some drunks and maybe a lady of the evening when we dropped you off."

"Maybe a couple, but they're not that bad, just misunderstood."

"Well, all right."

"Hey Ag, I hate to cut this short, but I'm a little late leaving for school. Tell me quick, though, are you and Dad all right?"

"We're fine. Dad just put in a new wood stove. It should save some money, but when it's hot, it's really hot. Well, I better let you go. I'll try calling you again this weekend."

"Okay, good talking to you. Tell Dad I said hi."

"I will. You have a good day at school. Goodbye."

"Bye, thanks again for calling."

"Goodbye, Michael."

"Bye, Ag."

"Bye, bye."

Mike hung up the phone and wondered how many times you were supposed to say goodbye on a phone. He shifted his thoughts to what he needed for school: notebook, marker, keys, and wallet. His last task before leaving was to see just how much he'd have to hurry. Normally, he left at twenty minutes to nine. "Quarter to, bummer." In his rush, he slammed the door to his room.

"Goddammit, can you keep it down out there!" an unknown voice complained as Mike hurried down the stairs.

CHAPTER THREE

Lessons

One of the first rules Mike had learned after losing his sight was to walk slower, which would reduce the number and impact of collisions. Unfortunately, his morning walk meant breaking that rule to be on time for class. After passing by the receptionist's desk, he heard a vague comment about slowing down. He agreed and kept walking at the same speed.

He hadn't been late to class all week, and if he made it today, it would be an entire week. He moved down the hallway and into the dayroom. Mike stopped at a clock that was on the sunny side of the skylights. It was a typical black-and-white round office clock, but it was hung lower than normal, about five feet from the floor. He put his face about an inch from the clock. "Cool, eight fifty-six."

"Hey, Mikey, that you?"

Mike was happy and surprised to hear George's voice at a time that was actually before the first class. Mike's surprise slipped out when he answered. "Yeah. Morning, George."

"Well, don't we sound cheerful this morning? You better be careful, being all bubbly at this god-awful hour. People are going to talk.

51

You either had an exciting night or a restful one. Personally, I hope you didn't sleep much."

"Funny you mention that," Mike replied. "I'd tell you all about it, but we both need to get to class."

"All right, but I still want to hear all about it. I'll follow you, since your eyes are in better shape."

George followed Mike down the hallway and continued talking. "That reminds me, you've mentioned a few stories that I've been wondering about. Snowmobile tag, cooking in the woods, and now this. All these stories, and you have yet to join me in one of Portage Bay's fine taverns."

"Tavern? There's a word I don't hear often. You mean a bar?"

"Yeah, I guess. Sometimes, I like to play with words. Anyway, you gonna buy me a beer or not? Seems only fitting for a Friday."

He smiled at George's effort to get a free beer. "Sure. What's a good time?"

"I've always been fond of enjoying the moment, although I don't imagine that sneaking out right now would be a good idea."

"I suppose," Mike replied.

George thought for a couple of seconds and said, "Speaking of words, I've noticed you say that before. I think you're saying 'I suppose' but you mumble through the 'up' part."

Mike smiled a little, remembered when friends had noticed the same thing, and replied, "I suppose."

"Thought you might say that. Anyway, how about having a drink after school?"

"Sure," Mike answered. He liked the idea of going out for a drink later, but he was more interested in what was going to happen next. "Any idea what's going on in class today?"

"Nothing nearly as fun as going to a tavern, but yeah, I heard something. There's good news and bad news. Which would you like to hear first?"

"I didn't think there would be much of either. It seems like it'll be another slow class, maybe more about organizing a kitchen."

"That's part of it, but life is always full of surprises."

"I have a suspicion that your life may contain slightly more surprises than others'," Mike joked. "No offense intended."

"None taken, none indeed. And you might just be right about that," George commented with a tone of proud reflection. He continued. "Back to the good news and the bad news. Which do you want to hear first?"

"I'll take the good news."

"The good news is that today you'll be getting a free lunch."

"Cool, how's that?" Mike asked.

"Some unlucky soul in our class is going to make the first meal, probably muffins."

"Really? I thought we'd still be learning more about independent living, not cooking yet."

"Nope, today's the day," George said. "Some other teachers told me Margaret was making sure we had all the ingredients handy. Ready for the bad news?"

"Is it that my cooking skills are lousy, so I'll have to eat my mistakes?"

"Even worse. Eating your mistakes could be uncomfortable. Eating mine could be painful. Margaret will pick a couple Sad Sacks to cook and the rest of us will answer questions, if this is the same as last time."

Mike smiled at the reference to Sad Sack, which was one of his favorite comics. They turned a corner and entered the kitchen, almost bumping into Margaret as they did.

Margaret spoke to both. "Good morning. As a matter of fact, George, you're right. We will start cooking today. Since you and Mike mentioned that you could use some practice cooking, maybe you could be the first ones to prepare a snack?"

Mike continued to be impressed how the woman's stature far exceeded her size.

"You want Mikey and me to make something?" George asked slowly. "That could give new meaning to the phrase, 'the blind leading the blind.'"

"Actually, I think it would be a great way to start the cooking section of our class. After all, you two obviously work well together, and you just admitted that you could use the practice."

"Michael," George said firmly, "I'm going to have to ask you to keep your voice down."

"He's not the person I heard," Margaret replied.

"Right. You really want to punish these fine people"—George motioned toward the other students, who were sitting at a large wooden dining table—"by having them eat anything that Mikey and I make together?"

"I admit there is some risk involved for the rest of us, since we'll have to eat what you make, but I think that could be just the motivation you need to focus your attention."

Mike heard a man clear his throat, a deep sound that could only be Norman.

"I don't mean to take over your class or anything, Margaret, but eating what they make sounds hazardous. Do we get any choice in the matter?"

"Good question, Norman," Margaret replied. "You don't have to worry too much. We've run the class this way for years. All students have cooked, and all students have lived. Besides, this is the most simple meal we'll make, so it's well suited for those with limited cooking skills. They will be making coffee and muffins from a premade mix."

"That's a relief," Norman responded, "although I'm still a little concerned."

"I can't blame you," Margaret said, "but we have some safety checks in place, for just these situations."

After realizing he couldn't get out of cooking, George's tone changed from playful avoidance to playful concern. "You folks really know how to make a guy feel confident."

"You'll be fine, George. Why don't you and Mike have a seat? There're a few things we need to cover before you begin cooking."

The two men sat with the rest of the students at the large dining table.

Margaret continued. "Back to our safety check, or comfort check. I will try any meal before the other students. The main reason is for my teaching. I want to give comments to anyone who cooks, so I can clarify what worked and what can be improved. If a meal reaches an extreme of *needs improvement*, I'll explain why and give you the option to eat it. Does that sound okay, Norman?"

"I think so."

"All right, we've gotten a bit ahead of ourselves today. I'm going to review some key points from past classes, and eventually, we'll be enjoying some carefully prepared coffee and muffins."

"You guys just wait. Mikey and me are gonna surprise ya. Life is full of surprises."

Mike heard a deep voice mutter, "Some surprises are better than others."

Margaret walked into the center of the kitchen. Mike could see a long counter behind her and a small counter in front. It was one of those modern kitchen islands with an oven in the middle, burners on top, and a small counter space. He wondered if there was a way to put one in his kitchen back home.

She placed her hands on the kitchen island and spoke. "We're looking forward to it with anticipation, George, but first I want to review a little." Her tone told Mike this was going to be one of her lectures, so he took out his marker and paper, just in case something good came up.

"We've discussed a few ideas for organizing a kitchen to make it easier to find things. What's the best starting point for organizing pots, pans, food, and everything else in a kitchen?"

"Big stuff goes low," Norman answered.

"Small stuff goes high," joked George.

"Brilliant, George," muttered Margaret. "Other answers?" There were none, so she continued. "I'm thinking of a more general starting point. Here's a hint: if you are saying that big stuff goes low, a reasonable question is lower than what?"

"You need a reference," Albert answered. "That's the best starting point. In a kitchen, the sink is a good reference, since it's usually in the middle."

"That's the answer I was looking for. Most of the organizing techniques we recommend use the general categories of high, low, left, and right. As Albert described, those categories work best with a central reference. The sink usually works, but it could be your stove or anything else in the middle of your kitchen. With a central reference, Norman's comment about putting big things in low places makes more sense. What's another guideline?"

"Food goes on the left side," said Mary in a soft but confident voice. "Things that hold food go on the right."

"Another good guideline. Many of these guidelines are arbitrary. Normally, it doesn't matter if food is stored on the left or right of the sink. In this case, we choose guidelines that are easy to remember."

Mike saw Margaret motion toward the right side of the sink. "This guideline is easy to remember because most people eat with their right hand. If you think of holding a fork with your right hand, you'll remember where forks go. Then, you'll know that other things that hold food also go on the right, like plates and cups." She brought her hands together. "Combining these three guidelines goes a long way in helping you remember where to find things in the kitchen. Any questions or comments?"

She waited a moment while she leaned on the counter behind her and crossed her arms. Mike looked down at the table and wondered about the organizing scheme in his kitchen back home. He tried to put different things in a good place, but it always took too long. That often led to a different guideline: Things go where they can most quickly be shoved. He smiled and thought how that was more of a *disorganization* scheme. He looked up when Margaret started speaking again.

"All right, I'll summarize the key points. First, the sink is your central reference. Second, big stuff goes low, and third, things that hold food go on the right. I want you to visualize that: Sink in the center, big stuff low, and stuff that holds food on the right. I mean it. Imagine that for a moment." She paused. "If you can visualize that much, you know that food itself goes on the left, and small things go high. Time for a pop quiz. Where would I find pots and pans?"

"On the lower-right side of the sink," George answered.

"Very good, George, and quick too."

"Thanks. I've always been proud of my kitchen skills. Although, it did help when you invited me to stay after class a few times last year. All that extra washing, drying, and putting away dishes left a lasting impression."

"I'm glad it had some benefit," Margaret replied. "Next question: where would I find a can of mushrooms?"

"Upper-left," Albert answered.

"Correct. How about a large bag of flour?"

"Lower-left," Norman added.

"You guys are doing great. What do you do when the guidelines don't work?"

Mike joined the conversation. "Remember that these are just guidelines. Actual performance may vary."

He may have seen Margaret smile, or maybe a cheerful change in her tone made him think she'd smiled. "Cleverly put, Mike. There will be exceptions, but like all organizational techniques, it's good to have some general guidelines as a starting point. What's an example where we break the guidelines?"

Mike heard the sound of pages turning as other students scanned the notes they'd taken in previous classes. He held his own notebook close to his face and read some notes in large letters, which he'd written with a marker.

Mary responded. "A can opener. It's small, but it doesn't go high. It's in the same drawer as other utensils, below the countertop. I think it's the drawer to the right of the silverware."

"Good point, Mary," Margaret said. "This kitchen has some exceptions, and your kitchen at home will have some. It's up to you to find a useful combination of general guidelines and exceptions. That's enough about storing and finding things. Are there other guidelines you remember for working in a kitchen?"

"Put big labels on cans or anything else that you can stick a label on," Albert answered.

"Or, for those of us who can't read a label, rubber bands on cans can go a long way, pardon the pun," George added. "But you gotta remember what one, two, or three bands mean, not to mention avoiding the temptation to shoot 'em at friends."

"Good answers, and George, can we try to avoid suggesting games in the kitchen? People can get hurt in here, especially at first, so we want to focus on safety and efficiency." Margaret looked around the table. "Some common options are masking tape, reusable labels, or rubber bands as George suggested. What are other suggestions you remember from past classes?"

"Add light, lots of light," Norman said.

"Another good answer. Many of our students have some functional vision. Adding light is the best way to make the most of the vision you have. Other suggestions?"

Norman again answered. "Look for places where glare makes it hard to see, like shiny surfaces. Then, do something to change the surface."

"Correct, glare can be at least as bad as low light for many students. Glare can come from shiny floors, tabletops, or mirrors. There are ways to reduce or eliminate it. You can use non-glare floor wax or a tablecloth, or move a mirror. How about some key points that focus more on the process of cooking?"

"Turn the handle of pots and pans," Mary added, "so they don't stick out where you can bump into them."

"Good answer, Mary. That's a simple effort to keep from getting burned by bumping a pot of boiling water or a pan used for frying meat. Others?"

"Memorize the phone number for Domino's?" Mike asked.

George chuckled and added, "Hard to beat a thirty-minute guarantee."

"Michael, I'm starting to think you're hanging around with the wrong crowd, or person. That's enough of a review. Now, it's time for the big event. George and Mike are going to make our first meal. It's actually more like a morning snack since we like to start simple. They will be making coffee and muffins, and the rest of you will add suggestions on how to proceed. What's the first step?"

There was no answer, so Margaret gave a hint. "Think about how you used to make breakfast."

Albert responded. "Well, a lot of the steps don't change, from when we made coffee and muffins with sight. I'd start by making the muffins, since they take longer than the coffee."

"Good suggestion, Albert. We'll start with the muffins. Anyone else have a suggestion?"

Norman answered. "When in doubt, read the instructions. That's another thing that doesn't change much from cooking with sight."

"Good. One of you should read the instructions, and the other will work in the kitchen."

Mike quickly replied. "I'll read the instructions." He knew that reading meant using the text-enlarging machine, which was off to the side of the kitchen. Following the instructions meant working inside the kitchen, directly in front of everyone. He enjoyed making an occasional joke, but he never liked being the center of attention for too long. Part of this feeling was the same response that many people have, sighted or not, to speaking in front of a group. Another part went back to being the only boy with glasses. Aunts had thought the glasses were cute; other boys had thought they were dumb; Mike had thought people should think about something else.

"Thanks, Mike," Margaret said. "The instructions are on the back of the box, sitting next to the toaster. Actually, there are two boxes, since we're making a double recipe."

He picked up a box and walked toward the machine. It reminded him of microfilm readers in public libraries, so Mike had quickly become familiar with the enlarger—zooming in on the text, focusing the camera, and moving to the right paragraph.

"While Mike is starting the enlarging machine, I'll mention that it would have been fine if George had chosen to read the instructions. His sight limits him from using the enlarger, but there are always options. He could have played an audio tape we have made where someone has read the instructions aloud."

Mike switched on the machine and put the box of muffin mix under the video camera to read the instructions on the back. He waited a few seconds for the monitor to warm up and moved his face close to it. "All right, the instructions say we should preheat the oven to four hundred and twenty-five degrees, but you've been telling us to do more than that whenever we heat up the stove."

"That's right," Margaret replied. "Do you remember any details?"

"Bummer. I thought you might ask that. Those gloves, the big ones. We should get them out whenever we switch the stove on."

"I think you mean oven mitts, Mike," Albert added. "We're also supposed to be careful about what we wear."

"Good answers, Albert. George and Mike, how does your clothing apply to the guidelines for working with a hot stove?"

"Well, personally," George answered, "I take great care in my attire. I always start by carefully selecting a pair of blue jeans, which usually means picking the cleanest. Then, I pick whatever T-shirt feels right for the day, which is no small challenge because I have several favorites. Or, I pick the one that's clean. Last, but certainly not least, I pick a matching plaid shirt, or maybe the one that's clean." George tugged on his plaid shirt. "If I feel ambitious, I tuck in the plaid shirt, but most of the time, I go for the born to be free look."

Mike smiled and thought about the difference between George's look and Margaret's neat dress.

"I never realized you considered this so carefully, George," Margaret replied.

"Oh, great care, great care indeed."

"This morning, it appears that you've gone for the born to be free look with both your shirts."

"Yeah, I woke with an enthusiastic spirit. To be honest, I'm still thrilled about our new president. I mean, how can you not like a president named Jimmy?"

Mike heard a deep grumble, followed by a gravelly voice. "I can give all kinds of reasons."

George looked toward Norman and asked, "Really, even when our very own Walter Mondale is now vice president?"

Norman flexed some of the muscle in his voice. "Yes, really."

Margaret used just as much strength in her voice. "I think we need to move away from a discussion about politics and return to our cooking. George, how does your carefully selected attire relate to working over a hot stove?"

"I'm not entirely sure, to be honest. Maybe I'll be warm wearing two shirts?"

"Maybe, but I was thinking of something else."

"It could burn," Mary added. "Wearing loose clothing is a burn risk when you work by a stove with low sight."

"Oh, yeah, that safety stuff. That's the other thing I always think about when I carefully select my attire."

"I suspect you should think about it some more," Margaret said. "We need to avoid wearing loose clothes when cooking. The safest option is to take off your plaid shirt."

"I'd be happy to. I've never been one to say no when two women ask me to take off my shirt," he said while pulling an arm out of a sleeve.

Mike chuckled, which made George do the same. Margaret sighed and spoke. "Mike, it looks like you're not wearing loose clothing."

Mike was still chuckling when the answer came out. "No, women have always told me that I look better in tight shirts."

"Showoff," George joked while taking the plaid shirt the rest of the way off.

Mike laughed harder. Margaret sighed again and spoke again. "Boys, we really need to focus on our cooking."

He knew she was right. He and George mumbled in agreement and faced Margaret to listen carefully, although they were still trying to hold back some laughs.

Margaret continued. "George, please set the oven to four hundred and twenty-five degrees. It's the big dial in the center. As I mentioned yesterday, we've placed plastic bumps at one-hundred-degree increments on the oven dial, so you should rotate the oven dial clockwise, just past the fourth bump. Then, get out the cooking mitts and place them about a foot away from the stove. The mitts are in the top drawer on the right side of the oven. Mike, please continue with the instructions."

"We need two eggs and a cup of milk."

"I think I can handle that," George said while getting the oven mitts. "I'll start with the eggs, so let me guess, a double recipe would be, something like, two times two eggs, carry the three, divide by four, minus seven …"

"George," Margaret said, sounding like a stern 1950s' grammar teacher again.

"Right, four eggs and a couple cups of milk," George said, sounding jolly. "Now, just to illustrate my vast cooking prowess, I'm going to apply one of the ideas we've talked about, in addition to some of my own special innovations. I'm not going to simply get the eggs out of the fridge and set them on the counter, since that can lead to an unfortunate experience."

Norman spoke over George's monologue. "Which I hear you've experienced a few times. Something to do with the combination of eggs and gravity."

"Yes, on rare occasion, an egg has escaped my attention."

Mike enjoyed the exchange and added, "An egg, like one? I heard it might have been more than that."

George looked toward him and asked, "Michael, whose side are you on? Sure, it may have been slightly more than one egg, but should we not make a stronger attempt at staying focused? I'm sure Margaret would appreciate it."

"You're always looking out for me, George, can't tell you how much that means."

"You're welcome," George said, enjoying himself. "Now, returning to our regularly scheduled demonstration, I am doing my best to follow the rules we discussed. One important rule is to have all your ingredients out in front of you before you throw them all together. My own bit of brilliance is to put the required number of eggs into a bowl, to keep the little buggers steady."

"Couldn't you just take out the entire carton of eggs and put it on the counter?" Albert asked.

"That might work," answered George, "but personally, I like the bowl idea." His tone changed from answering Albert to announcing to the entire class. "Unless there are further interruptions, I am going to continue thusly. First, I am going to get a bowl." He put his left hand on the sink to help find a cabinet with his right. "Not just any bowl, mind you, but an appropriately sized bowl, just big enough to hold four eggs." He opened the cabinet, felt around for a moment, pulled out a small bowl, and showed it to everyone.

"Carrying said bowl with me, I'm going to get four, not two but four, eggs from the fridge." He opened the fridge, felt for the carton of eggs, and took an egg. He showed it to everyone by slowly holding the egg high and waving it a little. "That's one." He then carefully put it in the bowl. He reached for another, showed it in the same way and said, "That's two." He reached again and commented again, in a confident and happy tone, "Three, and finally number four." His sentence ended with the sound of a crack as the last egg broke on the floor.

"Crap."

Everyone laughed. Norman's deep laugh was as rich as his voice. He was still laughing when he said, "Maybe the carton idea wasn't so bad after all."

"Perhaps," George replied.

Margaret's formal teaching tone faded when she held back a laugh and added, "You really had me going there for a moment, George. I was starting to think I was all wrong about your vast cooking skills." She walked toward the sink and returned to her normal tone. "You did, however, manage to show the importance of being careful and focused in the kitchen. This time, all we have to worry about is a mess on the floor. Next time, it could be something sharp or hot. I'm going to deviate from standard procedure and not have you clean up the mess. I'll clean it up, for the sake of having you quickly return to your first cooking activity."

Margaret opened a cabinet beneath the sink and took out a pail, rag, and bottle of soap. She squirted some soap into the pail, filled it with water, and kept talking. "Surprises like this are actually a good thing. They happen, and when you cook on your own, you can expect them to happen more often than they used to, especially at first. The best solution is to know where your cleaning materials are, clean it up, and get back to cooking."

Mike knew he had some pails in his garage but wondered if there was one in his kitchen.

Margaret continued. "The same idea applies for knowing where your first aid kit is, in case something worse happens. In these situations, you should make sure you have nothing cooking or boiling, which could overcook while you clean. This is another good reason to give yourself more time when preparing a meal." She focused on cleaning for a moment.

Mike wondered more about his kitchen. He could clean out one of the pails in his garage, bring it in the house, buy a first aid kit, remember to turn off everything when a small mistake happened, and turn it all back on again later. Or, he could eat cold food. It might be less tasty, but it would save a lot of bother. His thoughts stopped wandering when Margaret spoke again.

"That's about done. Mike, where were we?"

"We were getting all the ingredients out."

"We should probably get out all the containers and utensils too," Albert added.

"I was hoping someone would say that," Margaret said. "What are some of the items we'll need, Albert?"

He thought for a moment and replied, "I'd start with a muffin tin and paper wrappers. We'll also need a bowl to mix everything together and a big spoon to do the mixing."

"Good suggestions. George, please get these out. Is there anything else we'll need?"

Norman answered this time. "How about the milk? That came up in the instructions. And we'll probably need something to measure it with."

"Mike, you'll need to help here. You could get the milk and the glass measuring cup. The two-cup container will work best."

Mike moved away from the reading machine and walked into the kitchen. When he was almost there, he heard the sound of pots bumping against pans, from George feeling around inside a cabinet.

"Is this the right cabinet?" George asked. "I can't feel the muffin tins anywhere."

"It's the right cabinet," Margaret answered. "I think they're in the back, on the right-hand side. You'll need both of them."

"Ah, there you are," George said as he pulled out some muffin tins. He stood up, started looking for some paper wrappers, and spoke again. "I still wonder about all the hassle with getting everything out ahead of time. Is it really necessary?"

"It may seem like a waste of time, but it actually saves time and frustration. And occasionally, careful preparation saves a meal because things don't burn or boil over while you're looking for something."

George took the wrappers out of a cupboard and replied, "I guess so, but it all still seems like a lot of bother."

"Actually," Margaret said, "there's one more benefit to getting everything out ahead of time, like giving us time to replace something that was, shall we say, damaged? An egg, for example."

"Hard to argue with that," George said as he walked to the fridge to get another egg.

After Mike and George placed more items on the kitchen island, Margaret continued. "George, please arrange everything in a way that will make it easy for you to find what you need. I also want to remind everyone of a simple yet helpful characteristic of this kitchen. All of our countertops are white. This maximizes the light and makes it easy to see plates, bowls, cups, and utensils, since we chose darker colors for those items. All right, are we ready to continue?"

"More than ready," George replied. "With your permission, I'll get on with it."

"Since you're sure, please carry on," Margaret added. "But remember, you're making a double recipe."

"Right," George grunted. "Mike, read the ingredients to me again, so I get the double recipe right."

"Add the following ingredients to a two-quart bowl: two eggs, one cup milk, and contents of this bag."

"And, to double the recipe," George replied, "we now have two tricky parts. I have to measure two cups of milk. Then, I need to add four eggs and probably a few shells."

"Great," Norman said.

"George, please," Margaret added. "We prefer our muffins without shells, and we've already seen the risks of not taking this seriously enough. Can you focus on the task at hand?"

"All right, all right, just trying to identify my challenges and all that. Anyway, now that we have carefully prepared our ingredients, bowls, measuring things, and the rest of this important stuff, I shall undertake measuring the milk, with as little spillage as possible."

Margaret asked, "Is there anything you would like to ask the class before you measure?"

"Sure, would anybody like to go out for breakfast? Mike's buy'n."

"Not quite what I had in mind. The question I'm thinking of involves how you're going to measure the milk, something we talked about a couple of days ago."

"Oh, that question. Sure. Okay, everybody, since you're my guests and I'm making a meal for you, I'd like you to know that I have to touch the ingredients more than sighted folks. For example, when I measure milk, I'll have to put my finger in it, to know when it gets close to the top. If anyone is uncomfortable with that, please get your own damn muffins." George tried making the statement in a lighthearted way, but his impatience was still clear.

"George, please."

"Sorry, I'll try that again. If anyone is uncomfortable with that, let me know now or later, and I'll find something else for you."

There was a silent moment, and George opened the cardboard milk container, unfolding the spout on top.

"I don't mean to be a bother." Albert added to the conversation this time. "But, could you answer one small question?"

George sighed and replied. "I'd be happy to."

"I hope this isn't being too picky or anything, but something else we talked about is telling everyone that we washed our hands before preparing a meal for others, since we may have to touch the ingredients more often."

"Right," George said. "I can promise you that I have, in fact, washed my hands, but that was probably last week sometime, so I'd be happy to wash them again now."

"That was a good comment to make, Albert," Margaret said. "We hope all of you continue to have guests over for meals, and mentioning that you washed your hands is a small but helpful effort. I know some students would rather not say this because you didn't have to say it with normal vision, but in school, we ask that you try it."

The sound of running water started toward the end of Margaret's comment.

"There, all tidy," George concluded, wiping his hands on his shirt. "Is there anything else anybody would like to ask about?"

There was no response.

"Are you sure?"

Silence continued.

"Are you really sure?"

"George, they're sure. You sound a little impatient. Are you sure you'd like to continue leading? It's fine if you'd like Mike to take over."

Mike hoped he wouldn't have to take over. It still felt better being off to the side, reading instructions and adding an occasional comment.

"Oh, I'm fine. After all, we're just getting to the fun part. I will now measure two cups of milk using one of the insightful ideas we've learned. In one hand, I will hold the milk carton, and in the other, I will hold the glass measuring cup. Since this thing holds two cups, my plan is to fill it almost to the top. I'll know when it's near the top by putting my finger on the rim, and just slightly inside. When I feel the milk on my finger, I know there are two cups. I like to pour very slowly, especially at the end."

Norman chimed in, "Good idea. That means you'll spill milk slowly instead of quickly."

The joke was poorly timed, since George was already a little frustrated. Mike expected his friend to snap back with a clever insult. Instead, George paused a moment before responding.

"I couldn't have said it better myself. Just remember, Coach, you'll be cooking in a few days. Then it's my turn to be in the peanut gallery." A quiet moment passed while George poured the milk. "There, if I am not mistaken, that's two cups of milk, which I will pour into the big bowl." He felt around for the big bowl and poured the milk inside.

"I want to add one more reminder," Margaret said. "For those of you with some functional vision, you may not have to put your finger on the rim. If you want, you can put the glass measuring cup in front of the black paper we hung by the counter. When you pour milk into the glass cup, in front of the black paper, you can see the milk better. If you are pouring something dark into the glass measuring cup, put it in front of the white tile."

"And, if you're pouring water into the thing," George added, "you're right back to sticking your finger on the rim. Now for the final challenge, I need to crack the eggs and add them to the mix."

"It's probably easiest to use a butter knife to crack them, instead of the plastic bowl," Margaret suggested.

"And watch out for shells," Norman grumbled.

George cracked the eggs and dropped the yolks into the bowl, quicker and with less drama than Mike expected. "I do believe that went all right. Michael, why don't you have a look inside the bowl, just to let these good folks know they won't be chewing on any eggshells."

"Good idea," Margaret said. "Just to be thorough, use the magnifying glass. It's in the same drawer as the measuring cups."

Mike held the magnifying glass in one hand and the large bowl in the other. He moved close to the light over the sink and carefully examined the ingredients.

"I'm doing my best to not make a Sherlock Holmes joke," George said.

"Good," Margaret replied. "Any shells, Mike?"

"I don't think so," he answered slowly, while continuing to examine the batter.

"Are you sure?" growled Norman.

"Aw, come on, Coach," George chided. "A little bit of roughage is good for the system."

Mike couldn't resist having some fun with Norman's concern. "Well, maybe one small shell, maybe. Nope, there has to be more than one. Wait, wait, it was a floater, damn things. Yep, looks fine."

"Very funny," Norman replied. Some of the force in his voice came out when he continued. "I'm starting to think that the best thing about this meal is that you two clowns won't be cooking again. And don't call me Coach." His voice became deeper and stronger when he asked, "Another thing, Mike, have you washed your hands?"

The room went silent. Mike hadn't actually touched any food yet, but he didn't feel like clarifying that detail to Norman.

"Not exactly," Mike answered.

"Once again, I'd like to ask that we finally cut the chatter and get something cooked." Margaret grabbed one of the boxes and walked to the text-enlarging machine, telling Mike to wash his hands while she walked. She placed the box under the camera and continued speaking. "We're almost at the end of the instructions. The next part is to add the muffin mix and stir thoroughly." She picked up the box again, opened it, and took out the bag of muffin mix from inside the box. "You'll need this," Margaret said while holding the bag toward Mike.

He took the bag from her, pulled the second bag out of its box, and cut both bags open with a scissor.

"Mikey, you add the mix. I'll stir, which means I get to lick the spoon."

There were some sighs and a grumble that could only be from Norman.

"George, I just said we need to get serious. Are you going to do that or would you like to repeat some of the after-class activities from last year?"

"I'm guessing you mean the part where I actively wash dishes after class?"

"You're guessing correctly."

George's voice was subdued when he replied, "Right, much as I enjoy invitations, there are more pleasant ways to spend my time after class."

Mike wondered if the after-class activity also involved Margaret staying with George and giving a stern lecture he didn't want to hear again.

"Good. So, you're agreeing to be more focused today and in future lessons?"

"I'd be happy to. Michael, you heard the lady, we need to get serious." George started mixing the batter and continued. "You put the wrappers in the muffin tins. I'll finish mixing this stuff, and we'll put a couple spoonfuls into each wrapper."

The two men focused on their work. The only sounds in the classroom were some tapping as they put batter into wrappers. The only words were occasional mumbles about which wrapper should be filled next, and when some of the batter missed its target.

"All right," George said, "they're all filled up. Time to pop 'em in the oven."

"Don't forget the oven mitts," Mike added.

"I was just thinking of that." George put on the mitts, opened the door with one hand, and used the other to place the muffin tins in the oven. He closed the oven door and asked, "How long do these things cook for?"

"Fifteen to twenty minutes," Margaret answered.

"I'll get it," Mike said, knowing he could set the timer faster than George. Mike leaned close to a timer, which was almost the size of a wall clock. He turned the dial to 15 minutes, and it started ticking, a little louder than other timers he'd heard.

George spoke again. "Well, there we go. Now, all we have to do is wait."

"Aren't you forgetting something?" Margaret asked.

"Very likely. Michael, I've been answering all the hard questions. Why don't you take this one?"

Mike paused, thought, and guessed. "Plates?"

"Good idea, but we'll take care of those in a moment. I was thinking of something else."

"Coffee," Norman muttered. "You jokers need to make some soon. I'm dying for a cup."

"Well, the last thing I want to do is let the coach down, so ..."

"I'll make it," Mike quickly added, to prevent George from making another joke. Besides, Mike felt it was a good idea to keep things moving, and he could make coffee faster than George, or most students, because of his relatively strong sight.

"All right," Margaret said, taking control of the class. "It'll only be a few minutes until the coffee and muffins are ready. Does anyone have questions or comments?"

Nobody answered. Margaret walked in front of the kitchen island and leaned back against it. She crossed her arms and waited for an answer. Mike was impressed again how a short woman seemed to stand so tall.

"Come on, folks, work with me here. This is the first time we've made a meal. I'm certain you have something to say about it. How does preparing this meal compare to the many meals you've prepared over the years?"

Albert responded with some concern. "Things went a lot slower than I expected, even for a simple recipe like this one. Don't get me wrong, I like cooking, but everything took a lot longer."

"Not to mention looking for things like eggshells," Norman said.

"Exactly," Albert added. "That all adds up to a lot of time, for each meal."

George walked back to his place at the wooden dining table and asked, "Did I mention Domino's?"

"George, don't push it," Margaret replied. "You're right, Albert. It will take more time, especially at first. I admit that's unpleasant, even frustrating, but the alternatives are even less pleasant. You could memorize the phone number to Domino's, like George. You could also go to a fast food place. Lord knows, the 1970s seem to be the decade of fast food. But do you really want to eat that stuff every day? Of course, there are better restaurants. These days, the current rage is all-you-can-eat salad bars. But who knows if that's going to last, and even if it does, traveling to a restaurant also takes time."

"I'm not kidding about Domino's. I make a call, and thirty minutes later, I eat."

Margaret sighed and rubbed her head. "George, not everybody can tolerate Domino's every day, or even every week."

"What about those new electronic ovens that are coming out?" Mike asked. "They use something like X-rays to heat food. They're supposed to be fast."

"You want to eat food that's gone through an X-ray machine?" Norman asked. "Sounds hazardous."

"I've seen the machines Mike is referring to," Margaret replied. "They don't use X-rays. They use microwaves. I'm sure these gadgets are another dining trend, like pizza delivery and all-you-can-eat salad bars. Microwave ovens can cook a meal in minutes, but that is one trend I see going nowhere. For starters, they cost about three hundred dollars. That's about a week's pay, for most people. Then, there's the food that comes out of the things. I tried a microwave meal at a conference a few months ago. It was a combination of tasteless mush and tasteless mush. I'm always open-minded to anything that can make cooking easier for the blind, but meals from a microwave oven can make TV dinners taste like fine dining."

The coffeepot started gurgling as Margaret finished speaking. "Mike, would you get everyone a cup? There's a serving tray next to the pots and pans."

Mike mumbled, "Sure," and started looking for the tray.

"I'd like to ask about that—TV dinners, that is," Norman added. "Back home, my wife cooked most of the meals. We're still trying to figure out how things will work once I finish school. Anyway, I'm cooking for myself while I'm living here. Compared to other options, TV dinners don't sound like such a bad idea. They save a lot of time."

"But can you really eat that stuff?" Margaret asked. "I mean, on a regular basis?"

"I could," Mike answered, filling a few cups of coffee and a coffee cup full of water for himself. "I admit, they're not the greatest, but if we're trying to live independently, TV dinners can help." He carried the tray to the table.

Margaret sighed and glanced toward Mike. "Any strategy for independent living is going to include a variety of options." She moved her glance toward Norman. "However, we advise caution when considering convenient food too early, which includes TV dinners, fast food, and Domino's." Her face settled in George's direction. "If convenient foods are considered too early, they tend to crowd out other options, more nutritious options, and certainly more tasteful options."

George scratched his nose and replied, "Hey, I'm all about taste, and that nutrition stuff's important too. I'm just say'n that I didn't cook much before I lost my sight. Now that I can't see, I'll probably cook less."

"That's a reasonable starting point, George. One of our goals is to show you a few simple tasks to make cooking easier. Those of you who haven't enjoyed cooking might find one or two ways to cook more often, especially from this class. Those of you who *have* enjoyed cooking can continue what you enjoy. We haven't heard much from Albert and Mary."

Albert responded. "I like cooking, always have, but I admit this is tougher than I expected. It seems like we have to relearn everything, like measuring, mixing, and working around a hot stove. I want to cook again. I don't want to eat TV dinners or fast food. But this is more than I expected."

"You're right, Albert. There are new things to learn." Margaret's voice sounded tired yet determined. "But I want to say again, we're here to help you learn. How about you, Mary?"

"I like to cook." Her voice was soft. "I've been cooking for my husband and kids for about twenty-five years. I tried cooking again when my sight faded." Mike suspected her head tilted forward a little. After a moment, she continued. "It was harder than I expected. Things that used to be so quick or easy ..." Her voice became even softer. "I was really looking forward to this class. I thought it would bring back some of the easy and fun parts of cooking for my family, but there are a lot of new things to remember."

Margaret's voice became almost as soft as Mary's. "I wish I could tell you this class or this program will bring back all your cooking skills, Mary. All I can say is that I know it's a tough situation, especially after spending so many years cooking for your family. I can tell you this class can help, one small step at a time. You can cook for them again. It'll be different, especially at first, but we're going to do our best to help."

Mary didn't respond.

"All right," Margaret said, her voice returning to normal. "The muffins will be done soon. George, why don't you get a plate and napkin for everyone? Mike, see if anybody needs a refill on coffee."

The timer rang soon after the two men walked back to the kitchen.

"I'll put a couple of muffins on each plate, since I'm getting the plates out anyway."

"Thanks, George," Margaret said. "As I mentioned at the start of class, I'd like to try the meals first, just to add any comments that might help with your cooking." George took the muffins out, put them on plates, and handed a plate to Margaret. Mike expected him to add a joke, but instead, George continued handing out plates, with an occasional "Here you go" and "One for you." After taking a bite, Margaret told everyone the muffins were fine, could have been cooked for longer, but she liked them a little moist.

In a few minutes, the group sat together eating their muffins and drinking coffee. Some of them occasionally chatted. Mike thought about the effort involved with making the muffins they were chewing. He also thought about Mary and how her voice was unusually soft. She never said a lot, but he worried about her, at least more than the others. She did sound stronger sometimes, especially when she made cooking suggestions.

"I hate to rush all of you, but we only have five minutes left to eat. We still need to clean up. Anyone who didn't cook has to clean, at least when George doesn't volunteer. Albert and Norman, could you help out today?"

The two men agreed, and the rest of the class finished their muffins and coffee. Mike grabbed his books, cane, and half a muffin. He walked out the door and thought about the next class, which was about home finance. He liked the topic because it gave more ideas for spending less, but there was also a somber reason for the class. Learning how to fill out a checkbook with less sight was just the starting point. Balancing a checkbook with less money was the hard part, at least for most of his new friends.

He walked out of Room 5 and wondered about the value of being cheap, with any income. His thoughts were interrupted when he felt a crunch inside his mouth. A moment later, he heard a deep voice holler down the hallway, "Michael, I thought you checked these things!" Apparently, some eggshells had found their way into the mix. He smiled, chuckled, and walked faster.

CHAPTER FOUR

Happy Hours

M ike walked slowly into the dayroom. One reason for being slow was that his body and mind were tired after a full week at school. Another reason was to be careful, since the room was barely lit. Some of the sunset passed through the skylight, but it only reached one corner. He walked through the light to a less lit corner. It was more subdued there, more relaxed. He felt around for a soft chair and sunk into it. As far as he could see and hear, the dayroom was empty, which didn't happen often. He rested his shoulders and enjoyed a moment with his thoughts. It seemed like days ago when he'd rushed through this dayroom to be on time for class, instead of just this morning.

Mike rested his head on the soft back of the chair and gazed forward. He wasn't sure when it had happened, but school wasn't new anymore. It wasn't bad, just not new. A couple of months ago, school was something to look forward to, a way to find some answers to an unexpected and unwelcome change. A couple of weeks ago, it was a new place with new people facing the same problem, and best of all, there were solutions to some problems. Now, it was routine. The people were still good, and the solutions still helped, but he had also learned the depth of the problem. "I'm probably just tired."

He shut his eyes and rested his shoulders. George would show up soon. They'd agreed to meet here at five o'clock. "But, George does live in his own time zone." Mike wondered what time it was and rolled his head in the direction of the clock, which hung on a post near the center of the room. It would tell him the exact time, but that would require standing up, walking a few steps, and coming back again. Sitting felt like a better idea, at least for a while. Some students would be walking through soon when the last classes for the week ended. He decided to enjoy some silence until then.

Mike exhaled slowly. There may have been the sound of a motorcycle outside. He wondered how cold it would be riding a cycle at this time of the year, although he used to ride his Honda well past the cooler days of autumn. His parents thought those rides were unusual, but that made them ever better, since Mike enjoyed being a little unusual. Of course, he never told his parents about some of the stunts he did on his motorcycle. They were risky and had led to some close calls, but those stunts had never caused a crash.

That had only happened once, during some routine cycling. A few years ago, he'd been coming out of a parking lot and looked the wrong way at the wrong time. He didn't even know the pickup truck was on the road until it crushed his left leg against the motorcycle's engine. He was still surprised at how they'd almost had to amputate the leg, yet all that remained was a scar about the size of his hand.

He let his head roll farther back into the cushion. Another faint sound wandered into the dayroom, maybe someone crying. "I hope not," Mike said to himself. He didn't want to ignore someone's cry.

He'd just had enough drama for a week. The silence returned, and he almost dozed off. There were some faint traffic sounds, probably from the road leading to Mariner's.

Some other sounds gradually came into the dayroom. They seemed like typical school sounds, but Mike couldn't identify specific parts. The sound of a door opening came from the area of Room 5, one of the first rooms that had become familiar. He heard footsteps next, followed by muffled conversations. They became clearer. Someone commented that they were happy it was Friday. Someone else suggested going out for dinner or drinks. Others agreed. When they were under the skylight, he opened his eyes to watch them pass.

When most of them had passed, he heard some students call back toward Room 5, with a combination of "Thanks for filling in" and "Have a good weekend." A woman responded with a combination of "Thanks" and "Have a good evening." The voice was young, probably a few years younger than Mike. After some more people passed, most of the silence returned, but he could still hear the woman by Room 5. A door shut, and some keys jingled, probably to lock the door. Mike imagined her as one of the new teachers at Bridgman's. She most likely had that young professional look, a business outfit that was a little neater than outfits on older teachers. She would probably teach whenever she could and speak in an upbeat style, choosing her words carefully.

The woman walked into the dayroom and stopped under the skylight, using the brighter light to find something in her purse. The first thing he noticed was her red hair. Even with his limited sight, he could tell her hair was a brighter red than any he'd seen before. He recognized her. She was one of the teachers he'd met on his first day during a short tour of the school. Besides her long red hair, this teacher was easy to remember because she was friendlier than most, and his twenty-something mind couldn't help but notice her wonderful shape. When they'd first met, he'd tried not to look too closely, but Mike enjoyed quietly looking now, from a dark corner of the dayroom.

She rotated slowly, pulled some things out of her purse, and moved them close to her face. That motion made Mike think her sight was similar to his. She rotated a little more, and Mike scanned her a little more, squinting to see better.

"Shit. Shit!" she said and walked quickly out of the room. He rolled his head toward her as she walked out. When she was out of sight, he heard more comments from her. "Dammit! Goddammit!"

When she was out of earshot, he said, "Damn, nice shape, lousy language."

Mike thought he was alone, so he was startled when he heard a laugh.

"I have to agree with you there, Mikey, very nice shape, at least that's what I hear. You've just met Samantha, or Sam. She's definitely one of the more colorful characters in our little family."

"Damn, George, you sure know how to sneak up on people."

"Ha, I haven't been able to sneak up on anybody for twenty years, or maybe forty pounds ago. You were just distracted, or maybe focused."

"I was just watching people, one of my favorite pastimes," replied Mike.

"If I had your sight, I would spend more time watching Sam, or any other young, thin, and gorgeous women Donny hires."

"I suppose. Who's Donny?"

George chuckled. "That short question has a long answer, which is best told with a drink, maybe two. I may not have the best cooking skills, but I can get us to a good bar in no time."

"Sounds good. What's the name of the bar?"

"That depends. What time is it?"

"I don't know, maybe a little after five."

"Well, go find out the exact time, and I'll tell you the exact bar. I know a couple good ones, and I hate waiting for a bus. So, my standard procedure is to take the bus that shows up first."

Mike walked toward the clock and asked, "How many bus routes have you memorized?"

"All the ones that matter. You got the time yet?"

"Ten minutes past five."

"It's going to be close, but if we hurry, we can catch the three forty-one to one of my favorites, The Slowstream Tavern." George lifted his hand, just above his waist. "Gimme your elbow."

Mike knew George was asking, or telling, him to be a guide as they walked. Mike stepped forward and placed his elbow in George's hand.

"Good, now step on it."

When they walked out of the dayroom, George told Mike to get some change ready for the bus fare. That slowed Mike down a little, but the light inside was still better than outside, which made it easier to find the right coins.

After they walked out of the school, George directed Mike to a nearby bus stop, where a bus was just driving away. They walked faster, yelled, and waved. Mike saw the brake lights come on as the bus slowed. When they stepped inside, the driver called out, "Hi, George, I had a feeling I'd be seeing you tonight."

"Hey, good to see ya," George said, still holding Mike's elbow.

They stepped into the bus and gave their bus fare to the driver. Mike found a place for them to sit, and the bus started to move.

"You know the driver?" Mike asked.

"I know a few of them, but I admit, I couldn't describe this one in particular. They hired some new drivers, so I'm still trying to tell them apart."

"How will we know when we're at the bar?"

"It's four stops," George answered, "but hopefully, she'll let us know when we're at the stop for The Slowstream."

Mike glanced out the window and noticed the bus was on a street he hadn't explored.

After the bus stopped twice, George commented, "You've gotten kind of quiet."

"This is a new street for me; kind of curious what's nearby."

"This part of the route winds around a bit. The first half is kind of a tough neighborhood. We should be passing by your place soon." George looked at Mike. "Why'd you pick that motel, anyway? These days, most students live in the new place that just went up, supposed to be the biggest one in town."

Mike waited a moment to answer, as the lights of Mariner's passed by. "It's cheaper and closer than the new place. Besides, I grew up in the country. We used to go camping and sleep in tents or a cabin. I don't need a lot to be comfortable." The bus slowed and stopped again.

"I guess, but there are supposed to be a lot of hookers and drug dealers around that place."

Mike smiled and joked, "Maybe a couple, but they're not that bad, just misunderstood."

"Right. Well, the direction we're heading now takes us into a nicer part of town. Surprising how fast things change in a couple of blocks."

George made some more comments about the neighborhood, but Mike focused on the buildings outside. He was still talking when the driver called out, "This one's yours, George. Tell Shelly I said hi."

"I'd be happy to, and thanks again for the lift."

They had only taken a few steps into the bar when Mike heard a woman's voice and smelled the smoke from several cigarettes.

"George, it's about time you showed up. Wasn't sure if I'd see you this week. C'mon, I think your favorite booth's open."

George followed the waitress, and Mike followed George. The lights were dim, like most bars, so Mike couldn't clearly see the woman. He wondered what her age was, but it was hard to guess, since they were talking, walking, and avoiding obstacles. Some obstacles were chairs, and others were customers.

George called out to Shelly, "Maybe I'll make up for it this weekend. Lately, I've been spending more time becoming the fine student I aspire to be."

"Sounds like they're hassling you about your grades again," she said. "I've been trying to tell ya to bring your books here. That way, we could all help with your homework, but you never listen."

"I appreciate your gracious offer of help, again. But like I said before, we don't really have grades or much homework. I just need to show up on time more often."

"Or at all," she joked. "I'll never figure out how there can be a school without grades or homework, but I never was a very good student, as long as they're taking care of you." She led the men through the crowded bar, slowed, and said, "Here's your booth."

After they sat, Shelly asked, "Who's your friend?"

"This is Mike. He showed up at Bridgman's a couple of weeks ago. I've volunteered to lead his welcoming committee. And of course, the first order of business is coming here to meet you, and maybe have a drink or two." They sat and George continued. "Mike, this is Shelly. You won't find a finer, funnier, or feistier waitress in all of Portage Bay."

"Good to meet you, Mike. George is the right man to lead your welcoming committee, as long as you don't get caught in the binds he finds himself in."

"I'm the victim of a curious mind," replied George.

"Right, you and all the other guys who are still trying to be twenty."

"I'm not that far away from my twenties, and Mike is still officially a twenty-something."

"Good for you, Mike, and who knows, you may be able to keep up with George. What can I get for ya?"

"We were going to have a couple of beers, but I'm starting to wonder how Michael will do on the Sloe Screw gauntlet. Michael, you mind skipping the beers to try out the gauntlet?"

"Sure," mumbled Mike, wondering what the gauntlet was.

"It seems like you're making a tradition of welcoming new people with a walk down the gauntlet, which works for me. It's as good as anything else to get your mind off your worries. Last time, you had me bring out the first two drinks right away. You want that again?"

"Sounds great. The first two always go the fastest."

"Coming up."

After she walked away, Mike asked, "What's a Sloe Screw gauntlet?"

"A hell of a lot of fun, but you're probably asking about the drinks. It's a list of drinks, in order. The first one is the basic Screwdriver, orange juice and vodka. Then, we move on to something a little sweeter, the Sloe Screw, which is orange juice and sloe gin."

Mike recognized these drinks from the times he and some cousins had played pool in small-town bars. During most of these times, they were legally too young to be in a bar, but usually, that wasn't a problem.

George continued. "I'm not clear on all the details after that, which may or may not come as a surprise. Anyway, some of the drinks are the Sloe Comfortable Screw, a Sloe Screw with a Twist, and a Sloe Comfortable Screw with a Twist. Actually, you can add *with a twist* to most of the names. A few of the names add *against the wall* somewhere." George thought for a moment. "I think the longest name is A Sloe Comfortable Screw Against the Wall, with no Damn Twist. I rarely get to that one, but who knows, maybe this'll be our lucky night. Speaking of a lucky night, what was the deal this morning, when you told me you didn't sleep much?"

Mike didn't remember making that exact statement, but it was close enough. "You know, when you're as good looking as me, getting a full night's sleep once a week can be tough."

"Don't I know it," George replied. "Anybody I know?"

"Which one?" Mike asked with a smile, not sure if George was trying to call his bluff or get some gossip.

"Right, in other words, you haven't got any in many moons."

"Longer than that, actually."

Both men laughed, and George added another comment.

"Don't I know it. Well, that reminds me of something that'll give you another reason to drink. Sex is something that becomes even more scarce when you've lost your sight."

"Really?" Mike hadn't thought of that before.

"Yep. I saw some stats on it a while back, but I also see it around the school. More than one guy has lost his wife after losing his sight. Seems to happen most to the rich ones. I'm serious. One day, these guys are making buckets of money, buying all kinds of toys, and getting more sex than they know what to do with. Then a few days later, they lose their sight, their big paycheck, and just to add insult to injury, no nookie. Well, sometimes it takes a few months before the missus packs up, but you get the idea."

The conversation paused while Mike thought about George's comment. Mike didn't like the idea of less sex, like most guys in their mid-twenties, but he also didn't like the idea of less work. He started asking a question about less work when George continued. "So, what did you do before showing up at this little country club? Didn't you say something about making tractor parts?"

Mike cleared his mind and answered the question. "Yeah, I worked there for about three years. Good place, good pay." He also started to hope the drinks would arrive soon.

"What kind of parts did you make, engine parts?"

"Not too often. We made gears, so they weren't usually in the engine itself. Most of them were cylinders about two feet long. Others were a couple of inches or yards."

"Right, probably used in the tranny, power-transfer stuff. I used to help my friends fix their tractors. Kinda cool to think we may have worked with some of the gears you made. So what's involved with making a gear? Do you just set up some big lathe, throw in a metal tube, and push a button?"

"Exactly. Then we take a break. Union rules."

"Great," George replied. "So you're the reason spare parts cost so much."

"I like to think your hard-earned money went to a good cause—me." Both men chuckled. "How about yourself? What did you do before coming to Bridgman's?" Mike asked.

"I worked on cars, always liked tinkering with stuff. I'm lucky because I can still help with them."

"You still work on cars?"

"I wish," George answered. "I help by answering questions. People have all kinds of 'em."

"Like what?"

"That one's easy. The more people ask me questions, the more I give three answers. First, please don't kill yourself or bleed a lot. I hate seeing all that sticky blood splattered over a perfectly good engine. Second, car repairs can be like rabbits. It's amazing how more can show up if you don't show a little patience. And third, never, ever use a butter knife, no matter how tempting or brilliant it may seem. That takes care of about half the problems. I help with the other half by remembering back to my time in a garage or by asking around."

"George is the first guy I turn to." Mike was surprised to hear Shelly's voice. "He kept my old truck going for years. When it finally died, he told me to get a used Datsun. At first, I thought he was nuts, but now, I love it, especially with these crazy gas prices." She placed two glasses in front of each man. "Here are the opening drinks in George's famous gauntlet—two Screwdrivers and two Sloe Screwdrivers. Enjoy."

Mike looked at the glasses. It felt a little odd having two drinks in front of him, but they also looked unusually appealing.

"Thanks very much, Shelly," George said as she walked away. He lifted a drink and added, "Michael, here's to your first time at The

Slowstream Tavern, your first attempt at the gauntlet, and many more of both."

Mike raised his glass back at George, thinking that was enough of a response. Then he remembered that George was completely blind, so he added, "Thanks." Both men took a long swallow.

The drink tasted unusually good, especially since Mike hadn't had one in a few weeks. He rested back in the booth, scanned the crowd, and asked, "So, you came to the school about two years ago?"

George also rested back and answered, "Yeah. I'm not always the fastest learner." Then he returned to a previous subject. "It's pretty cool that you made parts, always wondered what that was like."

Mike suspected George didn't want to talk about repeating classes, which wasn't too surprising. Mike decided to share more about his work. "It's not that complicated. Actually, someone else made the parts. I was in deburring, so—"

George interrupted Mike and asked, "De-what?"

"Deburring. We took the burrs off of gears that had just been cut by a different group. Burrs are little bits of metal that stick to a part after it's made."

"I see. I imagine they'd raise hell in a tranny if you didn't take them off."

"Exactly. Those little burrs were probably the hardest part of the job. Damn things had a way of flying into your skin."

"Ouch," George said, cringing a little. "That sounds like mosquitoes with an attitude."

"That's about it."

Both men drank again.

"This may sound strange, but your work will change one of the classes you'll take. There's good news and bad news. Which do you want to hear first?" George asked.

"The good news."

George answered in a cheerful tone. "The good news is that you won't have to spend much time learning how to read Braille."

"Really, how do you know that?" Mike asked, wondering if his work gave him some unknown advantage.

"That involves the bad news. Your hands probably show that you worked for a living, if you'll pardon the expression. Folks who work in an office have hands that are soft, nice, and ever so sensitive. They have less trouble learning Braille because they can actually feel those damn little bumps. Guys like you and me can't feel the damn little bumps because we've worked with our hands a lot, and we have the calluses to show for it. I don't know all the details, but somebody here told me that working with your hands leads to thicker skin, calluses, and maybe something else that makes it hard for us to read Braille. It's a shame, really. I used to enjoy reading."

Mike took another drink and was surprised that the glass was empty. He moved it toward the edge of the table so Shelly could pick it up. It bumped into another empty glass with a clinking sound. Mike felt some comfort that they were drinking at the same pace.

"Me too," Mike replied and pulled his second drink closer. "There must be some options."

"Not many, at least not options that have worked for me," George said. "The teachers push the idea of books on tape a lot. I tried them, but I could never get into it. My mind wanders if I sit around listening to anyone for too long, even a book on tape. Maybe I'll try them again sometime."

"Bummer. I hope tapes work for me. I really like to read. With luck, I won't have to worry about them for a couple of years. I can still read with a magnifying glass," Mike added with cautious optimism. He was also starting to feel the effects of his first drink, which made him take another long swallow from the second.

"Really? Good for you. Not many people here can do that. Is your sight supposed to stay that way or get worse? I don't like focusing on sad stuff too much, gets addictive, but a lot of folks come here while their sight is changing, usually for the worse."

"I never thought about that. It must be tough being around people who are losing more of their sight."

George's voice became more serious. "You'll learn for yourself soon enough. Everybody here is dealing with some tough stuff, but losing more sight isn't the hardest part. The hardest part is rebuilding a life. It's easy enough for some. Others never quite make it. I'll tell you more about that later. You never answered my question. You gonna be able to read for a while or not?"

"They don't know for sure," Mike replied, still thinking about how his sight would fade.

"They never know for sure. What's their best guess?"

"I should keep this level of sight for six months, maybe a year," Mike said in a subdued tone.

"Sounds good to me, man. What I would give to have six months of eyesight, even what you're seeing. I never took very good care of my diabetes, and one day, my sight just faded. There wasn't much time to have a last look."

Mike wanted to say that something similar had happened to him, but George kept talking.

"Talk about a bad day. The good news is that most days have been better ever since," George said with an upbeat tone. He laughed a little and added, "Especially if you consider the hangover that soon followed." He laughed some more. "That sucker lasted for days."

"I suppose," Mike replied. He was going to add more, but he saw Shelly walk up. He slid an empty glass to the edge of the table so she could take it away.

Shelly added her thoughts. "Personally, I think a little hangover is a small price to pay to get away from your worries for a while. How're you guys do'n?"

George finished his drink, and Mike thought about the hangovers they'd have tomorrow.

"Better by the minute, Shelly, better by the minute. I was just about to tell Mikey about some ways to make the best of his sight, like the teachers at Bridgman's."

"Since you put it that way," she replied, "you're probably talking about how the teachers look, so you could be talking about Donny."

"Careful, I wanted Mike to figure that out on his own."

"Right. Should I get the next two drinks in the gauntlet?"

"That would be wonderful," George answered.

Mike finished his drink and handed the glass to Shelly. She took it and the three others.

After she walked away, Mike asked, "Who's Donny?"

"I'll tell you about him in a moment. First, I want to get back to some things you've probably seen. You're new to this place, and you're more legally blind than blind. Have you noticed a certain pattern among the teachers at Bridgman's?"

Mike was surprised at the question. Part of him wanted to find a cautious answer, since his instinct was to respect teachers and the

Women's Lib movement, but the drinks and George's style made him less cautious, and a little curious. "Well, compared to the vo-tech I went to, they're similar in some ways. Some teachers are easier to work with. Some at the vo-tech gave more homework than others, but we don't have homework here. Most of the teachers at the vo-tech were men, but that makes sense since I studied small engine repair."

"Give that a little more thought."

"You mean that there's more women here?" Mike asked.

"That's one way to ask the question. Another way is 'Are there many men?'—teachers, that is."

Mike shifted his glance, thought about the teachers, and answered. "Now that you mention it, I haven't met many."

"And, actually, the few men who are on the staff have a uniquely dorky appearance," George joked. "At least, that's what I'm told, but I think they sound that way too. Here's another question. Did you meet the school president when you first arrived?"

"Yeah, I remember he had on a lot of aftershave. I think his name was Harold, or maybe Donald. He introduced himself, some office staff, and some teachers."

"He goes by Donald, but the important part is the teachers that he introduced you to. Do you have any thoughts on them or the teachers in your classes?"

Mike considered the question for a moment and answered. "Well, they seem nice enough. I remember meeting Margaret. Even then, she seemed friendly but sort of businesslike. There were a few more. All of them were friendly, especially the one with bright red hair."

"The one with the red hair was very friendly. That's interesting, but a topic for later. Now, stop being a nice guy, talking about personalities, and start thinking like a typical guy, and talk about something far more fun."

"All right, I get it."

"Took you long enough."

"They're all women and young." Mike paused and lifted his eyebrows. "And fit."

"That's one way to put it. And who hires them?"

"Donald."

"Who you'll soon be calling Donny, I imagine. Don't get me wrong, I like being around gorgeous women as much as the next guy, even if I can't see 'em. But Donny takes it too far. He hires them one day, and soon after the next, he's on the pretty-boy version of a hunt, for yet another affair. One crummy part is that the guy has a decent wife. Another is that the weaker ones usually fall for it. Besides falling into the sack with the jerk, they usually fall in love with him. Then comes the real mess, after Donny returns to the hunt. He moves on to another young teacher, and the one he leaves behind feels pretty messed up. She just started a new job, slept with her boss, and thought it was a relationship. Most of them feel guilty about it, but Donny's the problem."

"Really, the president of our school?"

"Yep, a few teachers have mentioned it over the years," George said as he took another drink.

"Wow, he does sound like a jerk."

"He is, but it's complicated. I hate to give Donny any credit, but he's brought in a lot of grant money. If it wasn't for his money, we'd still be in a ratty old building making chump change, spending all day stuffing nails into bags."

"Nails?" Mike asked.

"Yeah, some company has been paying students to put nails into bags since the early days of Bridgman's. Then the company sells the bags, and probably gets a juicy tax write-off in the process. The evening news didn't make a breaking story out of that particular collaboration of business and government. They have prisoners make license plates, and they have blind folks stuff nails into bags. We still wonder who's better off. Anyway, that changed after Donny showed up—at least, it's a smaller part. He brought in a couple big grants, so we got a new building and more staff, and students started getting better jobs. I imagine some of this would have happened without Donny, but his grant money and contacts moved it along."

"Men who make a lot of money seem to mess around with a lot of women," Mike answered. He heard Shelly walk up and turned toward her.

"It sounds like you're still talking about Donny," she said while putting down four more drinks. "This time, you each have a Sloe Screw Against the Wall and a Sloe Screw Against the Wall with a Twist, which has a lime on the rim."

"Thanks again, my dear. Michael and I were just discussing what Donny gives and takes from the school."

"I'm not sure what to think of it all," she replied. "His money has done a lot for students and teachers. Still, if I were his wife, I'd kick his ass. Hell, I'd like to kick his ass anyway. A few of the women he's screwed over stop in here sometimes. It's not pretty."

George chuckled and replied, "Michael, did I tell you she was a little feisty?"

"You call it feisty. I call it clear," Shelly added in a tone that was friendly but firm. "Can I get anything else for you guys?"

"Not right now, thanks," George answered.

Mike thought Shelly nodded, then walked to another table.

"It's funny how a hunt doesn't change that much," George said while biting into a lime.

"Huh?" mumbled Mike.

George chewed on the lime and continued. "What I was talking about, before Shelly showed up. The hunt is pretty much the same in the woods as it is in the office." George chuckled again. "The animals don't change much either."

"You've lost me here, George."

"Sorry. I mean, when animals hunt in the woods, the weakest are the most common target. And, when Donny hunts in the office, he also goes for the weakest, the ones who need somebody and fall for his slick style. I don't think you've met many of the weaker ones. They usually teach workshops instead of the classes you're in. But you've definitely met one of the stronger ones. She's the one I caught you staring at in the dayroom. Her name is Samantha, talk about a pistol. She's younger than most teachers, came here fresh out of grad school." George laughed a little. "But she also has more personality than most, very quick with jokes and jabs. That turns off some people, but I get a kick out of her. Besides, Sam's one of the few people I know who shares my enthusiasm for exploring new drinks, while never losing interest in the old ones."

"Wow. Young, funny, and quick—I'm surprised Donny hasn't hunted her, even if she's one of the stronger types."

"I see what you mean," George said. He took a drink and continued. "But there is one side of her personality that may keep Donny away. If somebody pushes her too far, I try to quickly make the conversation calm. If that doesn't work, I recommend leaving the room, possibly the building."

"Sounds complicated. What sets her off?"

"Sam can get annoyed by a few things, unfortunately. One of them is people who carry on about driving their cars, or their damn little cocoons as she calls them. 'Hard on the outside and few brain cells on the inside,' she likes to say. She gets even more pissed off at cars with tinted windows."

That surprised Mike, so he asked, "What's the big deal?"

"It's just something she carries on about once in a while. She says drivers with those windows are intentionally sealing themselves off from any responsibility, on the road or off. One time, Sam was really carrying on about it after a few drinks. She said that it's fine if they want to be sealed off. We should seal them off in a jail cell or dungeon, according to her. She was really serious about it."

"I guess I can see what she means, but overreacting doesn't help."

"That's what I thought," George said, sounding confident. "For good, bad, and otherwise, I like to have a little fun with people who repeat a tirade. After hearing it a couple times, I told her that maybe some of those drivers had problems with their eyes, and the tinted windows cut back on the glare."

"Makes sense."

"That's what I thought, but Sam was having none of it. She became even more determined and said those drivers could wear sunglasses. Things got ugly after that."

Mike asked what happened.

"I still wanted to have some fun with it, not too bright on my part but what the hell. I said that she might want to have tinted windows if she could see well enough to drive. That's when she growled."

"Growled?"

George smiled at the question. "Most certainly. It's not often you hear a woman growl, so when you do, you remember. The words *I would not* were mixed in there somewhere, but mostly, it was a growl."

"Wow."

"Yeah, I figured that was a really good time to calm things down, so I told a joke or agreed, or something like that."

"That was probably a smart idea," Mike said.

"It is kind of bizarre, but like a lot of things, you get used to it. I've seen her go off on a few people. Eventually, most of them get used to her."

Both men took a long drink. Mike shook his head and said, "That's a new one on me. Haven't met many people who get that determined."

"Like I said, I like her overall, lot of fun, just got to be a little careful. She has a couple hang-ups, but who doesn't? I have to say, though, your comment about Sam being more friendly than the rest is unusual. She's normally more intense and sarcastic than the rest, instead of more friendly. Maybe she got laid the night before or something. Rumor has it she likes that too."

Mike smiled at the comment and replied, "Sounds like a typical redhead."

"You're not the first one to say so. Maybe even more lively than typical."

"Lively can be fun," Mike replied. "It sure beats dull, but it sounds like she gets too lively sometimes."

"Yeah, Sam can get pretty worked up," George said while leaning forward and resting his elbows on the table. "But like I said before, a lot of people at Bridgman's have a hang-up or two. People like Sam get pissed off pretty easy. Others cry a lot. I drink more than I used to. There's just no getting around the fact that losing your sight is going to get on your nerves. About half the people at school will be sorting through emotional stuff for a few years, maybe longer, and a little less than half get over the initial shock pretty well."

"A little less than half—what about the rest?"

"A small number do really well. They learn to use a cane, work with a dog, read Braille, compete in blind sports, jump buildings in a single bound, all that stuff."

Mike wanted to ask more about working with a dog and learning Braille, but George continued.

"In places like our wonderful school, you have them all. The really tricky part comes when school's out, but that's a topic for another story. There I go carrying on again, sorry about that. I do enjoy talking about our colorful cast of characters. As the unofficial coordinator of your welcoming committee, I should be asking you more questions." George paused, took a drink, and continued. "I've been meaning to ask, what brought you to our little school?"

Mike was still getting used to answering this question. A few days ago, other students had started asking him how he lost his sight, as they got to know each other better. It still felt awkward to answer, so he liked to start with a short reply. "Bad luck, mostly."

"That reason comes up a lot. Which version of bad luck took your sight?"

Mike sipped his drink, glanced off, and said, "I've always had a bad eye and a good eye." He was interrupted when Shelly walked to their booth.

"I'll say one thing for your trip down the gauntlet tonight. You guys are moving along at record speed. Glad you're having a good time."

George replied in one of his jolly tones. "What's not to enjoy? We've got good company, good drinks, and good stories."

Shelly smiled and added, "Some of which are actually true."

"Are you suggesting I may, on occasion, misrepresent the truth? You realize I would take great offense."

"I would never say such a thing, George. We all love your stories. I just wanted to say that I'm glad you're having a good time. That's all." She leaned toward Mike. "You just let me know if you wonder about any of George's stories. I'll set you straight."

"There you go again," George replied with feigned accusation. "Now, Shelly, my dear, you do know that one or two stories about a particular star athlete are very true, and very impressive I might add." Mike saw a satisfied smirk on George's face.

Shelly replied with feigned disappointment. "Aw nuts, you're going to tell the beepball story again." She looked at Mike. "I'm sorry, Mike. I really am. The rest of your evening will now be spent listening to George tell the story of his all-star moment this summer." She leaned close to Mike and spoke in a loud whisper, so George could hear. "I'll rush the next few drinks to make it more bearable."

"I suppose," Mike said and smiled.

The three laughed. Shelly told them she'd be back soon with the drinks and walked away.

"Well, now, I have to tell you the story, but I promise, this'll be the short version. I admit that I've never been the athletic type, as you can probably tell. I play a game sometimes, but usually, I'm happy to cheer from the bench. There's nothing like the sound of a good game. The crowds are cheering. The ball is beeping, and the players have a great time trying to find that little beep. How much do you know about beepball?"

"Only a little," Mike answered.

"That's okay. I'll explain more later. For now, you can think of it as another version of softball." Both men took a drink. George relaxed in the booth and continued. "Our team had a pretty good season. We won some games and lost some. But then, things got real interesting just before the last game of the season. A few days before that game, one player got hurt and another had to be out of town. That meant they asked me to get off the bench and actually play. That was fine with me, since I'm mostly there for the laughs." George sat upright and put his elbows on the table. "It turned out to be a pretty good game. Sometimes, we were ahead. Sometimes, they were ahead. And in the bottom of the last inning, it was a tie."

Mike enjoyed the story and how much fun George was having as he told it.

"After that, things happened fast. Our first batter got a hit but got out before reaching first base. Our second batter struck out, and our third batter made some people nervous because that batter was me." George smiled and pointed to himself. "Maybe I should have felt nervous too. After all, the game was tied. We were in the bottom of the last inning, and there were two outs. But, all that didn't really get to me. I play ball for the fun, the laughs, and an occasional beer." He raised his glass and drank from it to emphasize the point.

"I stepped into the batter's box and took some warm-up swings. I couldn't resist making some comments to my buddies on the other team. I asked them if they wanted to give up now or suffer through the way I was going to clobber the ball. We exchanged more great insults and laughs, only stopped when the ref suggested that we play some ball."

George pointed a thumb backward, over a shoulder. "I started joking with him too, but he encouraged me not to, something to do with throwing me out of the game. I thought it would be a better idea to get back into the batter's box, and I'm glad I did. The pitcher called out 'Ready, set, ball!' and I heard that little 'beep, beep, beep.'" He put his hands together, as if holding an imaginary bat. "I was more than ready to take a swing, and I swung hard! The bat connected with the ball in a way that felt downright magical. After clobbering it, I couldn't stop laughing, and when I did, I couldn't stop telling the other team how great the hit was. It was so much fun that I forgot to run. That was actually all right, since they had a great time telling me the ball was foul." George laughed, took a drink, and said, "That was strike one."

"This is the short version of the story?" Mike asked with a laugh.

"Oh yeah, this is definitely the short version, and it'll get longer if you keep interrupting me. Anyway, I smarted off for a while longer, but then, the second pitch came in." He held the imaginary bat again and looked past his left shoulder, as if a ball was coming in. "And I gave it another big swing! I can still feel that one too. It's a good thing there was some dust on the bat. Otherwise, nothin' would have touched the ball."

Mike smiled, and George continued. "The other team busted up in laughter. That's okay with me. Sometimes, they have a laugh at me, and sometimes, I have a laugh at them. Like I said, that's a part of the game I enjoy most, at least usually. Something changed this time. I started craving that hit. I even cut back on the jokes. So, I dug my feet into the batter's box, took a couple of practice swings, and waited for the third pitch." He held the imaginary bat, looked toward the imaginary ball, and spoke in a calm voice, at first.

"The pitcher called out again, 'Ready, set, ball.' The beep floated my way, and I tried clobbering it!" He swung the bat. Mike felt like ducking, since the bat would have come close to his head. After the swing, George paused.

"And?" Mike asked.

George laughed and took a drink. "And, all I hit was dust, but at least I swung harder than before. I swung so hard that I almost went down in a spiral after I missed. It could have had something to do with the beer. That wasn't the most dignified maneuver I ever performed, but it did get a laugh—from both teams."

"Bummer. That means you struck out," Mike said.

"Actually not, that's one difference between beepball and softball. We get four strikes instead of three. After all, we're swinging at a moving beep, not a softball you can see." George held up a pointer finger. "So, I had one strike left. Like I said, I've never been the athletic type, but this was one of the moments where I can see why people get into it." He slowly pointed left and right. "Both teams were standing. Both teams were yelling, all at me. Every once in a while, I enjoy having some attention, but this was a bit much." He laughed a little and pointed a thumb over a shoulder. "Eventually, the ref had to calm things down, so I could hear the pitcher." His voice became calm. "I decided it was just me and the ball. The people didn't matter. The game didn't matter. All that mattered was me and that damn little beep. If I missed, I missed, but I was going to give it my best shot."

George took another drink, but Mike didn't, since he was too interested in the story. George held the bat, swung slowly, and spoke calmly. "My fourth swing actually felt better than my first. I didn't even swing that hard, but damn, it was solid. I heard cheers, and I heard curses. I just knew the game was over."

"I suppose." Mike raised his drink toward George to give a toast. When George didn't reply, Mike remembered, again, that his friend was completely blind. He thought how easy it was to forget that. Maybe it was the drinks. He added, "Here's a toast to this year's beepball hero, George."

George raised his glass and thanked Mike. Both men drank. While setting down his glass, Mike said, "It sounds like a great game. I've played some softball, using the same priorities you mentioned. It'd be fun to try beepball sometime."

"Well, if you're going to do that, you'll need to know the rules. The ball is as good a place to start as any. It's a little bigger than a softball and, as you probably figured out, it beeps. Sometimes, it seems like the entire game is about finding a beep. Sounds strange, but there it is. Anyway, I'll get to the rules. First off, all players must wear a blindfold since most have some sight. That also allows all players to be equally frustrated in finding the damn beep. A team scores a run anytime a runner gets to a base, and there are only two bases, first and third. Softball has people who stay on a base. Beepball doesn't. Basically, a batter has to get to first or third base before anyone in the outfield holds the ball, which comes down to finding and holding a beep."

"Wow, the rules are really different. What about hitting? That has to be hard."

"It is, which leads to another difference. When you're hitting, the pitcher is on your side and tells you when he lets go of the ball."

"The pitcher is on the same side as the batter? That's kind of strange."

"I guess so, but you try hitting a beep that's thrown by someone who doesn't want you to hit it. It's hard enough when the beep is thrown by someone on your side."

"I suppose. All right, I think I get it. If I'm batting, the pitcher is on my side. He makes it an easy pitch and tells me when the ball's in the air. Then, I wait for the right moment and swing. If I get a hit, I run to first or third base. Hold it, if I'm blindfolded, how do I find the base?"

"Good question. You run to the base that starts buzzing. After a hit, someone randomly picks a base, by pressing a button somewhere."

"So there's buzzing and beeping. Any more sounds?"

"I like to heckle from the sidelines," George said with a smile. "But those are the main sounds."

"All right, so if I get a hit, I run to the buzzing base. I need to get there before someone in the outfield finds the beep. There are probably other details, but are those the main ones?"

"I'm impressed. That's about it. I hope you give it a try sometime, sounds like you might enjoy it."

"I suppose."

"Anyway, I'll move on to skiing, since beepball is months away. Skiing is coming up and a lot simpler, especially for me. My first rule is to find the chalet. The second rule is optional, but I have been striving for it more lately. After all, a guy has to stay ambitious. The second rule is to find a table by the fireplace in the chalet. After that, I pretty much call the event a success."

"Just out of curiosity, does anybody actually ski?" Mike asked.

"I've never understood why, but yes, most people do. I'm one of the few who doesn't. Some of the teachers are pretty good. It helps a lot that a local ski resort goes out of its way to help blind folks. They give us free lift tickets and bought some bright vests that blind skiers wear. Sometimes, legally blind folks ski like anyone else, but other times, they have a ski buddy with them."

"Sounds like it could work," Mike said.

"Actually, it works pretty well. They even have those zigzagging races where skiers turn by flags."

Mike was enjoying the conversation so much that he didn't see Shelly walk up.

He noticed her when she said, "I can hardly believe it when I watch those guys ski." She placed two more drinks in front of each man.

"Hey, now, there are plenty of women skiing as well, watch your language," George commented to Shelly, slurring the last few words.

"Yeah, yeah, you know I mean both. Like I was saying, I still get amazed when I watch those guys ski. I've been serving blind students for more years than I'm going to tell ya. I've always been impressed at how well you get on with ordinary stuff, not sure I'd be as good at it. But skiing when you're blind? It's hard enough for me to ski with sight. I don't know if they're brave or nuts, especially when they race. I mean, Jesus Christ, ski at full speed with no sight. That takes a lot of balls, for men and women."

"Makes me want to drink just thinking about it," George added.

"Well, that's what I'm here for," Shelly said. "This time, you have two drinks from our Sloe Comfort series, which have some Southern Comfort. One is a Sloe Comfortable Screw Against the Wall with a Twist, and the other is A Sloe Comfortable Screw Against the Wall with a Bump. The Twist has a lemon on the rim. The Bump has a couple of hazel nuts inside but no lemon. Other than that, the two drinks taste surprisingly similar."

"It all tastes good to me," George replied while reaching out for a drink and pulling one close.

"See you guys in a little while," she said and walked away.

"I have another question. If there are races, some things must be similar to beepball, like wearing blindfolds." George agreed, and Mike continued. "Do the flags buzz, like the bases in beepball?"

"Another good question. The flags don't buzz because buzzers need a battery, which don't do so well on a freezing ski slope. So instead, each racer has a ski buddy who calls out directions from behind. There's also a volunteer standing by each flag and shaking a tambourine. You could be asked if you're not careful. They need folks with better sight, since you only shake the tambourine when a skier gets about twenty yards from the flag."

"I'd like to help, but if a battery freezes, I probably would too."

"Oh, it wouldn't be that bad. At least you have an occasional adrenaline rush when a blind skier aims for your tambourine at high speed." George laughed and added, "I assure you that only a few tambourine shakers get clobbered each year."

"Great. It sounds better to join you in the chalet. I'm surprised enough people ski to have a decent competition."

"Well, that's the interesting part. A few are practically professional skiers, including some teachers. One or two went to the finals of some national ski race a couple of years ago."

"Really? I haven't met anyone who was that good at sports."

"Some are that good. Sometimes, people with other handicaps show up. One woman lost her legs as a girl. Now, she uses prosthetics to ski, very fast. I actually left the chalet once or twice when she was skiing. Even though I couldn't see how fast she was going, her skiing seemed to sound different. Maybe Shelly has a point. That woman has more balls than I'll ever have, or probably want."

Mike couldn't sort out the emotion that was in George's voice. That could be from the drinks affecting George's words, Mike's thoughts, or both. Regardless, Mike felt proud of these blind athletes but also felt sad about something, until a question came to mind.

"This is a little weird, George. Some blind or disabled people take skiing seriously enough to compete, at high speeds, with the best in the country. People you've met. But almost every week, I hear crying at school. What's going on with that?"

George's tone became somber, even though it wasn't sober. "I don't have that one entirely figured out. I've met blind people who amaze me. For the most part, they're just ordinary folks, but they don't stop. They may pause, but they don't stop. I've heard the amazing folks are just more determined, and I've heard they're obsessed, or nuts. All I can say is that they just keep going. You certainly don't compete in blind sports for the money or TV time. But it's still confusing. A lot of other ordinary folks end up crying a lot—good, hardworking folks."

George sipped his drink and gazed off toward the people in the bar. "In a lot of ways, I can't blame 'em. I mean, we can't drive anymore, can't watch a movie, and only about half of us ever work again. Then, there are the simple things that take about twice as long as they used to, like making muffins. Sometimes, it gets on my nerves too. Sometimes, I get seriously pissed off, but overall, I'm happy enough that I haven't let it clobber me. I still help with cars, find someone to have a beer with, and I still laugh, pretty hard sometimes." George smiled a little at the last few words, finished his drink, and added, "It's not exactly the meaning of life, but it works for me."

Mike was surprised at how thoroughly George answered the question. He wanted to think about everything his new friend said or ask a follow-up question, but George continued.

"Sorry about that, didn't mean to dump a lot on ya. There is one more important thought I need to share."

Mike leaned forward, hoping for an intriguing conclusion.

"I need to pee."

Mike leaned back.

"You mind guiding me to the men's room? I've laughed with half the people in this bar, but I usually annoy someone if I walk to the boys' room by myself. The path has too many moving targets, so I end up bumping into some schmuck. Then, he spills his beer. It lands on his girlfriend. She yells at him, and he yells at me. Then he feels bad since I'm a blind schmuck, which makes her feel bad, or else she yells at him for yelling at me. Meanwhile, I'm standing there nearly peeing in my pants while the whole thing plays out, again. It's a lot less complicated if somebody guides me."

Mike mumbled, "Sure, I need to go as well." The two men stood up.

"Leaving already?" Shelly asked. "I thought you were staying for a while, so I brought the next two drinks."

"Oh, we're staying, just need to get rid of the last few. Hey, since you're here, would you mind bringing a couple Cheddar Burgers and those Monster Onion Rings?"

"Coming up. I'll leave the drinks here and bring the burgers and rings in a minute."

"Wonderful. Michael, you're going to love the onion rings."

Mike led George to the restroom. They stopped a few times on the way, since people asked George how he was doing. George introduced his friends to Mike. At first, Mike tried remembering the names, but after meeting a few new people, he stopped trying to remember them all. Eventually, Mike's need to use the restroom became strong enough that he had to move George along, guiding him with more determination than ever before. When they finished, their walk back to the booth was similar. More people wanted to talk with George, and he wanted to talk with them. The conversations were good, but after a while, Mike became hungry and thirsty. So once again, he had to guide George back to the table with some determination. The burgers, onion rings, and drinks were waiting for them when they reached the booth.

"Try one of the Monster Rings first," suggested George.

Mike lifted one of the large onion rings and gazed at it. "I didn't know onions came this big. You sure it isn't a cabbage?"

"It does look that way, but once you take a bite, you'll know it's nothing but wonderfully deep-fried and battered onion. Some pleasures in life make it all worth it."

For a while, their conversation consisted of comments about how good the meal was and grunts of agreement. It was late for supper, so both were hungry.

Most of Mike's onion rings and burger were gone when he started thinking about some things they'd talked about earlier. "There's something I don't understand."

"Hell, I seem to find a few dozen new things I don't understand each day," George replied with a mouthful of hamburger. "What's on your mind?"

"I'm still trying to figure out how some blind folks spend so much time crying, and others practically become professional skiers. You said both groups are good, hard-working folks. What's different about them?"

George grunted a "Hmm" sound, swallowed, and bit into his last onion ring. "There is one difference between folks who get on pretty well and those who don't. It's age. For the most part, younger folks learn how to adapt. It goes back to what I said when we started the gauntlet, about rebuilding a life. Older folks have more to rebuild—how they take care of their kids, the job they know well, the places they like to drive to, or the food they like to cook. That's a lot of rebuilding. I can't blame 'em for not rebuilding all of it. Anyway, that's the best difference I can think of."

"So, where do you draw the line between you and old?"

George laughed, finished his drink, and answered. "Ha, there's a question that's been asked for a while." George turned his face toward the crowd in the bar. "When are you old? This little conversation does make the question more real. I go back to the classic answer." He looked straight at Mike and paused, just long enough for Mike to realize he was looking into his friend's blind eyes. George blinked and calmly said, "It's all a state of mind, my friend. It's all a state of mind."

CHAPTER FIVE

Cleaning Up

M ike didn't know what the dream was about, but he didn't want to leave it. Unfortunately, his right arm would no longer tolerate a lack of blood. After rolling off that arm and onto his back, he woke barely enough to feel blood pulse into the arm. The room was quiet, just what he wanted after the previous night of too many drinks. He resisted an urge to open his eyes, since that would take him away from the dream. He pulled up the blankets, took a deep breath, and enjoyed the silence. The pulsing in his arm faded with his consciousness. A dream seemed to start, maybe the dream he was enjoying a moment ago.

Images from the dream emerged, but one wasn't right. It was less of an image and more of a mist, or a hue, inside his closed eyes. The dream faded and the hue became a little brighter. It was red, a dull red hue. He rolled his head to the left and hoped the dream would return. The red hue became brighter, and his face became warmer. A conscious thought tried to tell him something, but he resisted it. He just wanted to sleep.

Mike's eyes were still closed, but the hue grew and filled his sight. A bead of sweat pulled at the hairs on an eyebrow. He didn't want to figure out which eyebrow. He sighed and rolled onto his left side. The tickle on his eyebrow faded, along with the red hue. Unfortunately, the dream faded as well. Seeing the dream didn't matter anymore. He just wanted to rest.

He knew he was now facing a wall that was a few inches away. This knowledge added a strange comfort. At least, it was harder for anything to bother his face. Mike enjoyed a long moment of silence. The hue seemed to return, and the conscious thought could no longer be stopped. "Why in God's name couldn't it be cloudy today?" Making that statement nudged him from sleep to consciousness. "Damn." He opened his eyes and saw sunlight reflecting off the wall. Then, he saw it dim as the sun went behind a cloud.

He gave up on trying to sleep, but lying in bed felt right, especially since he was starting to feel the unique pain of a hangover headache. His glance wandered toward the wall. Something was familiar about it. He scanned up and down, which made him wake a bit more. It was the block, the large cinder blocks. He'd used the same kind of blocks when he built his house. They were used for the walls in the basement.

Just a couple of years ago, he'd broken ground for that house. He hired contractors to build most of it, but he still carried many blocks, just like the ones he was looking at now. "Damn things get heavy." The sun and reflection returned, so he rolled onto his right side, which caused his head to ache. He wiped some sweat from his face and pushed down the blankets.

He thought about the shower in his house. That would feel great. Mike remembered how some cousins had helped him select the shower. They'd made jokes about how he needed to use it more often. He'd made jokes that water cost money. He smiled at the memory of those jokes. If he were home right now, he would coast through this hangover with a long shower, maybe even a bath. After getting cleaned up, he'd grab a cold Coke from the fridge and get outside. The crisp winter air would work with the caffeine to leave the hangover even further behind. Then, he'd finish the soda while walking on the five acres around the house. He was still getting used to the idea of having his own woods on his own land. Mike sighed. It was a good home.

He wondered what his cousins were doing now, Larry, Butch, and Kuba. "I still don't know where he got that nickname." He'd asked a few times, but Kuba always told a different story. "I hope they're enjoying a game of snowmobile tag right now." Mike looked across the room. His desk was easy enough to make out, but there was a stain on the wall he hadn't noticed before. He tried to analyze the details of the stain. "If I can't see that, I won't be playing snowmobile tag anytime soon. Crap." He squinted, but it didn't make a difference.

The thought of a shower returned. At the moment, it could be as satisfying as a game of snowmobile tag. Mike sighed. Unfortunately, that would involve getting his shower bag, robe, and a towel. "Damn, I've been meaning to wash the towels and other laundry." All the tasks involved with getting cleaned up felt unusually challenging. One task seemed even more challenging, and immediate, since his headache was getting worse. That challenge was standing up, or maybe sitting up. "Hey, just like George said, I'm a man firmly in my twenties. This'll be easy." Feeling confident, he quickly sat up in bed. "Oh, bad idea." Echoes of pain bounced through his head, ending in slow throbbing. "Bad idea." He hunched over and rubbed his forehead. When some of the pain faded, he sat up, slowly. "That's better." He rotated and carefully put his feet on the floor.

"Time for a break." Mike put his face in his hands, leaned forward, and rested his elbows on his knees. He decided that aspirin was now more important than a shower, but both would have to wait. Sitting still felt right and helped the pain fade. He was tempted to say he'd never drink that much again, but he didn't—no use repeating bold and meaningless claims. It had been a long time since he'd laughed that much, maybe even before he'd lost his sight. He smiled a little. "George can be pretty damn funny." His eyebrows lifted. "And Sam sounds like ..." He paused and rubbed his eyes. "I have no idea. It's probably best to keep my distance from that one, damn good looking, though."

Other parts of the evening came back to Mike. "So, my chances of getting laid just dropped off a cliff. My chances of getting a job are fifty-fifty, and making muffins takes forever." He gazed at the floor. "Crap," he mumbled. "Although, I don't really like making muffins, but I need to drive. My house is five miles from anything, or maybe twenty. Crap." Mike's eyes wandered to the window. After wiping more sweat from his face, he thought about opening the window to cool the room. Unfortunately, that would require standing, which still felt too challenging.

He stared at the floor again and wondered. If sex were less likely, would marriage be unlikely as well? He hadn't been in a rush to get married but had planned on it sometime. The thoughts made him feel lonely. What about work? He'd done okay making tractor parts, but that required sight. His dad had worked at a desk for a while. Maybe that was an option, but these days, it probably required a college degree. He'd never liked the idea of going to college.

One of his dad's comments came to mind, about not making a bad situation worse. Mike looked up, just a little, and mumbled something George had said last night, "I can't think about sad stuff too much. It gets addictive." He'd heard there were some work options after finishing at Bridgman's. Learning about those options in a few days was better than worrying now. "Or, I could roll over and spend the day in bed."

He took a deep breath and let out a long, loud yawn. That felt good. Then he grimaced. "What is that raunchy taste?" He answered his own question. "The onion rings. Yuck. Did I brush last night? Doesn't seem like it. I need to brush." The number of important tasks were piling up: open the window, aspirin, shower, and brushing. No, brushing came before the shower. He could probably finish everything in an hour, and right now, the result was practically luxurious, even worth standing up for.

"All right, time to be brave and bold." He moved his hands from his face to his knees and pushed himself up, slowly. He expected a sudden shocking pain in his head, but there was only a dull ache and a little lightheadedness. He stood still for a moment to make sure a sudden pain wouldn't surprise him. "One small step for man. Now to conquer the world, starting with some aspirin."

He took some slow, shuffling steps toward the closet. He lifted a hand just as slowly, reached into the closet, and felt for the shower bag. The hand bumped into a large bottle and dropped down to the shower bag, since the big bottle and bag were always close. Once the hand was inside the bag, it quickly found a small bottle of aspirin. With the help of the other hand, he opened the small bottle and shook out two, maybe three pills. Mike found an open can of Coke in the fridge and washed down the aspirin. The cold drink and caffeine felt unusually refreshing. He finished the can and threw it toward the garbage bin by his desk. He moved a little faster.

Mike pulled his shower robe off its hook on the back of the door and slipped into the robe. He reached for the towel rack, which was also near the door. He only felt a bare piece of plastic. A vague memory returned of resting his hand on the towel rack last night and slipping a little. Instinctively, he moved his foot around the floor below the rack. The foot moved into something soft. The thought of using an old towel that had fallen on this floor wasn't pleasant, but it was the only option. He bent down slowly to pick up the towel. After standing up just as slow, he picked up his shower bag and keys, and then walked out the door.

The shower was near the stairwell. Someone walked from the stairs and toward Mike, just before he entered the shower room.

"Hey, darling."

"Good morning, Ruby," he mumbled slowly.

"Honey, it ain't morning, and I hope you don't mind me saying, but you don't look so good."

Mike resisted the urge to think about a prostitute telling him he looked rough. He also didn't feel like talking, so he just replied, "I'll be okay," and pushed open the door to the shower room. He wondered if Ruby could smell his breath. "Might as well start with that," he said to himself while taking out his toothbrush. He brushed with softer strokes than usual, since any movement in his head seemed risky.

He finished brushing, rinsed out his mouth, and stood still in front of the mirror. "Thank God for small wonders." Another small wonder came to mind: a long drink of water from the faucet. He cupped his hands below the faucet, filled them with water, and drank it down. After repeating that a few times, it was time for a break.

He rested one hand on each side of the sink and leaned on them. His head slowly rolled up, close to the mirror. "You look like hell." A slow moment passed. "But that water was good, not bad for city water." He noticed the water was still running in the sink. His right hand wandered toward the sound and turned the water off. He slowly stood straight, or straighter. After another moment, he reached into the shower with his other hand to turn it on.

Mike let the shower water warm up more than usual. He was still in no mood for a cold surprise. Besides, it seemed right to undress slower than normal. "Now for the main event." He stepped into the shower. After the water sprayed over him, he felt his body move easier and stand straighter as the thin yet heavy coat of sweat washed away. He took a deep breath in through his nose, enjoying the steam and the absence of decayed onion rings. He finished the shower and wondered what to do next.

After returning to his room, he didn't have to wonder any more. He was particularly interested in wearing something clean, but there was little to choose from. His closet was nearly empty, and the pile of laundry was unusually high. The size of the pile had made it easier to pull clothes out in the last few days to see which ones could be worn one more time, but the time had come. He pulled the remaining clean shirt from his closet, which was the shirt he intended to wear for special occasions. He didn't want to wear dress pants, so he found the pair of jeans he'd chosen not to wear yesterday and slipped them on.

He grabbed handfuls of dirty laundry and shoved them into an Air Force duffle bag, which he'd borrowed from his dad. A clip on top of the bag could seal it shut, but using the clip would also reduce how much laundry could be stuffed inside. He kept the bag unclipped, gave the laundry on top an extra shove, noticed a couple of sleeves hanging out, and decided they were fine. Mike then grabbed a box of detergent and dumped a jar of coins into his hand. After dropping the coins into a front pocket, he walked out the door and down the stairs.

The laundry room was in the basement. He reached the bottom of the stairs, walked into the room, and heard the humming of washers and driers. Sunlight came in from windows near the ceiling. He suspected all the machines would be busy because it had been afternoon for a while. Mike realized that he hadn't checked the time all day. He walked in front of a clock hanging on the wall. "Damn, that's one dusty clock." It was a little past 3:00 p.m. He walked by the washing machines. All the lids were down, suggesting the machines were being used. He put his hand on a couple machines to see if one wasn't vibrating.

He found a machine that was still and opened the lid. There were clothes inside, so he had to choose between taking the clothes out and waiting for the owner to show up. Folks at Mariner's Motel were less likely than most to show up a few minutes after their wash was done. Showing up days after wouldn't surprise Mike, but he still wanted to avoid an awkward situation, in case someone showed up while he was moving their laundry out of one machine and on top of another. He walked toward the door and listened for a moment.

Someone was upstairs talking to the hotel receptionist in a tone that was getting louder, but it didn't sound like anyone was coming down to the laundry room. After returning to the still machine, he grabbed an armful of laundry and placed it on top of the next machine. He moved a second armful of laundry, and then felt inside the machine to see if anything was left inside. He pulled out a sock and a small T-shirt.

Mike noticed something red lying below the machine, by his feet. It was longer than the sock but smaller than the T-shirt. He picked it up and felt a small clip on one end. He held onto the clip and moved the garment close to his face. It was light, long, and red—with a couple of cloth circles. He scanned it for a moment longer. "Cool. Wish I could help take this off sometime. Then again, that depends on what's under it. Some women would look better in a parka." Mike chuckled at his own joke but stopped when he heard someone walking toward the laundry room. He tossed the bra onto the pile of clothes he took out of the machine.

"Well, hello again, darl'n. Seems I barely see you for a few days, and then I keep bumping into you. This could mean we're meant to spend more time together."

"I suppose. I could never afford to go out with someone as classy as you, Ruby. I'm just a humble blind guy."

"For a guy who can't afford a night out, you sure get dressed up when you do laundry."

"Huh?" Mike mumbled.

"Your shirt, very nice. I haven't seen many guys wear something like that with blue jeans, but it works."

Mike had forgotten about the shirt. He also wanted to keep the conversation brief, so he was relieved when Ruby changed the subject. "Sorry you had to take my laundry out. I ended up yelling at the manager. Bastard won't fix the heat in my room." She walked closer to the pile of laundry.

"No problem," Mike added as he glanced at the laundry pile. Most of the clothes were tangled together, except the bra. It was spread out on top, like a red stripe.

"Michael, Michael, Michael," Ruby slowly repeated as she picked up the bra and dangled it in front of him. "If I were the suspicious type, I would think you were enjoying my favorite bra."

Mike's instincts were to react with a witty phrase and gracefully exit this topic. He almost made a joke about a parka. After searching for something else to say, only one thought came to mind, which had nothing to do with Ruby. It was that his hangover headache had suddenly become worse. After an awkward silence, he replied, "It fell. I picked it up, just picked it up, and put it on the pile."

"Uh-huh," she said while tossing the bra back on the pile. "You don't have to be so shy, sweetheart. Everybody needs a little release once in a while." She stepped closer to Mike. He backed up but had to stop after bumping into a washing machine. He still wasn't used to a woman tall enough, strong enough, and who came close enough, to nudge him around. She leaned close and whispered, "If you like the bra, I can show you the rest of the outfit, and less."

He didn't know what was worse, the image of Ruby taking off that bra, and the rest, or the cigarette smell on her breath.

"Sorry, Ruby—I mean, thanks, or—"

She cut him off, whispering in his ear again. "Honey, you can have me or laundry. What do you want?"

"Laundry!" The words came out faster and more certain than Mike had intended.

Ruby pulled back half a step. "Well, if that's the way you want to be, that's the way it'll be." Mike could tell he'd succeeded for a moment, but Ruby wasn't about to give up. "For now, anyway. Some guys need a while before they can enjoy my kind of entertainment. I have a feeling you're going to be thinking about my favorite bra again. When you do, just let me know."

An awkward pause passed. The best response he could come up with was, "Okay." His hangover headache continued to get worse. He rubbed his forehead and added, "I should really start my laundry."

"Good idea. I've always said that men should do what they need."

"Thanks."

Mike took a deep breath and moved the dirty clothes from the duffle bag and into the washing machine. That felt good since he'd become especially interested in starting his laundry and returning to his room. He reached into a pocket for some coins. There were several types. Ordinarily, he would take out a few and look at them closely, preferably under bright light. If he did that now, Ruby would probably offer to help, which felt unusually unappealing. Mike could say that he'd forgotten the coins in his room, but she'd probably heard them jingle in his pocket. He remembered a teacher at Bridgman's describing how helpful it could be to have all coins sorted out and in different pockets or something.

He dismissed the memory to focus on the current problem. If he kept his hand in the pocket for much longer, Ruby would probably make another awkward joke. These little problems were some of the most annoying parts of being blind, and hung-over. He sighed and decided that asking for help was slightly less annoying than having Ruby offer it.

"Hey, Ruby, could you pick out some change for the machine?" Mike asked while holding out a fistful of coins.

"Sure thing, darling. Damn, if you have all these coins, you probably have a lot of bills. So much for your discount." She took some coins out of his hand and put them in the machine. "Cool, there's a couple bicentennial quarters. I like those. You want me to take out some more for the dryer?"

Mike nodded and mumbled, "Yes."

"All right, these are for the dryer. I added some extra quarters, just in case. Maybe you should put these in your left pocket and put the other ones in your right."

"That's what they keep telling me," Mike replied as he put the coins in each pocket. He appreciated Ruby's help but really wanted to start the laundry so he could leave and relax in his room.

He was about to start the machine when she commented, "You might want to put some soap in first."

"Right, soap. Soap is good," he said as he reached for his box of detergent, poured some into the machine, and pressed the start button.

"I don't mean to be a bother, but you just put in a lot of detergent, might want to measure it next time."

"I suppose." He collected his things and walked toward the door. "See you later, Ruby."

"See you later, darling."

When Mike returned to his room, he closed the door and leaned back against it. "I need to avoid complexity today." He switched on the light, since the sun was no longer shining inside. After dropping the duffle bag, he scanned the room. There were a few piles scattered around: books, papers, wrappers, and some things he couldn't make out. He rested a hand on top of the fridge and felt some crumbs. "It might be time to clean, or maybe go back to bed." He rubbed his head and sighed. "I better clean. Besides, it's simple, overdue, and I can do it alone."

The next couple of hours were strangely familiar, as he picked up something that was lying out, found a place for it, and wiped off the surfaces he used the most with the damp towel from his shower. Another familiar moment occurred just before he finished, when he thought about how much work was involved with cleaning, even in a small room. Mike knew his laundry would be finished by now, but he decided to wait a while longer to move the laundry from a washer to a dryer. Better to reduce the chance of bumping into Ruby again.

He opened the window a little by his desk, sat down, and felt some fresh, cool air flow in. After enjoying the short break, Mike realized he hadn't eaten all day. He walked to the fridge and started the routine of making some sandwiches. He paused after realizing there were just two slices of cheese left, three pieces of bread, and no mayo. "Bummer. I've been meaning to get groceries too. This is as good a day as any, maybe buy an ice cream bar or two." He made one and a half sandwiches, reached into the fridge, and pulled out the cardboard milk carton.

After sitting at his desk, Mike took a couple of bites from the sandwiches and gazed out the window. He could still see some light off to the right, but most of the sky was dark. It was a peaceful sight, but it also had a practical meaning. Most people from Mariner's would be out for work or play. That meant the practical task of finishing laundry should be easier, since the washers and dryers should be free.

He sighed and thought about how easy laundry used to be when the machines were in the basement of his own house. Of course, he'd never enjoyed laundry, but now, Mike liked the idea of having his own washer and dryer. If he still had them, he wouldn't have to hope there would be machines available, and there certainly would be no embarrassing moments with a red bra. He finished the last sandwich, drank from the carton of milk, and realized it was now empty. His glance moved to the window. Little light was left. Without thinking, he said, "Blind people can buy a washer and dryer too. Maybe I'll even buy a house to go around them, but right now, I gotta take care of some stuff."

A simple plan came to mind. He would fill the duffle bag with a second load of dirty laundry, trying hard not to forget all his towels. In the laundry room, he would move the first load of laundry from a washer to a dryer. Then, the second load of laundry could go into the washer he'd just emptied. Last, he would use the empty duffle bag to carry groceries from the grocery store he'd found on his recent morning walk. He finished his supper, stood up, and said, "Good to be a man with a plan. Besides, what better way for a guy firmly in his twenties to spend a Saturday night?" After filling the duffle bag again, he put on his coat and returned to the laundry room.

The laundry room was quiet and dark when Mike entered. He flipped on the light switch and moved the clean laundry to a dryer. Then he emptied the duffle bag into the washer, added some soap, and reached into his left pocket for the coins that Ruby had sorted out earlier. He put the coins into the machines and started them. After hanging the empty duffle bag from a shoulder, he noticed the clock and walked next to it. "Wow, almost seven." Before leaving, he glanced at the spot where Ruby's bra had dropped a few hours ago. He shook his head, sighed, and switched off the lights.

When he walked out of Mariner's, the street showed it was a Saturday night. Some of his neighbors were sharing a bottle from a bag, and others were quietly tending to their business. As he walked farther, people were carrying shopping bags and walking in groups, talking and laughing. The light from streetlamps came and went as he went under them. It was harder to see with the inconsistent light, so he applied lessons for walking in crowds. He looked around more to see things his peripheral vision used to show him. Sometimes, that showed obstacles like a fire hydrant or mailbox. Other times, it showed a person rushing down the street or cutting in front of him. He thought about taking out his long, white cane and just holding it. The cane would show people that he was blind, but he didn't feel like bothering with it. Fortunately, the grocery store was soon in front of him. After walking inside, an old cash register caught his attention. A clerk said, "Good evening," and Mike said the same.

The store was well lit, so Mike could see there were four aisles, which seemed well organized. The wooden floor creaked as he walked. There was a mild and familiar scent in the air, a combination of fresh bread, vegetables, and a butcher's shop. The place reminded him of the small-town grocery stores he'd gone to as a kid, which was surprising since Portage Bay seemed so much larger. He wandered into the first aisle and paused. Looking at a shelf made him wish he'd written down a grocery list or recorded one in a cassette recorder. He never was very good at remembering groceries or any kind of list. He settled for imagining the contents of his fridge.

Mayo was on the top. He would need a jar of that, a large one since they were cheapest. Ketchup was on top too. He wondered why he even bought ketchup. It was only good for hot food, like burgers, and making hot food was too much of a hassle in Mariner's. Okay, back to groceries, but more hot food sure would be tasty. "Stop it," he told himself. "Focus on groceries." Mike tried to imagine what else was on the top shelf of his fridge. There was Coke, bread, and maybe pickles. He didn't need pickles, should probably eat those soon. He could use Coke and bread, though. The top shelf probably had more on it, but he couldn't remember anything else.

Moving on to the middle shelf, it had bologna and cheese. The bologna was okay, but he could use some cheese. The margarine was also on the middle shelf, but that was probably okay. On to the bottom shelf, he usually needed milk, maybe some carrots, and something else. There was something else on the bottom shelf that he'd really been meaning to get. He shook his head. No chance of remembering it now.

After finishing the mental scan of his fridge, he tried remembering the list he just made. There was Coke, cheese, mayo, and "Crap, some other things." He decided to walk through the store and just pick up what looked good. Next time, he would write down or record a list, probably.

Mike walked through the store and looked at most of the groceries at eye level and some that were lower. He could move his face close to those groceries without looking awkward and still get a meaningful image. He picked out a few groceries, mostly those involved with making a sandwich, and some snacks. That seemed to be enough, so he started walking to the cash register. After a few steps, he remembered that he needed Coke. "And milk," he mumbled and walked back to the aisles. This time, he picked up a twelve-pack of Coke, a gallon of milk, and some doughnuts that looked good.

He decided it was time to stop shopping when his hands and arms couldn't hold any more. He walked toward the cash register again. On the way, he passed by a freezer. It was about waist high and had a sliding glass lid on top. Inside, bright lights lit colorful shapes. They were the right size to be ice cream bars. Since Mike knew he was within earshot of the clerk, he tried resisting the urge to say how good one of those would taste right now, or maybe two. "Or three," he finally mumbled.

"Can I help you with something?" the clerk called from the cash register.

"No, I'm all right," he replied while thinking of a way to open the lid on top of the freezer. Since his arms were full, he had to bend over and try to slide open the lid with a couple of fingers. He felt something move in his arms, like it would slip out. Mike stopped and instinctively bent further over the freezer, almost resting on top of it. If something was going to drop, he wanted it to drop a few inches onto the freezer instead of a few feet onto the floor, but Mike still wondered what the clerk would think of a guy who was almost lying on a freezer.

Something slipped out of his arms and made the clear sound of a heavy glass jar hitting the glass lid. It had to be the mayo. Fortunately, he was pretty sure it didn't hit hard enough to break. Unfortunately, he could see the jar slowly rolling away. Mike's arms and hands were clinging to his other groceries. "Bummer." He quickly thought about the jar rolling toward the edge, if he had time to ask the clerk for help, if he should drop the other groceries, how this was starting to be a bad day, and how the jar seemed to be gaining speed. He repeated these thoughts a few times when a hand stopped the jar.

"That was close," the clerk said.

"Yeah, it was, thanks," Mike replied while looking up at the clerk.

"Next time, you might want to use a basket. We have a stack of them by the door."

"Good idea. I must not have seen them." Mike stood up and took a deep breath. "Can I ask you for another favor?"

"Sure."

"Could you grab me an ice cream bar out of the freezer?"

The clerk sounded a little surprised at the request, or maybe he'd been watching. "Sure, what kind do you want?"

"Any will do, maybe pick your favorite."

"Are you sure you don't want to pick your own? I mean, it seemed like you were just looking at them."

"No, that's all right," Mike replied, not wanting to explain his limited sight. He walked toward the cash register to leave the awkward moment behind.

The clerk took an ice cream bar from the freezer and walked in the same direction. Mike placed his groceries on the counter and wondered if he'd made a bad impression.

When he saw the clerk walk behind the till, Mike said, "I hope I didn't look strange over there. I forgot my grocery list and ended up carrying more than I expected."

"You'd be surprised how often we see that here. People usually buy more than they think they will." The clerk smiled, and his voice changed to a joking tone. "We don't mind. It's good for business."

"I suppose. I also have a problem with my sight, so I move close to things to see them better."

"I was just wondering about that. With Bridgman's nearby, we're used to helping folks with limited sight—teachers, students, even a few former students." The clerk pressed keys on the old cash register, which made mechanical sounds.

Mike was relieved that he didn't appear awkward. Apparently, the clerk thought of him as just another customer who bought more than expected and, as a result, might need some help. That felt comforting.

"Well," the clerk said, "that'll be nine dollars and eighty-six cents."

Mike took out his wallet and lifted it close to his face. He could clearly see inside it because of the good lighting. He poked around and picked a ten-dollar bill. After handing it to the clerk, he took the ice cream bar and put it in his coat pocket. Finally, he put the rest of the groceries into the duffle bag and slipped the bag over a shoulder.

"Here's your change, looking forward to seeing you again some-time."

He thanked the clerk and walked outside. Mike took a couple of steps up the hill and reached in his pocket for the ice cream bar. While taking off the wrapper, he heard some people in front of him, laughing. They were walking into a building, just up the hill from the grocery store. He paused and took a bite of his treat. A few people came out of the building. They were also laughing. The pleasant sounds from both groups made him remember it was Saturday night. He also had a vague memory of the building they walked into and out of. He slowly walked toward it.

A gust of wind blew by, and something creaked above him. He saw a window, walked closer to it, and guessed what was behind the glass. "Yep, an X, made from fishing poles." He took another bite and thought more about how he really liked the name of this bar, The Tacklebox. He felt the presence of his dad, who would recommend that Mike not spend another night in a bar. Someone walked slowly out the door. This time, he could hear some music inside. He recognized the song, about a man who met a woman in a taxi. Mike took a big bite from the ice cream bar, finished it, and walked inside.

The wooden floor creaked, reminding him of the grocery store. At first, he thought this place would be like The Slowstream Tavern, but this bar felt different. This wasn't a place where you'd order a Sloe Screw Against the Wall with a Twist. It was simpler than that. It was also darker than The Slowstream Tavern. He could barely see the blurry image of a bar to his left and tables to his right. He felt like sitting on a barstool. The stools weren't visible to him, but he knew they'd be near the bar. After slowly walking in that direction, he reached out a hand. He felt a stool a moment later, sat on it, and carefully lowered the duffle bag to the floor. Mike used a foot to discretely nudge the bag under his knees when he heard a bartender ask, "'Evening, what can I get for ya?"

"Good evening. I'll just have a beer. What kind do you have?"

"We got Schmidt on tap. Otherwise, we have bottles of Grain Belt, Schlitz, Pfeiffer's, and a couple of others."

He thought of his dad again, since he usually drank Pfeiffer's. Mike liked joking with his dad that no beer was cheaper. His dad would calmly respond that only made it better.

"Do you have Red White and Blue?"

"Sure do," the bartender replied. He quickly turned away from Mike and walked to get the beer.

Mike put both elbows on the bar and leaned over them a little. He felt the comfort of resting on old wood, even if he couldn't see it very well. The day had gotten off to a slow start, but he'd made the best of it. His fingers started tapping on the wood when he recognized another song. It was about a man who met a woman in a van. Mike sung along for a few words and smiled at the images that the song conjured up. While he listened, his gaze wandered. Eventually, it settled on some colorful flashing lights near the tables, probably a jukebox. He watched the lights and kept a small smile as the song continued.

"Here ya go, one Red White and Blue. It's still happy hour, so that'll be a buck."

Mike knew he had quarters in his left pocket from the help Ruby had given him a few hours ago, but those were for the dryer, which he still needed to use tonight. He reached into his right pocket. After feeling a variety of coins, he brought a handful close to his face but couldn't see them well enough to quickly pick out the ones he needed.

Instead of taking more time looking for the right coins, he moved the handful toward the bartender. "Would you mind taking out a buck's worth? I don't see very well in low light."

"No problem," the bartender said as he took some money from Mike's hand.

Mike thanked him and reached for the beer.

While he took a sip, the bartender continued. "I was just talking with a couple of friends who don't see so well. One teaches at Bridgman's and the other finished a while ago."

"Cool. I just started."

"How's it going?"

"Pretty good, except learning how to cook." Mike smiled. "Even with sight, I always thought a toaster was too challenging."

The bartender laughed and agreed. "I know what you mean, half of my meals come from the grill here. Works for me, though. I'd rather spend my time outside than learn how to cook more."

"I'm the same way. That's actually how I found this place, after roaming around outside."

"In that case, you might be able to help me out with something. Do you have a few minutes to hear about it?"

Mike mumbled, "Sure."

"I was just trying to solve a little problem with the friends I mentioned, the ones from Bridgman's. We're setting up another ski trip for blind folks who live around here. Have you heard of blind skiing?"

"Yeah, they mentioned it at school."

"Well, a lot of the planning takes place right at this bar. Quite a few blind folks stop by here since we're close to Bridgman's and since our drinks are affordable. Usually, we have plenty of people to plan the trip, but we're a little short this time. Would you mind kicking around some ideas with us for the next ski trip?"

"Sure, but does it matter that I don't ski much?"

"Not really, we just need to talk about some options right now. Mind joining us?"

Mike shrugged and mumbled "Sure" again.

"Great, come on over," the bartender said as he waved his hand toward the end of the bar and walked away.

Mike grabbed the duffle bag and moved down the bar, stopping when he heard the bartender again. This place was more comfortable to sit at, since there was a bar light directly overhead.

"Fred, I found someone who might be able to help."

"Good to hear it. Howdy, I'm Fred, happy to meet you."

Mike set the duffle bag down by a barstool next to Fred and replied, "Hi, I'm Mike, good to meet you too."

Fred offered a handshake. Mike shook the man's hand and sat on a stool.

The bartender continued the introductions. "Mike's a new student at the school. Fred finished there a few years ago."

"That was back before they had the new building," Fred added. "I haven't been to the place for a while, but some teachers keep me updated on things." He pointed away from the bar. "One of them just stepped away to use the john but will be back in a minute."

"Well, I'll tell you more about the ski trip we're planning." The bartender put his palms on the bar, leaned on them, and explained. "A small problem is getting in the way of a big ski event we have coming up."

"What's the problem?" Mike asked.

"This might sound a little strange, but the small problem is that we don't have enough people to shake tambourines."

"I heard something about that," Mike said. "Is that where somebody stands in the middle of a ski slope and shakes a tambourine to help blind skiers?"

"Yeah, that's part of it."

"Doesn't it get cold out there?" Mike asked. "I mean, I can take a little cold, but it's always the wind that gets ya." He smiled and continued, "There's not much on a ski slope to block the wind."

Fred chimed in. "But there's always a bright side. Anybody who shakes a tambourine gets a great view of the race."

"That's a good point," the bartender added. "It really is a great race. That's the big event I mentioned. A couple times each winter, we organize a race between blind skiers and any sighted folks who want to give it a try. All the skiers wear a blindfold and have a guide, who gives directions from behind. To be extra careful, a volunteer stands at each gate and shakes a tambourine, so the skiers know where to turn."

"It's a pretty short race, though," Fred said. "Only about four gates. This is all for fun and to raise money for local blind folks. If we had more gates, there's a chance somebody could get hurt, especially one of the sighted skiers. They're not used to skiing with a blindfold on."

"Wow, it sounds like a great time," Mike added and took a drink from his beer.

"It really is," Fred commented while looking toward Mike. "But the whole thing depends on having a few volunteers to shake a tambourine by the gates. We've thought about having the racers only work with a guide and skipping the tambourine shakers, but the racers didn't like that idea. They're used to turning by a sound."

The bartender rubbed his forehead. "And that goes back to the small problem I mentioned. Two of our volunteers just decided to leave early for Christmas. They're married, and her dad just took a turn for the worse."

"Sorry to hear that," Mike replied.

"Thanks, we're all hoping for the best, but we also need to find a couple of volunteers to fill in. What do you think? Is this something you'd be willing to try? It's all for a good cause."

Mike needed a moment to think about the question, so he took a drink from his bottle of beer. After setting it down slowly, he answered. "I'm sure it is, and I might be able to help. Would like to think it over for bit, though."

"Well, that's all I'm asking for right now," the bartender said.

Mike wanted to help, but there were just enough risks to make him nervous. If he could have watched a race just once, it would be easier to volunteer, but he'd never tried or even watched skiing. To him, standing in a winter wind seemed stranger than snowmobile tag, and shaking a tambourine wasn't going to create much heat. The only experience that came close was standing still on a frigid day when a school bus was late. And in that case, there weren't skiers coming right at him who might be a little competitive or might be getting used to a blindfold. He was still thinking of the combination of shivering and being clobbered by a racing skier when the bartender raised his voice and directed it away from the bar.

"Hey, we might have found someone to help with that problem we were just talking about."

Mike looked in the direction the bartender was talking. A woman walked toward Fred and sat next to him, on the other side of Mike. The bar light above them reflected off her bright red hair, which Mike instantly recognized. He took a long drink from his beer to settle a sudden surge of shyness. He finished the bottle, waved it at the bartender, and dropped a pile of coins on the bar. The bartender replied to his request in a quick, single motion. He reached down, pulled a beer from a cooler under the bar, popped off the top, and slid the bottle to Mike.

"Really? I step away to pee, and when I come back, you've solved everything?"

"Service with a smile," Fred responded. "Mike, this is Samantha Smothers, the teacher friend I mentioned. Most people call her Sam. Sam, this is Mike. He might be able to help with the little volunteering problem we're having."

Sam looked at Mike. "Well, hello again," she said with a smile. "I remember meeting you a couple of weeks ago when Donny was showing you around. How's school going?"

Mike felt happy she remembered him, impressed with how she looked close up, and uncertain how to respond to the simple question. He also tried remembering what George had said about her. He repeated these thoughts a few times before answering, "Pretty good." He took another drink.

"What do you think of Portage Bay? I know when I first got here it took me forever to get comfortable."

Fred added a comment. "I think I remember that. At first, you were a little, well, shall I say *unsettled.*"

"That's one way to put it," the bartender added in a teasing tone. "Once or twice, you were a little unsettled and maybe a little tense, like the time I almost threw you out of here."

"All right, all right," Sam replied in a similar tone. "You guys both know I'm enthusiastic, but you also know I'm worth any small bit of trouble I may cause."

While the others spoke, Mike tried again to remember how George had described Sam. He'd mentioned that she was funny. That part was clear.

Fred and the bartender laughed and replied by saying "Yeah" and "Sure" a couple of times. Everyone in the small group took a drink.

Sam set down her drink first and led the conversation. "Now, if you don't mind, I would like to learn more about our new friend. Mike, before these jokers distracted me, I was trying to ask you about Portage Bay. Does the place still seem new and exciting, or is it already part of your routine?"

Mike remembered thinking about that question a day or two ago. He decided to give an answer that was more appealing than accurate. "It's actually still new and exciting. I always like exploring new places." He was happy about the answer, since it gave a hint of exploring with her sometime.

"I like that," she replied. "It's always fun to check out new places, like this ski trip. You'll love White Pine Ridge. The forest up there is amazing. The skiing is also good, and there's a chalet with a huge fireplace."

"That's the part I like best," Fred added, "after the skiing of course. It's made from small stones, some as small as a golf ball. Others are as big as a beepball. They're from a stream that runs down the ridge, which makes all the stones real smooth. I like the way they feel, and you can't beat an open fire."

"That reminds me," Sam said, "when are we going to call the ski resort to take care of the final details?"

"That's a good question," answered the bartender. "We got so wrapped up in getting the word out that we lost track of stuff like that. Anyway, I'll give 'em a call." He looked below the bar and reached for a pen. He then took a napkin from a pile in front of Sam and started writing. "There are probably two types of questions: the ones involving the race and the ones involving the rooms."

Sam gave the first ideas. "We'll need seven rooms, four with four beds and three with two beds. We should also learn if they can keep one more double open for us again. We'll cancel it a week ahead of time if we don't need it, just like last time."

Fred chimed in. "And try to get rooms that are farther away from the bar. One lousy part of last time was hearing people party till some god-awful hour."

"Got it, quieter rooms," the bartender said and wrote some notes.

"Or, we could just tell George to keep it down," Sam said.

"Especially his blasted singing," Fred added.

Mike gave a surprised laugh when they mentioned George singing.

"It sounds like you may have heard him sing," Fred said.

"Actually, I haven't, but we have enjoyed a few drinks. Now that you mention it, I can imagine him trying to sing after having a few."

"You're right about that, although *try* is the important part. He doesn't sing often, but getting out of town does seem to bring out his jolly side. That's all fine and good. I just wish he'd keep it down a little."

Sam added her thoughts. "And maybe realize that singing louder doesn't make his voice better." She took a drink and added, "Okay, I think we should get back to planning."

"I agree," the bartender said as he wrote more notes. "We also need to check into food for about twenty people. It can probably be the same as last time—breakfast, lunch, and dinner for two days."

Sam confirmed the suggestion. "That sounds about right. They only want an estimate. We'll get there on Friday night, but it's fun to stop some place along the way."

The bartender lifted his pen and looked up. "I think that does it for rooms and food. For the race, I'll make sure they have all the standard stuff—like gates, timers, and staff ready to help. All that should be fine, though, since they hold a few races a year." He looked down again and wrote. "I'll also double-check they have enough tambourines and those bright vests they give to blind skiers. And just to be safe, I'll make sure the price is about the same as last time."

"I think that's enough for now," Sam said. "Other ideas may come up during the phone call. Is there anything else we need to do around here? I think we've made enough announcements at school, since we already have enough people."

"Well, the most important thing is finding a couple of people to shake tambourines," the bartender added. He shifted his gaze from Sam to Mike. "That comes back to the conversation we had with Mike. What do you think, want to give it a try?"

Mike felt uncomfortable. He was hoping his offer to help could involve finding someone else or at least taking a day to decide. With all three of his new friends looking at him, it seemed like he had to decide now. "I want to help," he said with a serious tone. He continued with a lighthearted tone. "But, let me see if I got this right. You want me to stand in the middle of a freezing ski slope and shake a tambourine while blind skiers head right for me?"

Fred answered, in a similar tone, "Well, if you put it that way, it sounds a little uncomfortable, but yeah, that's about it."

Sam added some comments. "You don't need to worry too much. I've competed in some of these races, might even join this one. We really don't want to hit the tambourine shakers." She laughed a little. "Besides, we're a competitive bunch, and hitting you would raise hell with our speed."

"I suppose," he said with a nervous laugh. "But, I'd like to watch just once before helping out."

Sam persisted. "Aw, come on, this is one of those times when you just need to jump in. We can even throw in a free lift ticket."

Mike also persisted. "I appreciate it, but I've never been much of a skier."

"In that case, I'll throw in a free ski lesson. You'll be flying down the double black diamonds in no time."

Mike liked the idea of a personal ski lesson with Sam but still felt cautious. Besides, he was starting to enjoy this battle of wits. "I'm more of a bunny-hill kind of guy."

"We can do that too," she said. "It's a great place to start."

"Actually, I'm more of a bunny-hill kind of guy who does best sitting in an inner-tube."

"Okay, so skiing isn't your thing. There must be something I can bribe you with."

After thinking of a few things he would enjoy doing with Sam, Mike glanced away.

"Except that," she replied.

Mike wasn't sure if she saw a change in his face or if she was just having some fun with the pause he took.

Sam tried again. "All right, I'll go with a trusty old favorite, food. The chalet at White Pine Ridge has a great menu. We'll pay for one meal while you're up there."

The thought of some good, warm food appealed to Mike, and this lively conversation made Sam even more appealing. He would probably agree to her request, but not yet. "Just one? I mean, all the work involved with shaking a tambourine could make a guy really hungry."

Sam smiled, "Oh, so you like to bargain?" She leaned toward Mike and looked into his eyes. "Good, so do I." She held the gaze for a moment.

Mike could clearly see her eyes but couldn't tell what color they were. At first, he wondered if his eyes were having one of their bad moments, but then he realized her eyes were grey, a soft grey. He started to look at them more, but she shifted her gaze away from the group and thought aloud.

"Our group doesn't have a lot of money, so we need to keep things cheap. A meal isn't a problem, since it's about the same price as a lift ticket." Sam looked back at Mike. Her voice changed from contemplative to upbeat. "But, I'm sure my very good friend here could help." She pointed at the bartender. "He would be more than happy to throw in some free meals."

"I would, would I?" the bartender asked.

Sam leaned toward him and spoke in a loud whisper, "Work with me here, we almost have him."

The bartender smiled. "I'll match you, one meal. I'll give one meal and don't tell anybody, or else they'll all be asking for a freebie."

"All right, Mike, there's the deal," Sam said with playful confidence. "You better take it before he changes his mind."

"I don't know. You want me to stand in front of a bunch of blind skiers for two meals?"

Sam gave him a determined look. "You drive a hard bargain. There's just one more thing I'll say." Her expression softened, and she calmly said, "Please."

The word had an instant effect on Mike, especially since all he really wanted was to please Sam. He smiled and said, "Okay, I'm in." He also wondered about having the meals with her.

Sam raised her hands and called out with an excited, "Yay!"

"Good to have you with us," Fred added as he raised his beer in a toast. After taking a drink, he asked in a teasing voice, "Hey Sam, I don't remember getting a free lift ticket *or* meal when I volunteered."

Sam paused, which was different from the quick replies she'd just given Mike. She took another drink and answered. "I guess you didn't bargain hard enough. Besides, it was a long time ago when you volunteered."

Fred let out a little laugh. "It was last year."

"Things move on fast in this world, Fred. Now, we better get some planning done."

Fred agreed with a chuckle.

Sam took a notebook out of her purse and read some tasks to the bartender and Fred. The two men agreed on completing the tasks or said they knew someone who could help.

Mike tried following the conversation, but they were using names and jargon he didn't know, so his mind wandered to some questions. Was Sam giving him special treatment, or did she just like to bargain? Like every school, Bridgman's had an active rumor mill. Most of the rumors about Sam were about some trouble she'd gotten into for being too enthusiastic. Sometimes, she wandered from the lesson plan and taught lessons that were meant for other classes, and other times, her enthusiasm led to classrooms that were too loud. Other rumors came from her time out of the classroom. Apparently, her enthusiasm continued after school with a variety of guys. He could see why. She knew how to capture a guy's attention. Mike was thinking more about the rumors when he heard Sam speak up.

"Crap. That still leaves us one volunteer short. Are you sure there's nobody else you can think of?"

Fred answered. "I'll ask around again, but the people I talked with told me they already have plans."

"Same here," the bartender said.

"How about you, Mike?" Sam asked.

Mike quickly shifted his thoughts and listened to her.

"Could you ask around to see if anyone else will shake a tambourine? We really need one more person."

"I might know of someone," Mike said slowly. "But we'll probably have to bargain with him too."

"I do like bargaining, but I also like to be cheap. What did you have in mind?"

"A couple of drinks might do it," he answered.

"We can probably do that," she said. "Who are you thinking of?"

"George. He'll do a lot for some free drinks."

The bartender laughed a little and replied. "Free drinks with George could also burn through all the money we raise on the race. Seriously, though, anyone who shakes a tambourine has to have pretty good sight, since they only shake the thing when a skier is about twenty yards away. George can't see well enough."

"Okay," Mike said. "I'll still try to find somebody."

Sam grabbed a napkin, took a marker from her purse, and started writing. "That'd be great. I'll write down the date for you. The trip starts after school on Friday, December tenth and finishes Sunday night, December twelfth. If you find someone, talk to me at school."

"You can also stop by here and let me know," the bartender added.

She handed the napkin to Mike. He thanked her and took it, making sure to brush her fingers a little. He may have felt her fingers brush back. That made him curious if there were any other signs from Sam. He wanted to look into her eyes again or hold her hand for a moment, but their hands were touching between the bartender and Fred. Instead of thinking of just the right move, he felt his hangover return. He pulled his hand back and rubbed his forehead.

"You okay?" she asked.

"I'm all right. I was just out with George late last night, and it might be catching up with me." He wanted to put the napkin in a front pocket of his jeans, so Mike stretched out one leg. That led to kicking the duffle bag, by his stool.

Everyone heard the sound of glass hitting the floor. The thought *Damn mayonnaise jar again* entered Mike's mind. He hoped the jar didn't break.

"What was that?" Fred asked.

Mike hoped a clever response would come to mind, but instead, traces of his hangover continued. He decided to give a simple answer. "If I had to guess, I would say it's a jar of mayonnaise hitting the floor."

"Of course it is," the bartender added.

Fred took his turn. "Mike, this may seem like a strange question, but I'm just a little curious. Do you always bring a jar of mayonnaise with when you go to a bar on a Saturday night?"

He still couldn't think of a clever response, so Mike offered another simple one: "Of course."

"Oh, I see it all the time," the bartender said confidently.

Fred slowly nodded. "Yeah, the more I think about it. That's perfectly normal."

"You guys can be really strange," Sam added.

Mike enjoyed the moment of appearing a little unusual. He also wondered about making a graceful exit soon. It had been a good night, but his hangover was clearly making a comeback; better to exit before he appeared a little too unusual.

He rubbed his forehead again and decided a simple and straightforward response was best. "Stopping by here was a little unplanned. Since I went out with George last night, tonight was going to be for busywork, like laundry and groceries. I should really get home now. There's still some laundry to take care of."

"Makes sense to me," the bartender said.

"I guess it makes sense," Sam added. "But I still think you need to have a little more fun on your Saturday nights."

"I suppose. Well, I'm going to head out. It was good meeting you, and I'll see you later."

The small group said goodbye to Mike, and just as he reached for the door, Sam yelled out, "Let us know if you find someone else!"

Mike smiled, waved, and walked out of The Tacklebox.

Snow was gently falling when he stepped outside. Mike wondered if the sidewalk had become slippery. After testing it with a couple of careful steps, he realized it was safe. Actually, this kind of snow made the sidewalk safer, since the thin layer of soft snow made things a little brighter. After walking for a while, he heard the sound of a double bell, which had become strangely familiar. He glanced to his left and saw the lights from Tank's gas station. He also heard a group in front of him. They sounded like young men who'd had too much to drink, but he still used them as a guide, walking a few steps behind them.

His thoughts wandered to his new friends. They were a lot of fun, but he was still nervous about standing on a freezing ski slope with skiers headed right for him. It was too bad that George couldn't help. They could have had a great time sharing this little adventure, or misadventure. Norman might be interested since he was into sports, but asking him could also be challenging. He still considered many blind sports to be hazardous.

Norman had become both easier and harder to talk with. Sometimes, he was very relaxed and even friendly, but other times, his bullying side came out, especially when he was uncomfortable. Mike remembered something his dad used to say about such people: "He's the kind of guy who can really make the worst of a bad situation." Maybe Albert or Mary would be interested in volunteering, but they didn't seem like the type. Mike turned a corner and recognized some bright flashing lights. "Home sweet home."

"Hey, hey, new guy. How the hell are ya?" Ruby asked as she stepped out of a car. She looked back into the car and spoke to the driver. "Now this guy, he's a good one, not an asshole like some people."

"Go to hell, bitch," the driver yelled as he spun the tires and drove off.

Mike hadn't seen Ruby like this before. She wasn't walking or standing very steady. When other cars drove by, their lights helped him see her better. It looked like her hair and clothes were messed up.

"You okay, Ruby?"

"Me? Hell yeah. Things just got a little rough, happens sometimes." She pulled out a cigarette and lighter. "I always take care of it, though." She lit the cigarette.

Her words were slurred and contained none of the streetwalking voice, which Mike had noticed before. She reached into her bag, grabbed a tissue, and pressed it against her face. She took the tissue off and looked at it. "Damn, I was afraid that bastard was wearing a ring."

"Are you sure you're okay?"

"Yeah, yeah, I just need to get cleaned up. It always pisses me off when someone draws blood, especially on my face. The worst part is it can be bad for business. I wonder if he messed anything else up." She looked down and scanned her body. "Goddammit, I just bought this blouse. Now it's got blood on it and half the buttons are gone." Her voice changed, sounding less frustrated and even friendly. "But you know what, new guy, this does give me a chance to show you something. Come a little closer."

Mike paused and wrinkled his forehead.

"Oh, come on, I'm not going to bite, and I'm certainly not trying to get any more business tonight, so just come a little closer." Mike took a half step toward her. Ruby forced a smile, rotated toward the flashing lights of Mariner's, and pointed at the top of her unbuttoned blouse. Mike saw the red bra.

"I thought it would bring me luck tonight. So much for luck."

"I'm sorry, Ruby. Are you sure there's nothing I can do to help?"

"I appreciate the offer, but I'm shot. All I want to do is get cleaned up and watch some TV. Ha, that's the same thing you do to relax, right? Besides, you've already helped. Sometimes, all a girl wants is someone to care a little."

Mike thought about asking if she wanted someone to watch TV with, but he suspected Ruby really did want to be by herself. Maybe she had a routine for this kind of problem. Besides, it was only this afternoon that she'd offered her services to him, so watching TV together could be awkward. "All right, it sounds like you have everything under control."

"One thing I always do is keep things under control. Come on, we both need to get home." They crossed the street together. "You're still carrying that duffle bag? Do you always take your laundry with you when you go out on a Saturday night?"

"Most of the time, but I'm trying something different tonight. This time, it's full of groceries. Want a doughnut or maybe a sandwich?"

Ruby laughed. "Michael, we need to talk about your choices on a Saturday night. You're never going to get a girl if you keep this up."

"I suppose."

They both chuckled and walked into Mariner's. Mike could hear the TV by the reception desk.

"Sure, why not." Ruby said.

"Huh?" Mike mumbled.

"I'll take the doughnut. That sounds great right now."

Mike took the duffle bag off his shoulder, set it down, and felt around inside it. "Here, have a couple." He handed the box of doughnuts to Ruby with one hand and searched inside the bag with the other.

"Thanks. Are you looking for something inside your bag? I could help you find it."

"No problem, I found it. Have a Coke to wash it down."

"You are a good one, new guy, a very good one."

Mike couldn't think of a reply. He wanted to give Ruby something to feel better, but he also didn't want to give the impression that he was being more than friendly. "No problem, what are friends for?"

"Hey," a man called from behind the reception desk. "I'll take a couple of those, if you're handing them out."

"Sorry, only one handout a day," Mike called back.

"In that case, I'll talk with you tomorrow."

"I suppose."

Mike and Ruby walked into the hallway and toward the staircase. When Mike started walking down the steps, she asked, "Aren't you going to your room?"

"I still have to finish some laundry. It's my favorite way to spend a Saturday night."

"We need to talk, Michael. We really need to talk."

"Good night, Ruby."

"Night, new guy."

Mike walked down to the laundry room and put his dry clothes into the duffle bag, on top of the groceries. Then he moved the wet clothes into the same dryer. He started the dryer and walked to his room.

Something about climbing the steps was unusually tiring. After Mike stepped into his room, he shut the door, leaned back against it, sighed, and spoke with calm frustration. "Ruby wakes me up before sunrise and gets beat up after sunset. I'm going to stand on a freezing ski slope in front of a bunch of blind skiers, racing at high speed, and I need to find someone else to do the same, mostly for a girl who is probably too intense for any normal guy to consider." Mike shook his head and wondered about how complex life could get.

"I know exactly what I'll do. I'll put away the groceries." He pulled out the clean laundry from the top of the duffle bag and put it in a pile, close to where the pile of dirty laundry used to be. He thought about the uncomfortable issues while putting away the groceries, hoping to find something more comfortable about any of them. "One thing is for sure. Sam's gorgeous, and as long as I don't piss her off, I might even get laid. Cool."

He grinned, grabbed his toothbrush, and walked to the bathroom. When he returned to his room, Mike sat on the edge of the bed and remembered sitting in the same place this morning. At that time, he'd felt very hung-over, worried about getting a job, and annoyed about the low chance of having sex. At least one of those issues was now less of a problem, maybe. Some parts of the day had been tougher than expected, and some were better. "Sometimes, that's what you get."

He turned out the light and dozed off.

CHAPTER SIX

Challenges

Mike opened the door to Bridgman's, waited for the receptionist to say "Good morning," and replied with the same. After
passing her desk, he scanned the reception area for traces of bright red
hair, as he'd done for a couple of weeks. No traces appeared. He
walked into the corridor and kept scanning, with the same result. He
felt disappointment and relief. Disappointment came from the hope
to talk with her again. Relief came from something they would probably talk about—whether he'd found anyone else to shake a tambourine. He'd spoken with Sam briefly since telling her he'd look for
another volunteer, but so far, she hadn't asked him about it.

In the last week, he'd casually asked some students if they would
help. They'd casually said they weren't interested or said they would
get back to him and never did. This week, he'd directly asked some
students, and they'd directly said no. He'd almost tried the same technique with Norman, since he was showing friendlier moments. Just
before Mike was going to ask, somebody started joking with Norman
about how the Vikings were going to lose another Super Bowl. Norman didn't think it was funny and used his deep voice to say so. Mike
still enjoyed talking with Norman but had learned to keep things calm

when Norman used that tone of voice. The best option now seemed to be asking George. He knew more people than most, so he could probably find a volunteer.

Unfortunately, asking George was risky because the conversation could quickly become complicated. He might ask how, or worse why, Mike had ever volunteered to stand on a freezing ski slope and shake a tambourine in front of blind and blindfolded skiers, especially since he didn't ski. With most people, Mike could probably reply with a little joke and move on, but George could ask some awkward questions with his own jokes. Eventually, Sam's name would come up, and George might figure out that Mike volunteered to impress her.

If he figured that out, George could easily have too much fun with the topic. Of course, he would admit she was attractive, but he would also enjoy a few, or many, laughs. Some of the laughs could be simple, like dealing with Sam's lively side if the flirting continued. Other laughs could be complicated, like the challenges of flirting with a teacher. That could get Mike expelled and Sam fired. Mike could handle a few laughs at his expense, but since George laughed louder and longer than most, others might join in and learn about Mike's hope with Sam. That could put a quick end to the hope.

Mike sighed. There were problems with asking Norman because he could be too grumpy. There were problems with asking George because he could be too playful, and there were problems with being attracted to a teacher. All these relationships and rules reminded him of the gossip he used to hear at work a few months ago at the tractor parts factory. Eyesight hadn't been an issue there, but issues with relationships were more similar than different. He decided to stop worrying so much. He'd found a way through messy problems before, at least well enough. He'd do it again, hopefully better than well enough.

Maybe George wouldn't ask why he'd volunteered to help. After all, it was for a good cause. Maybe George would just say he knew somebody and solve the problem in seconds. Maybe he wouldn't suspect that Sam was the reason Mike chose to volunteer, and even if he did, maybe he would have a couple of laughs about it and be discreet. Mike sighed again. He was trying to worry less, but discretion wasn't one of George's strengths, and curiosity definitely was. Maybe asking Norman was the easier option after all.

He felt a small relief after stepping into the dayroom. That meant a simple part of his morning routine was coming up, checking the time. He walked to the post in the dayroom, put his face close to the clock, and saw it was 8:45. He took a few steps toward the corridor that would take him to the kitchen for his first class. Mike then saw a familiar shape leaning against the wall. It was the shape of a man with a beer belly, and as Mike got closer, he could see an untucked plaid shirt.

"Hey, George, how ya doing?"

"Mikey, good morning, sir. I'm doing just dandy, thanks. I might also add that this is the third morning in a row that I'm here on time. One more makes four, and four makes for a free burger and monster rings."

"I suppose."

Mike had forgotten about that deal. He'd suggested it on Monday, after George had received another lecture from Margaret about being late again. The deal was that Mike would buy supper if George was early for the rest of the week. To help with this, they'd decided to meet in the dayroom before class. Mike had thought about buying drinks during a night out, but buying a meal was almost as motivating and much cheaper. George's comment also clarified to Mike that it was

Thursday. The week was going by fast, so he should ask for another volunteer soon.

"Hey, George, I was wondering if you could do me a little favor."

"I'd be happy to. What's on your mind?"

"It's about the ski trip that's coming up. Have you heard about it?"

"Sure, you thinking of going?"

"Yeah," Mike said while leaning against the wall. In a small way, that felt better since it took the conversation further away from the center of the dayroom.

"Well, that sounds great. We'll have a blast in the chalet. I can probably get them to come up with their own gauntlet of drinks, like the one at The Slowstream. I bet we could finish the whole thing."

"Actually, I might need to spend some time outside of the chalet."

"Really? Don't tell me you're going to be skiing. I thought your only winter sport was snowmobile tag."

"No, I'm not planning on skiing."

"All right, what else are you going to do?"

Another voice came from behind the two men, a deep voice. "Hey, guys, mind some more company in your little morning meeting?"

Mike turned toward the man. "Hi, Norman."

"I meant to stop by when I heard you yesterday," Norman said. "I've always liked getting to work, or class, a little early. It lets me ease into the day."

"We'd be happy to have you join our little group. Michael was just about to ask for some help with something."

"I may be interested in helping too, if I can," Norman replied. "I've been bored out of my skull around here. I actually wish we had homework."

"Funny you mention that," Mike said. "I thought about asking you too."

"Hey, before we get into that," George added, "we better start walking to the kitchen. I would rather be a little early than late. I don't want to lose my bet with Michael on a technicality."

"You can't say I didn't try," Mike added sarcastically.

"I always knew I should never entirely trust you, Michael. That's one of the reasons I like you; you keep things unpredictable. Gimme your elbow."

Mike moved his elbow toward George's lifted hand. He held Mike's elbow, and the three men started walking toward the kitchen.

"Sounds good," Norman replied. "I should be early anyway. Today's my big day to cook."

"Oh yeah, I forgot about that. What's on the menu?" George asked.

"Well, Margaret's spent the last few weeks telling us to start with what we know, so I'm making the meal I know best: meat." The last word came out as a slow, low grunt.

Mike smiled a little at the way it was said and couldn't resist a joke. "When you put it that way, I have to wonder if it's going to be alive at the start of class." All three chuckled.

"That is tempting, makes me miss mornings in the woods during deer hunt'n season. But no, I need to keep it simple. I bought a package yesterday and put it in the fridge."

"Pardon me for going out on a limb here," George added, "but if I had to guess, you'll be serving the meat with potatoes?"

"Pardon me for saying," Norman replied, "but that's a silly question."

Mike suspected Norman was trying to tell a joke, but it came off with an edge.

"Well, sometimes," George said. "I quite like being a little silly. Other times, it's fun being serious. I've even been known to seriously talk about a few metaphors for life. We could chat about that for a while, if you'd like."

The comment impressed and concerned Mike. He was impressed because George had brought up something that had annoyed Norman a few weeks ago. It was Margaret's question about sports being a metaphor for Norman's life, instead of his football players'. Mike was concerned because Norman wasn't the kind of guy Mike liked to tease or bait, as George just had.

Norman didn't take the bait, or at least didn't respond verbally, but there was some tension. Mike decided to keep things calm with a safe reply. "We don't have time to talk much more anyway. We're almost at the table." George sat just to the right of Mike, and Norman sat two seats to the left.

"Good morning, gentlemen," Margaret announced.

The three men mumbled a response. Mike was relieved that Margaret would be talking for a while, since it could remove the tension.

"I'll get started since we're all here, even though it's a few minutes before nine." Mike could see she was looking toward him. Her tone was more upbeat than usual, maybe from seeing George on time again.

"I'm looking forward to today's class for a few reasons. First, I want to say that everyone has done a great job cooking so far. I might even say that things have gotten better in each class." Mike saw her smile this time, and she was clearly holding her glance on George.

He must have sensed her lighthearted tone or the glance in his direction, since he replied in the same way. "You wouldn't, by chance, be suggesting that there was room for improvement after the brave souls who took the risk of going first, would you?"

"Not at all, George," Margaret answered with a similar tone. "I have nothing but respect for your cooking skills."

"That's what I thought you were going to say."

"And," Norman said, "I have nothing but respect for the way you can handle an egg." He finished with a small but sarcastic laugh.

George laughed in a way that mirrored Norman's tone and replied, "I'm glad you liked it, Coach. Just remember, today's your turn."

Mike started feeling nervous about sitting between the men.

Norman laughed again, tapped his knuckles on the table, and then spoke slowly. "Yes, it is."

Mike felt more nervous.

Margaret returned to her normal teaching voice when she announced, "I get the impression that you guys have had a chance to get to know each other. That's good. As your classes have shown, there are a lot of challenges for blind folks, so we're all better off when we get to know each other and support each other. Wouldn't you agree?" The group's response was so light that Mary's voice was the loudest.

"George and Norman, do you agree that we all need to help each other out?"

"Oh, I'd be happy to," George answered, in a way that was too familiar.

"I'd be happy to, too," Norman responded, mocking George's phrase.

There was a pause that Mike couldn't figure out. Maybe Margaret wanted the guys to think things over, or maybe she didn't know a good way to proceed.

"As you know, I like to review some key points before most classes. This time, I'm going to go way back to our first class. I mentioned that people have to work through a lot of challenges when they come here. They respond in a lot of different ways. We can handle most of those responses, even encourage them. But ..." She paused and took a couple of steps in Mike's direction. He'd come to respect how this small woman could sound so strong without becoming angry. This time, her voice was stronger. "If students start behaving in ways that interfere with learning, I *will* manage the situation so we can continue learning." She stopped about an arm's length from George. "I hope that I've made myself clear."

Margaret walked back toward the center of the kitchen and sounded less firm; at least, she tried to. "I mentioned that I'm looking forward to today's class. The reason is that I'm a woman who enjoys a good steak, and that's what we're having. Norman and Mary will be cooking today, and the meal is a great American favorite, steak and potatoes. Norman, Mary, why don't you get started? Is there anything you need before you begin?"

Norman answered in an upbeat tone, "Nope, we prepared a lot of it yesterday." He stood up, stepped toward the kitchen, and continued in a tone that was a little too upbeat. "I've always believed that being early is the best way to be."

Mike heard George let out a quiet cough or laugh, as if he were holding back a joke.

Mary also walked to the kitchen and said, "I agree with Norman. I think we have everything ready." She continued when she was near the stove. "Norman, if it's all right with you, I'll organize things, at least at first." Mike was a little surprised at the sound of Mary's voice.

It had more confidence than before. Maybe she'd just needed more time than others to get comfortable at school.

"I think that's a good idea," Margaret said while walking out of the kitchen, toward the text-enlarging machine. "What do you think Norman?"

"Sure, why not. She knows what she's doing."

Mary moved around the kitchen with an ease that impressed Mike. Right now, she seemed about as comfortable in this kitchen as Margaret. Mary also had a nonthreatening way of asking Norman which tasks he wanted to do. At first, she made short requests in her soft voice, starting with, "Norman could you." Norman's replies slowly changed from clear words like "Yes" and "Sure" to more relaxed mumblings like "Uh-huh" and "Ya." In contrast, Mary's requests gradually became more direct. Mike wondered if she was used to being a peacemaker in kitchen conflicts, or kitchen table conflicts.

"I hate to be a bother," George called out. "But I have a question."

"What's on your mind?" Margaret asked.

"I'm a bit *late* in asking this question." He continued in a roguish tone, which didn't quite fit this situation. "But I figure it's still worthwhile. From a public health perspective and from a personal perspective, I hope you don't mind me asking. Have you washed your hands?"

Mike remembered that Norman had asked the question a couple of weeks ago when George was cooking. Norman rotated toward George and paused before answering. Mike wasn't sure if it came from frustration or from the chance that the answer was no. Mike also thought he heard some knuckles tapping from the kitchen.

"My hands are clean," Norman finally answered.

There was a moment of silence. Mike suspected Margaret hadn't seen this situation before, but she eventually spoke.

"That's a good point. I should have mentioned it sooner. Norman and Mary, I would appreciate it if you would wash your hands now." She looked toward George. "Thanks for your helpful question, George. I'm looking forward to any more questions and comments that are *helpful.*" The last word came out in a way that told George and Norman that she had enough of their thinly veiled insults. Mike wasn't sure if the two men would stop their little jabs at each other, but he did hear the sound of running water after seeing Norman walk to the sink.

A few minutes went by, as Mike watched and listened to the activity in the kitchen. Cupboards opened. Water started and stopped, and pots bumped against pans. His thoughts wandered toward the idea of finding a volunteer to shake a tambourine, until he heard Margaret's voice.

"You guys are doing great. I want to pause for a moment, so we can all learn from your cooking. What are the main steps in what you've done so far?"

Mary answered. "Well, I started by getting out the things we need."

"Could you tell us what they were?" Margaret asked.

"We just finished getting the potatoes ready. We peeled them after school yesterday and put them in the fridge. I just took the potatoes out of the fridge and set them on the counter. I've been trying to put things in groups more often, like you taught us. So, I asked Norman to put everything together on the counter—the potatoes, a big pot, and the masher. I also set out a pack of instant gravy and a small pot for it."

"Norman, I noticed you took care of the steaks. Could you tell us a little about that?"

His voice was civil but still had some tense, gravelly tones. "Sure. There's not much to tell. I took the meat out of the fridge, pulled the plastic off, and set it on the counter. I also added my secret spices. We wanted some veggies, so I just started warming up a can of corn and a can of green beans."

"It sounds like you have everything under control. Does anyone have any questions or comments?"

"I just thought of one," Norman said slowly.

Mike wondered if Norman was going to add another jab at George.

His voice was deep but calm. "How do you want your steaks? I think rare is best, but for reasons I'll never understand, my wife likes them crispy."

George was the last person to answer. To Mike's relief, it was simple. "I'd like mine medium."

Norman and Mary returned to their cooking. Mike's gaze wandered toward the table. He could still hear the sounds of steaks sizzling, pans moving around, and Mary giving instructions to Norman, but Mike's thoughts focused on getting a volunteer.

He might be able to ask for volunteers when the meal was ready, while everyone ate their steaks. The best options were asking Norman to be a volunteer and asking George to find one. Unfortunately, Norman was probably in one of his impatient moods. If Mike asked while they ate, Norman's most likely response would be that it's too hazardous to stand in front of competitive skiers. Asking George also had problems, especially in a group. If George suspected that Sam was part of the reason Mike had chosen to volunteer, George could quickly make some jokes and ruin Mike's hope with Sam. Mike decided that he would try to ask each man individually, unless a very good opportunity came up during the meal.

"Bummer," Mike mumbled in response to his own thoughts.

"You say something?" George asked.

"No, sorry."

George grunted an acknowledgment.

"All right," a voice boomed from the kitchen. "We're almost done." Norman's voice had the same calm tone from a moment ago. "I'll call out each steak depending on how it was cooked. Raise your hand and call back when it's yours."

He called out rare, medium, or well. The first couple of calls were in his normal voice, but the rest sounded like a coach calling out the names of his football players. Norman delivered each steak after each person raised a hand and called back, usually with the word "Here." After Norman delivered a plate, each person thanked him, including George. Norman replied to each person with a "You're welcome" or "Hope you enjoy it." When everyone had their steak, he and Mary put bowls on the table with corn, beans, mashed potatoes, and gravy.

When everything was ready, they sat at the table, which meant Mike was sitting between George and Norman again. It was still a little uncomfortable. His two friends seemed to have a truce right now, but Mike could only hope it would hold.

He thought about challenging situations that occurred before in this and other classes. Usually, George would lighten things up, but in this case, he was part of the challenge. Mike decided to stop pondering and start eating like everyone else.

"Norman, this is really good," Albert commented, chewing on a piece of steak.

"Thanks," Norman grunted and scooped some potatoes onto his own plate.

Albert chewed some more and continued. "I mean it. I used to go to some of the best steakhouses in Minneapolis, and this is different, even better."

Norman grunted another thanks and reached for the corn.

Mary spoke next. "He's right, Norman. This is really very good. Can I have the recipe for your sauce?"

"Sorry, can't do it. It's a family secret." His words were clearer this time, and Mike suspected Norman enjoyed holding firm.

Mike was also enjoying the steak and added his own comment. "Wow, that's not bad. If I can't have your recipe, can I have your steak?"

A few people at the table chuckled.

"Fat chance," Norman replied with a little laugh of his own.

"It sounds like a very nice tradition," Mary said. "Could you at least tell us how long it's been in your family?"

"Sure," Norman said while cutting off a piece of steak. "My dad used to cook steaks for as long as I can remember. He taught me how to do it, just like his dad taught him." He jabbed a fork into the piece he'd just cut off.

"Has the recipe stayed the same?" Margaret asked.

"I wish," he said, chewing on the steak. "My doctor told me to cut back on salt a few years ago, so I had to change it a little." He cut into another piece and continued. "I never asked my dad if he changed it or if his dad did."

"Could you tell us if you marinate the steak?" Albert asked.

Norman chewed for a moment and shook his head. "I don't think so. If I say much more, I could let out important details."

"That's fine, Norman, thanks," Mary replied.

During the rest of the meal, most of the people in the group chatted with each other, except George. Mike suspected George felt awkward about the comments he'd made earlier. Mike didn't feel very talkative either, since he was still trying to figure out how to find another volunteer.

When everyone finished their steaks, Margaret gave a summary. "Once again, I'm impressed with our meal. We've made a few different ones now, so in tomorrow's class, I want to spend some time talking about what was similar and different in preparing the meals so far. I'll ask each of you to describe what was easy or not with the meals you've made, so give that some thought. Tomorrow's class is also going to involve some cleaning. We'll review what we learned about cleaning a room with less sight, and then we'll all help in giving this kitchen a good scrubbing. That will prepare us for next week's class, which will focus on other types of cleaning, like laundry, and everyone's favorite, cleaning the bathroom. That reminds me, we need to pick someone to clean up after this meal. Mike and George, you haven't washed up for a while. Do you have time today?"

Both men mumbled a yes.

"Good. I have to leave for a meeting, but you know the drill. Does anybody have questions before I leave?" There was no response, so Margaret continued. "All right, I'll see you tomorrow. Mary and Norman, thanks again for a great meal."

Margaret carried her dishes and set them next to the sink. Mike and George stood up and started organizing the pots, pans, and other dirty dishes. Mike scraped food off of some plates into a wastebasket. George started filling the sink with water, added soap, and moved some dishes into the sink. Other students placed their dishes near

George as they walked out. In a few minutes, Mike and George were alone in the kitchen. For a while, the only sound came from pots, pans, cupboards, and water as the men worked together.

Mike suspected George was wondering about the jabs and jokes he'd exchanged with Norman. George might think that he shouldn't have added as many, or he might think that more would have been better. In either case, Mike hadn't seen George act this way before, so he chose a safe comment to find out. "You're kind of quiet."

"Yeah," George said. He paused before continuing. "I've been wondering if I was out of line, but the guy got on my nerves, has been for a while." He put a soapy plate into the sink for rinsing and moved the plate around the clear water. "I've never liked bullies or knuckle-draggers like Norman. If somebody doesn't push back, they just keep pushing other people around."

Mike scraped food off some more plates and into a wastebasket. "Yeah, I see what you mean."

George continued washing after putting the clean plate in a drying rack. "Thanks, and here comes the but."

"*But.*" Mike emphasized the word. "Margaret's already been getting on your case, and you want to finish this class."

Another moment of silence went by as Mike organized some dishes by the sink. "I'm stacking the rest of the plates closest to the sink. I'll put the glasses to the left of the plates, close to the wall," he said to George.

"Okay," George said while putting some glasses in the water. "I hate it when you're right. The knuckledragger still gets on my nerves, though."

"I know he does, and I'm not adding a but this time. I'll rinse and dry."

"Thanks. How many more dishes do we have left?"

"We're about a quarter done."

"Hey, you were going to ask me something before class started and King Kong showed up. What was it?"

Mike wiped a glass, sighed, and decided to tell George as little as possible. Maybe he wouldn't figure out how Sam was involved. "Well, I tried a different bar the other night and ended up talking with a couple of guys who plan the ski trip." Mike put the glass away and felt good about how the word *guys* came out in his description, knowing it might help avoid saying that Sam was there.

"Sounds like a good time, and if I had to guess, you were probably at The Tacklebox. I haven't been there for a while, but that's as good a reason as any to stop by sooner than later. Was Fred around?"

"Yeah, I enjoyed talking with him." Mike moved dishes from the rinsing sink to the drying rack and smiled a little. He had an idea that could focus the conversation on George and hopefully away from Sam. "Actually, Fred mentioned you, about how much fun you had on the last ski trip."

"Well, I always strive to make the best of any situation, and there's plenty of opportunity on a ski trip."

Mike responded in a lively tone. "This one had something to do with a talent I didn't know you had."

His friend gave a cautious reply. "Well, I've always been too modest to describe all my talents, but since you put it that way, I have to admit that I have a few."

Mike put away a dish and pressed on. "This one has something to do with singing."

George smiled. "Oh yes, *that* talent." He chuckled while saying, "On certain occasions, the urge to carry a tune does come over me."

"Fred also said something about how that occasion seems to occur later in the evening rather than sooner."

George put some dirty bowls and silverware into the sink and smiled. "I never thought about it that way before, but Fred may very well have a point."

Mike chuckled and couldn't resist having more fun. "You know, George, I feel a little left out. All the time I've known you, and I've never been able to enjoy one of your live performances."

George wasn't about to lose this battle of wits. "Well, Michael, as I've been saying, a man with all my talents has a tough time sharing them with everyone, so all I can do is advise patience. I'm sure you'll have a chance to enjoy one of those moments soon and hopefully participate."

"I suppose," Mike said with a laugh that continued until he finished drying a plate.

"Now, you were going to ask me about something, and I don't think it was for a live performance."

"You're right," Mike said while dropping a washrag into the soapy water. He wrung it out and added, "I'm a bit ahead of you with the rinsing and drying, so I'll wipe down the counters and tables." He stepped away and started wiping a counter, a little harder than usual. Mike realized this was the moment he'd been worrying about, where he would have to ask George to find a volunteer.

"All right, so what were you going to ask me about?"

"Well, I just wanted to ask about something Fred mentioned. He was wondering if you might know somebody who could volunteer to shake a tambourine." Mike hoped he didn't sound as nervous as he felt.

"Sure, I could probably find someone. I just need to ask around," George said while taking a pot out of the sink and wiping it slowly. "Now, you have me wondering. If they asked you to find a volunteer, they probably asked you to *be* one." He put the pot in the rinse water. "I have to give you credit for finding a way to look for a volunteer instead of standing in the wind on a freezing ski slope. Fred and his planning buddies can be pretty persistent. You're lucky Sam wasn't there. She can be relentless."

Mike stopped wiping the counter and decided to start wiping the kitchen table. It felt good to put some distance between him and George. When Mike reached the table, he tried finding a response that would return the conversation to George getting a volunteer. Before he could find one, George continued.

"Hang on a sec, didn't you say that you were going to be busy during the ski trip?" Then, he answered his own question. "Yeah, in the dayroom before class, you said that you couldn't spend much time in the chalet."

Mike continued looking for a good response.

"Don't tell me you volunteered to shake a tambourine?" George laughed while holding up a plate and shaking it slowly.

"Well, yeah, I did."

George laughed some more. "You're going to stand on a freezing ski slope and shake a tambourine while competitive skiers head right for you?"

Mike rubbed the table harder. "Sure, it's for a good cause, and besides, I do all right in the cold."

"Wow, that still surprises me. I mean, most of the volunteers are the sporty type, so it kind of makes sense. *But*, you've been telling the coach that the only sport you enjoy is snowmobile tag."

Mike worried George was getting close to figuring out the real reason. He finally thought of a response and hoped it was good enough. "You like to surprise people with singing. I surprise people in other ways."

"Yeah, I guess," George said. "This does surprise me, even amaze me. You've never skipped an evening of drinks and laughs before, especially to freeze on a ski slope. How did they talk you into it? Did they throw in some free drinks or something?"

"Actually, they did. I'm getting a couple of free meals."

"Really? That surprises me even more. Normally, they run the ski races on a pretty tight budget. Where are the meals at?"

Mike felt nervous. He hoped to find answers that would make George ask fewer questions instead of more. "One is in the chalet and the other is at The Tacklebox." Mike looked for ways to change the topic. "The kitchen table is clean, so I'll get back to rinsing and drying."

George pulled a fistful of silverware out of the soapy water, gave them a token wipe with the washrag, and dropped them into the rinse water. Mike picked up the silverware and rubbed off something George missed, which led to another way to change the topic.

"Damn, George, I like leftovers, but not when they're on the silverware."

"Everybody's a perfectionist these days."

Mike felt relieved they were talking about something else, until George spoke again.

"There's still something I can't figure out. The Tacklebox has great prices on drinks, but I've never known them to give away meals. I'm impressed you and Fred were able to pull that off." George started washing a small pot. "Or, were there others? Usually, a few people plan the ski trips."

This is exactly what Mike hoped would not happen. George had put some pieces together and asked a question that Sam in the answer. He took more of the silverware out of the rinse water. "Yeah, there were other people, but you know me. I've always been lousy with names." Once again, Mike wondered if he sounded nervous.

"Well, maybe I can help. I could mention some of the people who usually plan the trip. There's Sharon, Johnny, and like I said before, Sam usually helps out."

Mike cringed again while putting the plates in the drying rack. He really needed to end this conversation. "Yeah, those names sound a little familiar, but I can't remember exactly. The next time I see them, I'll do a better job of remembering names."

He found another way to change the topic. "I'm going to see what time it is. We don't want to be late to our next class." He walked to a nearby clock and was relieved to see that they really did need to finish soon. "We have about fifteen minutes before the Home Finance class starts. If we hurry, we should be all right."

"Sounds good," George mumbled. He dropped the pot he was washing into the rinse water. "Hey, I wonder if we could turn this into a trade. I'll get your volunteer, if you help me with something from the Home Finance class."

Mike was nervous about getting back to the topic, but it sounded like George might help. "Sure, but I always thought you didn't like that class."

"You're very right about that. Finance has always bored me to tears, but the class might solve a problem for me. It involves some of my own volunteering at a car parts store that a buddy owns." He carefully reached to the remaining dirty dishes next to him, pulled them closer, and put some in the soapy water. "I already help by hanging out at the store and answering questions, but we're trying to see if there can be an actual job in it. One tricky part is that other staff do some math once in a while, simple stuff with a pencil and paper. It's for inventory or giving a price to a customer. That's where the Home Finance class comes in, especially the abacus." He started scrubbing a frying pan.

Mike thought about the abacus for a moment while drying off some bowls. He'd learned how to use it at Saint John Cantius Primary School, the same Catholic school his dad had gone to. Back then, the device had captured his attention because the beads and shape were clever, simple, and useful. More recently, he'd been surprised to be taught how to use it again in the Home Finance class. An abacus was helpful because many legally blind adults couldn't see well enough to do math with a marker and paper, and math with Braille was even harder than reading with Braille. His thoughts shifted to a newer device. "Too bad those new electronic calculators are so expensive."

George dropped the frying pan into the rinse water. "Yeah, and even if they weren't a few hundred bucks, I still can't see the numbers, which brings me back to an abacus. I noticed you're pretty good with the things. Mind giving me some lessons?"

Mike wiggled the pan in the rinse water to get some soap off. "Sure, when were you thinking of?" He took the pan out and started drying it.

"Well, I was thinking of heading off to the shop tonight for a couple of hours. It gets slow sometimes, so I could probably practice there." He pulled out the last of the silverware, gave them a quick wipe with the washcloth, and dropped them in the rinse water.

Mike smiled and replied, "George, are you actually *asking* for homework?" He pulled the silverware out of the rinse water, dried it, and put it in the drawer.

"I prefer to call it *practice*, and I would greatly appreciate it if you would not put that word and my name together again, especially in public. I have a reputation to keep."

"I suppose." Mike walked away from the sink and continued. "Well, I think we're done. I'll just take one last walk around to make sure we have everything." He also felt relieved that George had agreed to find a volunteer without learning about Sam.

"So, could you show me more about the abacus and give me some things to practice?"

"Sure, we'll just stop by the dayroom later. That's all the dishes, go ahead and let the water out of the sink." Mike walked back into the kitchen and asked, "Do you have an abacus with you?"

"Yeah, I liberated one from our Home Finance class yesterday."

Mike smiled at the remark, knowing that the school encouraged all students to take an abacus home to practice. "How about meeting in the dayroom after school?"

"Sounds good," George said. "We better head off to Home Finance now. Between you and this possible job at the parts store, I may even show up on time a bit more. And besides, being on time would give King Kong less to talk about. Hard to beat that."

Mike smiled and walked out of the kitchen with George.

.   .   .   .

"Fifteen past five," Mike mumbled to himself as he stood in front of the clock in the dayroom. He knew George was trying to be on time more often, but Mike wasn't too surprised his friend was late. He walked back to the comfortable chair in the corner, which he'd been sitting in a few minutes ago. He sat down again and looked forward. From here, he could see down one of the corridors leading to the day-room, the one he used to come and go from Bridgman's. He rolled his head back into the soft cushion of the chair, shut his eyes, and listened for sounds of George.

He heard other sounds, traffic from outside of Bridgman's and someone crying from inside. He wondered what the crying was about. He'd heard more stories about students who were having a tough time. One guy had worked at a typewriter for a couple of decades, lost his sight, came here, and could barely find keys on the home row. Another student had diabetes. She had the choice of losing weight or more sight. The student spent some time on an exercise bike but tended to gobble down a candy bar while riding. Both were known to cry a bit, and Mike had gotten to know them. They were good people, just having a tough time living with less sight.

"Michael! You here somewhere?"

"Right over here, George, how ya do'n?"

"Very good, sir, very good. Sorry I'm a few minutes late."

"That's all right, George, but I'd like to get started. Feeling a little tired."

"That's just what I was thinking. The sooner we start the better." George felt around the chairs next to Mike and sat down in one. "I admit that I'll need a little review of the basics," he said while taking an abacus out of his coat pocket.

"No problem, the multiplication we learned this week can take a lot of practice."

"I may have to go back a little further."

"Okay," Mike replied. "We'll review some addition and subtraction."

"That'd be great, but maybe we could go back just a little more."

Mike finally understood what George meant and couldn't resist having some fun. "All right, did you know that an abacus has beads for counting?"

"Very funny. I can feel that."

"Just checking," Mike said with a chuckle. "It helps to have the basics down anyway, so we'll start from there. Tell me what you know about the beads."

"I'd be happy to. The bottom has four rows of beads, and the top has one row of them. The bar between the top and bottom is where I move the beads to, for counting."

"Cool, now count up as far as you can."

"Will do, but first, I have to zero this thing out," George said while moving all the bottom beads down and the top beads up. He then counted out loud to four, moved a bead while he did, and paused. "This is the first tricky part. I always want to move the top bead in the second column down when I reach five."

"That's an easy mistake, but moving that one will make it forty-five."

"Yeah, that's the part I mess up. So, I need to move the first, top bead down, like this. But that still ain't five."

"You're right, what is it?" Mike asked.

"It's usually time to put this thing down and pick a beer up."

"We don't have a beer."

"Unfortunately."

"Since we don't, why don't you try setting it to five. All you have to do is be smarter than the beads," Mike said with a chuckle.

"Very funny." George sighed and moved some beads down. "All right, this must be five." He held the abacus in front of Mike. Two beads in the far-left column were moved toward the center bar, one above the bar and the other below.

"You're close, but that makes six, five from the top bead and one from the bottom."

"Yeah, okay, beads touching the center bar are the ones that count. How about this?" he asked while sliding down the lower bead.

"Congratulations, now keep going to ten."

George did and Mike asked him to count to ten a couple more times. Then he moved the lesson on a little. "Now, show me fifty-five."

"Right, I remember that from class, sort of. There are only four beads on the bottom, so fifty-five only uses the top beads." George moved the beads and asked, "How's that?"

"Perfect. Now, show me five hundred fifty-five, and then five thousand five hundred fifty-five."

"Well, aren't we getting ambitious?" George moved the beads on the top row down, one at a time, and showed the abacus to Mike.

"Cool, now show me sixty-six."

"Okay, that'll use beads on the top and bottom," George said while moving the beads. "How's that?"

"Perfect once again. Now try seventy-seven and seven hundred and seventy-seven."

"Hold on, tiger, one at a time."

George started moving the beads around when a new sound came into the dayroom. It was a moan, with some grunts. The sounds became louder. Mike suspected they were coming from two people in the corridor in front of him.

George sighed. "I heard they might be coming by school again."

Mike wanted to ask what that meant, but he was more curious about the moans and grunts, which were coming closer. Finally, he saw something move in an arc. Something else moved just like the first. They were arms, outreached arms, waving around. A moment later, Mike could tell there were two young men walking toward him. They continued, waving their arms and making the sounds.

"What's going on, George?"

The reply was subdued. "Deaf-blinds."

Mike didn't understand George. The sounds from the men may have been too loud, or he may have been too focused on figuring out their movements. "What did you say?"

George leaned close to Mike and spoke in the same tone. "They're deaf-blinds. Once in a while, the State sends them here for workshops."

When the two men were a few steps from the dayroom, a teacher walked near them and took their hands. She led them by the hand because the wall the men were using for guidance ended when they entered the room. Each man waved his free hand around, looking for hazards nearby. Mike became curious what they were like, wishing he could see their faces. Unfortunately, they were too far away and too unsteady for him to see much. They walked out of the dayroom, in the direction of Room 5.

The sounds faded, and Mike thought about the men. Of course, he'd heard about people who couldn't see and hear, but he never tried to understand what their life was like, or even how they would simply walk through a school. Maybe the thoughts were too complex to even try and understand—or maybe too uncomfortable. He sighed and finally said, "I haven't seen them before."

"Yeah, we hear about them sometimes, but the first time they walk by can make you think. I tried striking up a conversation once, figured what the hell. Maybe I could be their welcoming committee. It was tough, though. They communicate with tactile sign language. A teacher translated for a little while, but we could only talk for a few minutes."

"Wow," was all Mike could think of.

"Yeah, they can put things in perspective. I don't want to pity them. They're still men, who deserve dignity, but damn, no sight and no sound." George held up the abacus. "I've heard some of 'em can use these things pretty well, though. Actually, I've heard similar stuff about Laura Bridgman."

Mike was still thinking about the two men who'd walked by. The name George mentioned was familiar, but as a school, not a person. "Who?"

"Laura Bridgman. She's the woman this place is named after."

Mike remembered the brief history lesson about the woman and this place. "Oh yeah. I don't remember a lot about her, do you?"

"I know a little. She was a deaf-blind over a hundred years ago, even before Helen Keller. Back then, they thought people like her weren't smart enough to communicate, instead of simply being deaf and blind. Eventually, Laura did communicate, even wrote some stuff. When she was a kid, a guy used to take her on walks. He saw her respond to some things, and that became her lucky break. A while later, somebody taught her to communicate."

"Lucky? You're saying she was lucky?" Mike asked, as much of a statement as a question.

"Beats the alternative, especially back then, but I know what you mean."

Mike mumbled an acknowledgment.

"Hey, I'm sorry for cutting this short, but I'd like to stop by the shop for a while tonight. Mind guiding me to the bus stop?"

"Sure."

Mike and George walked down the corridor where they'd seen the two men and teacher a few minutes before. When they were outside, they talked a little more about the men and Laura, but soon, George changed the topic. He described some new car parts that were coming out at the store he hoped to work at. When Mike left him at the bus stop, George called out, "I'll see you bright and early tomorrow morning, when I win our bet. All I have to do is be on time once more."

Mike had forgotten about the bet again. "I suppose," he said and walked toward Mariner's.

CHAPTER SEVEN

Night Lights

After Mike left George at the bus stop, he started thinking more about a life where you were deaf and blind. He never did get a good look at the two young men who couldn't see, hear, or speak, but in important ways, he didn't have to. They were young men, just like him, just like a lot of people. Mike usually described his vision loss as bad luck, but the amount of bad luck those guys had to live with was hard to understand—and harder to accept.

He sighed and realized his acceptance didn't matter. It was their very real world, whether anybody accepted it or not. It was still tough seeing those two young men, but he couldn't think about their life now. The day had been more tiring than most. Seeing the deaf-blind students had been the hardest part, but it was also tiring to think about the bickering between George and Norman and about the risk of being attracted to a teacher.

He decided to focus on something simple, his evening routine. The first part was seeing what traffic was like and if there were any people he could follow. After scanning the busy road, he was surprised how many lights were on, streetlights above and headlights moving nearby. He then scanned for shadows moving on the sidewalk. These

183

shadows would be people to follow. They could help avoid hazards at crosswalks and surprises on the sidewalk. A couple of weeks ago, he was surprised after a close call with a drunk sleeping on a warm vent, and Mike still wondered what it would be like if another blind person walked toward him.

No moving shadows appeared, so he wandered close to the buildings. They could guide him on his walk, safely away from the street. Now that he was underway, he fell into the next part of his routine, letting his thoughts wander while he walked. The temptation returned to think about the deaf-blind students. His tired mind wasn't able to resist this time.

He wondered what it was like to see nothing and hear nothing. What kind of world was that? It would be days and nights of darkness and silence, but even then, they were still young men. Since he worried about finding work again and having sex again, they must have had the same worries. What else would they think or worry about? The only answers he could think of were pitiful, probably because he was tired.

George was right, pitying them was the wrong response. Laura Bridgman would want ordinary conversation instead of pity, although Mike didn't know much about her. "Should learn more." He also remembered the crying that was part of school and about the people who skied competitively without sight. It was hard to put them all in the group called "blind." That group was just as diverse as the group called "sighted." An unusual question occurred to him. Did sighted people think about him in the same way he thought about the men who were deaf and blind? He sighed and tried harder to dismiss these thoughts for a while. They were just too complex for a tired mind.

Mike scanned the headlights and streetlights again. "Sure is getting dark earlier." He felt a shiver and shoved his hands deeper into the pockets of his parka. It certainly was getting cold enough to be moving closer to the darker days of winter.

A few steps later, he realized how full this new life had become. He'd only been here for about a month, and it already filled his time and thoughts, too full in some ways. Memories of life away from Bridgman's came to mind, like what his parents were doing. He couldn't remember the last time he'd talked with them. His mom had called the front desk at Mariner's and left a message a couple of days ago, just asking how he was doing. That meant she really wanted to talk with him, since she was also paying for a phone in his room. He'd meant to call her back yesterday, maybe the day before. A car horn distracted him for a moment, but he'd become so used to the sound that his head barely turned.

Mike thought about what he'd be doing right now if he'd felt the same way on a Thursday night a year ago. He would probably be driving home after work, through the country. Back then, being tired from work would lead to roaming around his house and finding something to do that was more fun than important, like tweaking the new booster for his TV antenna. Reception had improved within five minutes of installing it, but Mike enjoyed improving reception just a little more, which often led to hours of fun.

If that didn't capture his attention, there was something else attached to his TV, the coolest piece of electronics to come out in years, probably longer. That was his Atari game system. He was surprised how much time had passed since he'd thought about it. Before it came out, Mike and his cousins had enjoyed the new Pong games that had showed up in cafes and bars, but with the Atari, he had all that in his own home. He'd learned about the gaming systems before they were on sale in Minnesota, and like most cool gadgets, they would be sold in the Twin Cities before St. Cloud. That was all right with Mike, since he didn't want to take money out of savings to pay for it. He liked the idea of putting a twenty-dollar bill aside for a few paychecks, at least until the game system was on sale in St. Cloud.

Mike smiled at the efforts he used to make to save money. One of them was keeping the heat so low that he had to wear a parka inside his new house. For Mike, it was a reasonable effort to save a few bucks, and almost as good, wearing a parka inside gave his dad a chance to have a laugh. He liked to ask Mike if there was a heater in his new house. A couple of times, Mike turned the heat down even lower before Dad came over, which gave Mike another laugh.

The Atari came to mind again, especially the clear memory of when he'd actually bought it. He'd pushed his cash forward at the register at Sears, and the clerk had pushed the box to Mike. The next memory was strapping the box to the back of his motorcycle. He didn't drive the cycle with the throttle wide open very often, but that was one of the times, on the ride home from St. Cloud.

Setting up the new Atari was better than the best boyhood Christmas. The only distraction he allowed himself was getting out the two bags of nacho chips, salsa, and Coke he'd bought for this special occasion. He stayed awake most of the night, and what a night. He was one of the first people in Stearns County to have Pong in his own home. He smiled at the thought. A semitruck blared its horn. That sound didn't happen often, and it was too loud to ignore. One of these days, he might look for a place in a better neighborhood as long as it was still cheap.

He hadn't brought his Atari to Portage Bay. The reason he usually told himself was that his room was too small for many extras, but there was something else. Soon after buying the game, he'd become pretty good at it, through many late nights of intense play. He'd tried it again a couple of months ago but couldn't come close to the scores and levels he used to reach. Maybe it would still be worthwhile to bring his Atari up here. He'd learned to do more with less sight, and maybe the game could be fun again.

His gaze wandered to the street and the lines of light from cars passing by. Their speed and power made Mike decide that it would be better to focus on the next few feet, instead of the last few months and years. Suddenly, instinct told him about another hazard. There was some laughing nearby. It was strange to think of laughter as a hazard, but he needed to learn where it was coming from to reduce the chance of bumping into the people laughing. Mike stopped walking and looked around more carefully.

The wall next to him was a little brighter, from a window a few steps ahead. The laughing didn't come from the window, so he walked slowly and scanned past it. A door opened, and he heard music. Mike remembered there was a bar around this point in his walk. Some shadows moved out of the door and onto the sidewalk. As the shadows moved more, Mike could tell they were two men. They stopped a couple of yards in front of Mike and laughed again. He stopped to see which direction they would walk. If they walked toward him, he wanted to give them plenty of space in case they'd had a few drinks. If they walked away, they would be going toward Mariner's, so he could use them as a guide, even if they'd had a few drinks. The men laughed louder, staggered toward Mike, and spoke some slurred words. He stepped toward the wall and leaned against it, close to the door.

He watched them pass by and continue down the sidewalk, laughing and stumbling as they went. He looked forward and almost started walking again, but some other lights caught his attention. These lights had been part of his evening routine for weeks, but they were still mysterious. For a moment, he watched the neon signs blink. He'd always been certain that one sign was orange, but he'd wondered if the other was blue or purple. Since he was leaning against a wall near the signs, his view was close and steady. The other sign was definitely purple. He also noticed that the signs were different shapes. The orange sign was rectangular, and the purple sign was round. Each had more details, but they weren't clear from a few feet away.

He'd always been curious about the signs but never looked closely at them. That would mean standing a few inches from them and slowly moving his face left and right. He hadn't done that because other people might think he was strange. Tonight, he was too tired to care. If other people could tolerate some young drunks stumbling down the sidewalk, the same people could tolerate Mike standing near some neon signs.

He stepped toward them and moved his face close to the window where they were displayed. The orange one was simple. It was the word BAR in block letters. The purple one was harder to make out. It was a circle with a face inside, might have been one of those artsy moon faces, but that didn't feel right for this neighborhood. Mike thought about moving even closer to the purple sign to figure out exactly what the image was, but he started craving a cold beer. He'd never gone into this bar because it seemed too rough to relax in, but something felt right about stopping tonight.

After pulling the door open, he smelled cigarette smoke and saw very little since the light was lower than other bars. He didn't have the energy to let it bother him. Right now, all he wanted was a beer and a cozy barstool. After taking a couple of steps, he suspected that low light wasn't the only reason he couldn't see much. No light bounced off the floor—might be old wood that was dark, dirty, or both. More of the bar appeared as he got closer, but it also seemed to be a dark color. Finally, he found something to guide him behind the bar. Some colors were brightly lit, almost shoulder-high. In bars like this, that was usually a collection of bottles with different colors of booze. They seemed to be lit better than anything else.

He walked slowly toward the bright bottles, since a clear line of sight to them should mean a clear walking path. The unexpected challenge of this dark bar made him want to relax on a barstool even more. Unfortunately, he could barely see individual stools, so he walked even slower and reached out a little. Eventually, he would feel a barstool, hopefully with his hands.

Mike heard the dull sound of two hard surfaces knocking together and, an instant later, felt an ache in his right knee. Since he'd been walking so slow, the pain wasn't too bad, but it was enough to cause a comment.

"Dammit!"

"You better watch yourself," a woman called out from behind the bar. "Them barstools have been kicked around for quite a few years, and I'm pretty sure they haven't budged. You okay?"

"Yeah, I'm all right," Mike answered while rubbing his knee.

"It's probably nothing a cold beer can't solve. What can I get ya?"

"Do you have Red White and Blue?" Mike asked while sliding onto a barstool.

"Oh yeah, you want a bottle or tap?"

"Whichever's cheaper."

"You're my kind of guy. One tap of Red White and Blue coming up."

Mike continued to rub his knee and glanced around the bar.

He could see more now, since he was staying in one place and his eyes had started adjusting to the low light. Mike was sitting at the corner of an L-shaped bar, with the short end off to his right. He glanced toward that end. Some light appeared just past it, and Mike saw the blurry image of a door opening, followed by a man walking out the door. As he walked closer, Mike noticed the man had an unsteady walk. "At least I know where the bathroom is."

Mike's gaze wandered back to whatever was in front of him. It settled on the sight of the bright, colorful bottles. He wondered about all the laughs those colors had caused, even—or especially—in this place. There wasn't much laughing now, just an occasional murmur.

His glance moved left, slowly exploring the long side of the bar. That showed him where the murmur was coming from. Two or three people were talking, a few barstools away. The small group didn't keep his attention, since they appeared as hunched-over shadows. Mike guessed their heads might turn toward each other as they quietly spoke, but that was more detail than he could see.

He kept scanning down the long side until some other lights appeared. There was a dull white light over a green hue. Something seemed familiar about the green hue, but he couldn't remember what it was and felt too tired to try. He scanned further to the left, to the edge of his view.

There was a row of shapes against the wall that were close to being boxes, about the same height as Mike, with a light above each. He guessed they were booths. His glance jumped back to the green hue when he heard a loud crack, followed by a man saying, "Nice break." The shape of another man was bent over the green hue.

"Hmm, a pool table."

"If you like pool, we have tournaments once a month," the woman said from behind the bar.

Normally, Mike was startled when someone heard him talk to himself, especially when they added to the conversation. He was still too tired to care, which led to a simple response. "I like watching pool sometimes." Mike slowly shifted his glance toward the bartender. "But I like relaxing in a bar a little more."

"I know what you mean," the bartender said as she slid the beer in front of Mike. "I enjoy people more than games myself. That'll be a buck ten."

Mike reached into his jeans and searched for the right coins, something he'd become faster at. He'd also become used to forming an impression of someone from a voice, especially in dark bars like this. The bartender's voice was friendly but also rough, maybe from smoking. His first impression was that she'd seen more hard times than most but could also enjoy a laugh, probably a deep belly laugh.

He put four quarters and a dime on the bar and said, "I think that's enough."

"Yep, that's it." She took the coins and continued. "I don't think I've seen you stop by my bar before. Been here much?"

"I've walked by a lot, but this is the first time I've stopped in," Mike said and took a drink.

"In that case, welcome to Speakeasy."

He enjoyed her voice. It reminded him of the small number of determined women he used to work with at the tractor parts factory. "Speakeasy?" he asked. "That's a cool name."

"I wish I could take credit for it. This place has been in my family for a couple of generations, including the years when you had to give a password to get in. When Prohibition ended, my grandpa decided to use the name to show how he managed to stick it out during the dry times."

"Good for him. My grandpa stuck it out as well," Mike said and took another drink. "Sometimes he would tell us that he had to leave for a while to *go cook* in the woods."

The bartender laughed and replied, "That's a good one. So he was going to cook at his still, hidden in the woods."

"That's about it."

"Maybe he sold some to this place. Was it around here?"

"No, it was in the center of the state in Stearns County," he answered.

The bartender leaned forward a little, put her hands on the edge of the bar, and said, "Oh, so then it was Minnesota 13. That stuff was famous."

He was impressed that she knew about the moonshine from his home. "He only made it for himself. My uncles used to call it Minnesota 12.9."

The bartender laughed a little, and Mike continued. "Sometimes, it didn't turn out so good. Then, they called it Minnesota 0.9," he said and took another drink.

The bartender laughed some more.

"And if Grandpa made it while drinking the last batch, then it could be pretty hard to swallow. In that case, they called it Minnesota negative one."

The bartender laughed louder, and Mike ended with one of his favorite lines. "Little humor, not too much."

After enjoying another laugh, the bartender said, "Since you have some history with moonshine, maybe you'd like to try some of the stuff we have here."

"Really? You still sell the stuff?"

"Of course, we have a long and proud reputation to keep."

Mike paused to consider his history with moonshine. He enjoyed telling stories about Grandpa, but he also had some brief but memorable moments drinking the stuff. "I don't know. That stuff carries a punch."

"Ah, come on, one little sip to toast your grandpa."

Mike smiled and replied, "All right, give me a little one."

"Coming up."

He watched the bartender walk away and formed a clearer image of what she looked like. Her movements and build were solid. It seemed like she'd been lifting kegs of beer herself for a long time, instead of asking for help. Mike's gaze shifted after hearing other people laugh down the long side of the bar. He glanced in that direction and noticed more moving shadows. Some women may have giggled.

He looked forward again after hearing the tap of shot glasses on the bar in front of him. Then he watched the bartender step toward the colored bottles. She pulled one off the front row and placed it next to the shot glasses. The bottle and contents were clear. There was a simple label in the middle and a cork on top.

"I think I'll join you, if that's all right," she said while pulling off the cork and filling the shot glasses without spilling a drop. "It's been a while since I had a taste and even longer since I met someone with family in the business." She put the cork back on the bottle, tapped it down with her palm, and slid one of the shot glasses toward Mike.

"Here's to our grandpas and their stubborn ways," the bartender said while raising her glass.

Mike raised his glass and moved it slowly in her direction, worried he might hit her glass too hard and spill the respected whisky. He carefully stopped moving his hand after hearing and feeling the glasses touch in a toast. She downed her shot, but he cautiously sipped his.

"Wow!" he quickly called out. "That's really ..." He wanted to say horrible but stopped himself to avoid insulting her and her family. "That's really strong."

"You're right about that, but I suspect you could be out of practice with corn whisky. It's not something to sip. You pretty much have to throw it into the back of your mouth and wash it down real quick."

She was right about him being out of practice. He'd only had the stuff once or twice. That was a few years ago, when he and some cousins had found a bottle on their grandpa's farm. He didn't want any more but also didn't want to appear ungrateful or unable to finish the small glass. "You're right. It has been a while." He raised the glass again and said, "To Grandpa" before quickly swallowing the drink. It felt like a drop of lava was sliding down his throat. With all the grace he could muster, he said, "Yeah, that's all right." But his rough voice and cringe said more.

The bartender laughed in her rough but friendly way. "Thanks, but I have a feeling you might want to stay with beer for a while."

His response came out as a coarse whisper that resembled the burning in his throat. "Yeah, maybe."

"I still enjoyed sharing a shot and a story," the bartender said with a friendly tone. "I better take care of some other folks right now. Let me know when you need another beer."

He thanked her and took another drink from his cold beer. It relieved some of the sting in his throat. He glanced to his right again when some light appeared as more people walked in and out of the bathroom door.

His gaze returned to the colored bottles. He wondered about one of the shapes in the front row. It might have been the bottle of moonshine. He squinted to try and see more detail. A thought wandered back about the taste of the stuff. He cringed and quickly said, "Yuck," hoping the bartender was too far away to hear.

He thought about all the trouble people went to for that horrible flavor, the effort and reasons. The effort involved giving up a respectable amount of corn, carefully hiding the still, and probably dealing with a wife who didn't like her husband spending so much time on something that could put him in jail or worse. The reasons obviously weren't for the flavor, so they must have been for a little alcohol escape.

"I can relate to that," he said and took another drink of beer.

His thoughts focused more on his grandpa. He was basically a proud Polish peasant who had moved to the US for the chance at a better life. That life involved farming, without the fancy tractors and modern machinery available these days, in the 1970s. Mike thought about the calluses that were a permanent part of Grandpa's hands. He also wondered if modern farmers had calluses so thick. After working that hard, it made sense that Grandpa would like a little alcoholic escape. Mike smiled at another reason why Grandpa might have enjoyed that escape. It could have been Grandma. Working with her could be at least as hard as farming without a modern tractor, especially given her disgust with alcohol.

Another loud crack came from the pool table. He looked toward it and saw the green hue. It flickered in and out of sight as the shadows of people moved around the bar. He wondered how these people were similar to Grandpa. If you could put aside Grandpa's calluses and the lifestyle that made them, these people also wanted to relax after a hard day at work. Some women giggled again. Mike was looking toward them when he heard the bartender's voice.

"I have something for you," she said while sliding a small glass toward Mike.

He raised his eyebrows a little and cautiously replied, "I'm not sure if I'm ready for another taste of corn whisky. I mean, I really appreciate the offer, but ..."

"No problem, this one isn't corn whisky," the bartender said, interrupting Mike. "It's a lot sweeter. A friend of mine asked me to bring it to you. She said you might recognize it."

Mike didn't know what to think. After being so focused on his own thoughts, all he could do was look at the drink. After a moment, he looked up and asked, "Really?"

"Don't sound so surprised. I'd probably do the same thing if I was twenty years younger."

He was still surprised and tried to figure out what to do next. Instinctively, he felt like thanking the woman who had bought him the drink. More consciously, his feelings were mixed with caution and excitement. After a few seconds, excitement took over, probably from the beer and moonshine.

"I guess I can't argue with you there," he said with a smile. "I should say thanks. Could you tell me where she's sitting?"

Mike saw a hand lift a little, gesturing past the long side of the bar. "She's right over there, in a booth. It's by the pool table and has a bunch of papers on it."

He glanced toward the booth. There were more shadows moving around the dark bar and more people talking. That made Mike wonder about the challenge of walking across the room. He thought about asking the bartender for suggestions but decided not to, since she might offer to guide him. That felt like having a chaperone when asking a woman to dance.

"Aren't you going to try it?"

He was a little embarrassed at spending a moment lost in thought and not trying the drink. Instead of answering, he took a sip. The bartender was right. It was sweet and had a familiar flavor, from a few trips down George's gauntlet and from the days when he and some cousins had snuck into bars. "Sloe gin and orange juice," Mike said confidently, "with a bit more sloe gin than usual."

"That's it, otherwise known as a Double Sloe Screw."

"That's very good," Mike said while taking another sip and thinking about how the name could also be a suggestion. That could be great, depending on who'd bought the drink. He smiled at the memory of a joke he'd told himself a few days ago. It was about how some women looked better in a parka than a sexy red bra. He was still smiling when the bartender spoke again.

"Glad you like it. I have to go help some other customers, unless there's anything else I can get for ya."

"I don't think so, thanks." Mike looked at the glass, sipped it again, and tried to remember the last time a woman had bought him a drink, if ever. His head moved up quickly after realizing that he should have asked the bartender for the woman's name. Unfortunately, the bartender wasn't visible, merged with the many other moving shadows down the long side of the bar.

"Bummer."

His gaze moved right after hearing a loud laugh coming from the bathroom. Two men quickly walked behind him, still laughing. Mike realized that figuring out her name was now less important than the next challenge, walking across the dark and crowded bar with a drink. That could lead to a problem George mentioned sometimes—bumping into a guy who drank too much, spilling a drink on the guy's girlfriend, and having a larger problem to deal with. Mike stopped thinking about what might happen and started thinking about options.

He could take out the long, white cane, which was folded up in his back pocket as usual. He'd found some uses for it lately, more as a symbol of his sight than a sensor for his surroundings. Like most people with some sight, using that sight was easier than understanding each small sensation from the long cane.

He sighed and wished he could just walk across the damn room and see who'd bought the drink. Part of him wanted to dwell on that frustration, but a larger part wanted to find out who the woman was. He decided to look for more options.

Another option was doing the same thing he used to do with normal sight. That involved holding the drink close to his chest with one hand and holding the other hand a few inches away, to nudge through the crowd. He could also unfold and carry his white cane, so people could see it. Mike took another sip and decided to try both options. He would carefully hold the drink with one hand and use the other to nudge through the crowd and hold the cane. It would be unfolded and straight up, instead of sweeping.

That plan was as good as any, and he already felt a little late with trying to find the woman. He slid off the barstool, unfolded his cane, and set off for the green hue of the pool table. He decided that short steps were best, in addition to repeating the words "Excuse me" and "Sorry" whenever one of the moving shadows came close.

The process was unusually similar to driving through rush hour traffic. Some parts moved along at a steady but slow pace, and others contained delays where progress was actually disappointing because of how quickly it stopped. Mike tried to ignore one difference between rush hour and walking across the bar. Rush hour in a car could cover a mile. He was trying to walk across a room with no view to gaze at. Another difference was that rush hour usually gave people time to double-check where they were going. He hoped to go toward the pool table, but it kept coming in and out of view as the crowd moved.

He sipped the drink again, and another open space appeared. The open space quickly closed with a group. Based on the sounds, it was probably two or three couples. They were laughing and almost yelling at each other while slurring their words. Both of Mike's arms were pressed against his chest, since the open space was now very closed. He tried repeating "Excuse me" and "Sorry" a little louder, but the group was too loud and focused inward to hear, or maybe to care. Mike decided to move around them.

After taking several steps around the group, he wanted to see the pool table again. He found another open space and scanned the area near it. The green hue appeared a little to his right. It was larger than before, which meant Mike was close. If the pool table was on his right, the booth should be somewhere on his left. He looked in that direction and saw some lights behind two or three people. That could mean the people were standing in front of the lights that were over the booths. He walked slowly in that direction. He was just about to say "Excuse me" to a small group when they walked away.

A booth appeared directly in front of him, with several white shapes on the table. After realizing the white shapes were papers, he felt surprised and nervous from another shape—a familiar, bright, red shape. There was also a familiar voice.

"Well, hello there."

His mind buzzed with thoughts and questions. The clearest thought was to have another drink, hopefully a long one, but another thought demanded that he answer quickly, gracefully, and with just the right words. He waited for a joke or clever phrase. After feeling that too much time had passed, he settled for the best reply that came to mind.

"Hi."

The next thought focused on how miserable that reply was. He ignored the thought after noticing all the details he could see in the booth due to the hanging light. He glanced at her long red hair, moved up to her smile, and stopped at the eyes he'd enjoyed a few days ago.

"It looks like you enjoyed the drink," she said, still smiling.

"Yeah, I did," he replied and noticed his glass was almost empty. He wanted to reply more, but only one thought came to mind: *So, this is what speechless really means.* Finally, Mike remembered to thank her. "Thanks for buying it." He felt another long pause and loss of words. He forced some out. "I've always enjoyed this drink."

Sam's voice changed from friendly to teasing. "Are you saying you've always enjoyed a good slow screw?"

"Yeah, exactly."

She giggled, and Mike realized what he'd just said.

"I mean—"

She cut him off. "I know what you mean, sorry for having a little fun. I've been working on a conference presentation, with a few drinks to relax. I decided to take a break when I heard you laughing at the bar." She gestured across the booth and asked, "Mind joining me for another one?"

"Sure," Mike said while folding the cane. After sitting on the other side of the booth, he spent a moment enjoying the sight of her, especially her soft grey eyes. A few seconds later, he thought it would be good to start a conversation. That was easier now, since the initial surprise and adrenaline rush were over, but he still took another sip to calm some nerves. Unfortunately, intuition told him there was another problem. His glass was empty. He really wanted to buy another drink for himself and Sam, but the journey to and from the bar would reduce, or remove, the momentum and excitement. He stopped worrying when he heard a woman's voice, which was loud, strong, and familiar.

"Coming through! Sorry about that! Thank you!"

Some people moved out of the way of the woman, and she moved others with a shoulder or hip.

"Here you go, Sam," the bartender said. "Two more of the same. The place is getting a little crazy, so I'll just bring a couple more over in a while, which will save you the hassle of walking through the crowd. That sound all right?"

"Sounds great, thanks," Sam replied.

Mike saw the bartender shoulder her way through the crowd again and finally felt a clever thought come to mind. "She showed up with two drinks right after I sat down; what an interesting coincidence."

"Isn't it, though?" Sam asked with another smile. She then raised her glass toward him. "Here's to the very interesting coincidences life can bring."

With a light so close, he had a good enough image of where Sam's glass was, so Mike comfortably raised his until the glasses gently touched. "I suppose."

More thoughts and questions finally came to his mind. He decided to ask a question that felt safe, since one of the thoughts reminded him that she was still a teacher at Bridgman's. "It looks like you've been busy. What kind of presentation is it?"

Sam glanced down at the papers. "Oh, it's just stuff for work. I'm giving a presentation in the Twin Cities next week."

"Really? What's it about?"

"It's pretty dry stuff about some laws that were just passed."

"I didn't know you worked with laws. Are you a lawyer and a teacher?" he asked, enjoying the thought that Sam might be very attractive, smart, and ambitious.

"No, my degree is in Blind Rehabilitation, but I took some classes in how legislation needs to consider the blind," Sam said and took a drink.

"Cool, what parts did you find most interesting?"

"Are you sure you want to know?" she asked. "I mean, this isn't exactly the kind of conversation that usually happens in this place on Thirsty Thursday."

Mike recognized the phrase about Thursdays from bars back home and from nights out with George. It also explained why the place was so crowded on a weeknight. "Sure, why not? I've always enjoyed a variety of topics. Besides, talking about legal issues isn't too different from you writing about them on Thirsty Thursday."

"Fair enough," Sam replied. "Well, the main reason for my presentation is that our beloved legislature has a long history of ignoring the blind. Usually, it's just annoying, but this time, the new laws move beyond annoying and into the more irritating area of killing several blind folks a year."

Sam made the statement in a calm, matter-of-fact tone, which was different from George's description of her passion. Maybe she really was trying to make a good impression. That was probably obvious, since she'd just bought him a couple of drinks, but it was still hard to believe. Mike realized he should reply, instead of letting his thoughts wander further, so he made another simple response. "Oh?"

He listened to Sam make some comments about how stupid the government was, but his thoughts still wandered to a question. What would George say if he knew who Sam was talking to now? He smiled and tried to focus his thoughts on listening.

"So, in all their wisdom, they made another law that spoils drivers yet again. This time, those spoiled brats can turn at a red light. Waiting a few precious seconds is more than drivers want to tolerate when turning right on red. Of course, drivers choose not to believe that many idiots don't stop at all, turn right as fast as they can, and create a random deadly moment for the blind."

The comment made Mike's thoughts wander again. He thought about moments when cars turning right on red had nearly run into him, sometimes with the drivers accusing Mike of reckless walking. "Yeah, I know what you mean. That's happened to me a couple of times."

She leaned forward and rested on her elbows, as her hands moved to emphasize some points. "It has or will happen to all of us, and depending on simple luck, it'll kill some of us or just put us in a lot of pain. The government seems to think that the majority is never wrong, even when some of the minority gets killed." Sam took a drink.

Mike did the same and then asked, "You mentioned a couple of laws. What's the other one?"

"That one is a case where the legislature tried to help disabled people but missed another deadly detail. This time, they helped people in wheelchairs by putting down-ramps on sidewalks. Unfortunately, blind folks can wander right down those ramps and not notice they are now walking on the road, which leads to the little problem with death I mentioned."

"Wow, I hadn't thought of that before."

"That's probably because you can see the ramps, or at least rumor has it your sight's pretty good."

Mike wondered about what other rumors Sam had heard about him or which questions she might have asked about him. This conversation had captured his attention, though, so he focused back on it. "Well, what can the legislature do? If they take out the ramps, they piss off people in wheelchairs. If they keep the ramps, they piss off the blind."

"That's what a lot of people think," Sam replied. "But there's a third and fourth option, probably more. One option is to put bumps on the down-ramps. Another is to paint the things in a bright color, so people with limited sight have a chance at seeing them. Even better, the legislature could do both."

"Interesting. Those are good ideas, probably cheap too."

"A little thought can go a long way to keep blind folks from getting killed by the cars drivers cherish so much. I still get amazed at how drivers find reasons to spend more money on their cars. And of course, there are always reasons to drive faster, but they rarely put any thought into how their precious cars can kill." She took a drink and added, "Sorry, this stuff does get me riled up."

Mike was impressed by Sam's analysis and passion to solve serious problems. "No problem. Who are you presenting to?"

"It's at an academic conference down in the Twin Cities. One way to get ahead in teaching is to give presentations. I gave a few in grad school, but this'll be my first one here." Sam paused and organized some of the papers. Mike was about to ask another question when she continued. "You ask some great questions, but I've been working on this stuff for hours. I could use a little distraction, and there's something I've been meaning to ask you." She took a drink, held her glass up for a moment, glanced over the top, and spoke in a quieter voice. "How do you like to sleep?"

Mike was impressed with how she could change from telling him about the latest laws to teasing him again. He had the urge to take a drink but didn't. Instead, he laughed a little and replied, "I sleep great, curled up under the covers, very cozy." Then he took a drink and asked, "Mind if I ask why you ask?"

She smiled and said, "You can always ask me anything you want. I was just asking to give you a choice of how you want to sleep."

Mike enjoyed her wit. "Well, if I had my choice, I'd go with one of those new waterbeds that are coming out."

"Waterbeds? That sounds like something straight out of *Playboy*."

"Actually, I did see it there. A cousin gives me his copy sometimes. It has great articles." Mike smiled at the reply. He would never mention *Playboy* to a woman, but if a woman mentioned it, he enjoyed giving that reply.

"I'm not sure if I agree with your choice of magazines, but your choice of beds is interesting." Her tone became closer to the voice she used when describing laws. "The reason I'm asking is for the ski trip. The ski resort just sent us the final room reservations, so now we're figuring out who will be in what room."

"Any have waterbeds?"

"Sorry, wish they did, though."

Mike tried to come up with a joke about how they could share a room, but that was going too far, probably. He decided to play it safe. "Bummer. In that case, what are the options?"

"We have some with four beds and some with two. Rooms with four beds cost a little less."

Mike thought about the large scar on his right leg from his motorcycle accident. He didn't like others seeing and asking about it, even if most people in this group couldn't see well. This was one case where he didn't go for the cheap option. "I'll take one of the two-bed rooms." And even with one roommate, he liked to stay with somebody he knew, maybe George. "Can I pick who I sleep with?" The question was barely out of his mouth when he realized how it sounded.

"Is that an invitation?" Sam asked with a smile.

"Sorry, sorry, that's not what I meant. I just …"

She interrupted him. "That's all right."

"Really, I meant that I like rooms with less people. That's all."

"No problem. I'd do the same thing if I could afford it. I love being a teacher, but the pay isn't that great at first."

"I guess we both enjoy our privacy more than most," Mike replied.

"I guess."

A few seconds passed before either spoke.

"Speaking of the ski trip," Mike said, "I think I have a volunteer lined up to shake a tambourine."

"Great, who'd you find?"

"Well, I don't have the exact name yet, but I should have one by this weekend." Mike suspected he shouldn't mention that George was helping out, since his friend's reputation might precede him. George and Sam seemed like different people, at least when it came to following through.

"Maybe you could tell me who you're thinking about. I might be able to encourage them."

"At the moment," Mike said, "a friend of mine is sure he'll find someone. He knows a lot of people and owes me a favor."

"Now, I'm getting curious. Who's your friend?"

Mike took a drink. "George."

There was another pause.

"Okay, you're right. George does know a lot of people," she replied in a subdued tone and sipped her drink. Her tone picked up when she continued, "But hey, I've heard that he's trying to make a job for himself. That surprised a few people, but this place has a lot of surprises, like you helping with the race. So who knows, George could save the day this time."

A loud crack came from the pool table, which made Mike and Sam glance toward it. She looked back at Mike and changed the topic. "We always have a great time at White Pine Ridge, but I can't remember. Do you ski?"

"Not really," he answered, looking for a response that would show a similar interest. "I do enjoy being outside in the winter, though, so I'm looking forward to the ski trip." He smiled to himself, wondering how she would have reacted if he'd mentioned snowmobile tag. "I enjoy snowmobiling with friends and just being in the woods."

"I haven't tried snowmobiling since I grew up in California. We'd go skiing in the Rockies sometimes, but that's about it. What's it like to drive a snowmobile?" Sam asked as she slid down in the booth a little.

Mike thought about how she changed from confident teacher to comfortable friend, a very attractive friend. He took a drink and replied, "Well, I think snowmobiling and skiing are similar in a lot of ways, if you set aside the small issue of a screaming engine." She smiled at the remark.

"There are times when I enjoy full-throttle power across an open field, and other times when I like to slow down or even stop in the middle of the woods just to take it in and relax." Mike was happy how the phrase came out and that the tension he'd felt earlier had passed. A playful tension returned, after hearing the familiar voice of a strong woman.

"Thank you! Pardon me, coming through! Thanks."

Sam and Mike watched the bartender walk toward them, making a path through the crowd with her voice and shoulders. Mike smiled and thought how the bartender could serve people and command them, several times a minute when necessary. She placed two more drinks on the table.

"Here you go, two more Double Sloe Screws." She smiled and continued, "That has a nice ring to it. How you two do'n?"

"It does have a nice ring to it," Sam said with a smile. "We're doing good. Mike was just describing how he enjoys relaxing in the woods."

"Well, damn, ain't that romantic. All my old man talks about is his snowmobile."

Mike was surprised at the word romantic and felt a little awkward about it. Apparently, the bartender's directness in getting through a crowd carried on to her directness about two people having a drink. Then again, Sam had bought him a couple, and he'd had several thoughts about being romantic with her. It just felt strange to hear the bartender use the word. He couldn't sort that issue out right now, so Mike finished the last drink and pulled the next one closer.

"I'll get that out of your way," the bartender said as she took the empty glass from Mike. "Should I stop by with two more in a little while?"

"I'd love to, but it depends on the time, since tomorrow's going to be an early one." Sam moved one hand to the wristwatch by her other hand, opened the hinged cover, and felt the watch face. "I better stop at this one." She then reached into her purse and took out some cash.

"I'll take care of these," he said, reaching for his wallet. Mike took out a bill, handed it to the bartender, and asked, "Will this cover it?" He hoped it wasn't a one-dollar bill.

"Absolutely," the bartender replied while taking the money and giving back some change. "You have a good night. I enjoyed meeting you, Mike. Let me know if you want to try some corn whisky again."

The comment about corn whisky made him feel awkward, since it didn't seem like something that would impress an attractive and ambitious woman like Sam. He simply replied that he would stop by again. Then he watched the bartender turn toward the crowd, heard her make a small opening, and saw her fade into the moving shadows.

"Corn whisky?"

Mike sighed, took a drink, and then answered. "It's a long story."

Sam rested back in the booth and said, "All right, then tell me about the woods on a snowmobile."

Mike was relieved she'd changed the topic, but nerves still got in the way of finding the right words. "I'm not sure what else to say. It's just ordinary stuff, really."

"Not for a California girl who grew up in the city. I've only been through one winter here and not much of it was in the woods. What's it like?"

"Well, the woods are different in winter. Technically, the snow absorbs most of the sound, but there's more to it than that," Mike said as he rested back a bit. "Most of the birds have left, and other animals aren't as active. That pretty much leaves the wind, and the quiet sounds it makes blowing through the trees and bushes. There's really nothing like it."

He took another drink. He saw Sam do the same and continued, feeling he could wander into a topic that was a little romantic and true. "Well, there is something else that's even better. If you're in the woods at night, you might get lucky. When there's a full moon, everything glows in blue because the moonlight bounces off the snow. That's pretty cool."

"Or pretty cold," Sam joked. "Sorry, I couldn't resist. It really does sound like a great sight."

"No problem, and actually, you're right. It can get very cold. The best thing I ever bought was one of those new snowmobile suits, and I still never get on a sled without my trusty long johns. Sorry, that's probably more than you want to hear."

Sam smiled and said, "That's fine. I have a love-hate relationship with the cold. I fell in love with skiing when I was a kid, after family vacations in the Rockies, but the cold wasn't as bitter, maybe because we were skiing for a few days. The cold here lasts for months, and you don't warm up by walking or waiting at a bus stop. I've been amazed at how cold it can get, so I pile on long johns and anything else that helps." She took another drink and added in a quieter tone, "Anyway, I haven't seen the blue light you mentioned. Tell me more about it."

Mike took a drink and replied in a similar tone. "Well, there really is nothing like it. When you're out there for a while and your eyes adjust, it's amazing how much you can see. The whole place is filled with blue light. I mean, the trees actually cast shadows from the moonlight onto the snow, and then there's the quiet winter sounds I mentioned. It really seems like a different world."

Sam leaned forward in the booth and rested on her elbows.

Mike continued in a slightly playful tone. "You still have to be careful, though. One time, it was so peaceful, and the moon was so bright, that I got off my sled and walked deeper into the woods. It was great walking out there with the bright moonlight and winter sounds." His tone became more playful. "But then, one of those lessons from high school came back. It's the lesson that the moon sets just like the sun. In high school, you learn it, think about how useless the idea is, and forget it. If you happen to be standing in the woods at night and the moon sets, you remember that lesson pretty fast," Mike said with a laugh. "When the moon sets and you're in the woods, it's dark. And, I'm not talking sort of dark. I'm talking about as black as dark can be." Mike knew he was exaggerating, since starlight and nearby farms provide some light, but Sam seemed to be enjoying the story, so he didn't mind exaggerating a little.

Sam smiled, and he continued. "But fortunately, that problem becomes less important because, a minute or two later, you stop thinking about the moon above and start thinking about your toes below, since you can't really feel them."

She laughed, which made him enjoy telling the story more.

"Around that time, you become unusually motivated to find your snowmobile, but in the dark, in the woods, it seems like a really small target."

"Oh no, what did you do?"

"The first thing I did was shiver, since the cold was moving up from my toes. After that, I swore for a while. It didn't help me find my snowmobile, but it did warm me up."

They both laughed, and Mike added, "Little humor, not too much."

Both took another drink, and Sam asked, "Seriously, how did you get out of the woods?"

"It was actually pretty simple. I had to walk somewhere, since it was too damn cold to stand still. I started off by trying to follow my footsteps, but they were really hard to find in the dark. I think my footsteps crossed paths with a deer trail, which threw me off. I knew there were fields nearby, so I headed for a place where there were less trees to bump into. Once I was in a field, I hoped to find something familiar like a fence or road. It also feels better just to be moving, since it warms your body up. Eventually, I felt some snow that was harder than the powder I'd been walking through. It turned out to be my snowmobile track, so I followed the track to my sled."

"I guess that's all you could do, freeze in the woods or find something better."

"That's about it," Mike said as he rested further back into the booth. "Sorry for carrying on so much. What's it like growing up in California? I've never been there."

"No problem, I've enjoyed your stories." Sam leaned back into the booth and answered, "In some ways, it's not so different from here, if you set aside the small issue of a few months that never get above freezing. I mean, my hometown is Davis, which is right next to Sacramento. Many things are the same here as there, just different names. You have Pizza Hut here, and Davis has Straw Hat Pizza. You have Dairy Queen. Davis has Vic's Ice Cream. You grew up enjoying the woods. I grew up enjoying the desert. I mean, there are some great forests nearby, but my dad always loved the desert. He taught geology at UC Davis. He'd go to the desert for work sometimes. Other times, he'd just take me there for the weekend." Sam took another drink and looked at Mike, maybe to see if he showed an interest.

He instinctively raised his eyebrows, and she continued. "My light skin makes it tough for me to be in the desert sun. It's all part of being a redhead. I used to coat myself in sunscreen, wear long sleeves, and still get burned. But that didn't stop Dad. We'd drive around during the day, and he'd point out rock formations and colors. Then, we'd go for hikes just before sunset. This may sound strange, but hiking in the desert is about the same as your description of the woods in winter. It's just so peaceful."

Sam smiled a little and spoke with a teasing tone. "But we never had an adventure like getting lost in the dark." She took a drink and gazed at him, subtly daring him to reply.

Mike enjoyed the gaze, just like he did when they first met, but this one was different. It challenged him for a quick, clever response—and more. Moments like this didn't happen often, a subtle but direct battle of wits. This kind of challenge also mixed well with a few drinks, since they helped him enjoy the challenge instead of worrying about it.

He responded by intentionally slowing down. She would get her reply, but not with the speed her look asked for or demanded. He smiled, held the gaze for a moment, and looked at his drink. He sipped it and slowly put down the glass. After a pause that felt right, he replied, "Well, in that case, you've only had half the fun. Life's always better with a little adventure."

Sam took a drink in the same way Mike had. She looked at him and said, "I couldn't agree more."

He slowly nodded in agreement and thought about the beauty of her grey eyes, carefully examining and enjoying them. She tilted her head slightly, in a way that seemed to mean something. He wondered what it was. Then, a feeling below the table surprised him, a soft rub of a foot brushing up against one of his ankles. He tried to keep a confident look, but Mike suspected the surprise showed in his eyes. The soft feeling moved up toward his knee and back down again.

"I see you do like a little adventure," he replied after the feeling faded.

"It always makes life a little better."

He smiled and remembered something George had said about Sam. The memory wasn't clear. At first, Mike thought about how Sam could growl when she was really upset, but that wasn't it. And at the moment, it was hard to imagine that reaction. He tried harder to find the correct memory. That effort made him forget about the gaze they'd been holding, and he looked down at the table.

A clearer memory came to mind. George had mentioned something about Sam and romance, or maybe just sex. Mike thought about that comment from George a couple of weeks ago, what Sam had said a couple of seconds ago, and the papers he was looking at now on the table. All that amounted to a teacher who could be interested in having sex with him. He looked up at Sam and saw she was looking at the papers.

She looked at him and broke the silence. "I get the feeling you also have a responsible streak."

"Sometimes."

"Good, I like that too. I suppose adding some caution to an adventure can't hurt, might even be fun. I should be going anyway. Waking up early tomorrow is already going to be tough." She started putting the papers into her purse.

Mike worried he'd blown his chance with Sam and tried thinking of a good reply. He was relieved when she said something first.

"There is one more thing I would like. Would you walk with me to the bus stop?"

Mike was relieved and replied that he would. She put the remaining papers into her purse. Both of them stood up and put on their coats. To show his manners, he motioned for her to go first. He also suspected that Sam knew this bar better than he did. That would make it easier for her to find the best way to walk out. It seemed like she did, since she followed the line of lights and booths to the door without pausing. While she walked, Sam nudged people and firmly called out "Excuse me" and "Sorry," just like the bartender. A short while later, Mike saw the two blinking neon signs from inside of the bar.

Sam and Mike walked outside, and he wondered what to do. He could walk next to her, put his arm around her, try to hold her hand, or something else. She seemed to guess his thoughts again.

"You were right, you know. We should be careful. I do want to tell you more about what I would like, but we should keep it friendly when we're close to Bridgman's."

Mike wondered about the word *friendly*. He'd only known her for a few weeks and had never had to think about how to act. What a difference a day—or an hour—makes. Of course, he was still excited, just getting used to the change. He nodded to Sam and started walking with her to the bus stop.

As the two walked away from Speakeasy, the conversation reflected the cautious style they'd agreed on. He asked more about California, and she enjoyed sharing some stories from home. When they arrived at the bus stop, she checked her watch again.

"A bus should be here any minute. I hope you can make it to the next ski planning meeting. Maybe we can have another drink after it." Her voice sounded less confident than it had before when she added, "There's something else. I really do think you were right about being careful. Sometimes, I can be a little impulsive when I'm enjoying a conversation, like when we were talking in the bar. I want to continue that conversation, but when you see me at school, I'll probably act more like a teacher again."

Mike heard the bus coming. He wanted to explain how he'd also enjoyed the conversation, didn't have a problem with being cautious, and wanted to see her again. The bus came closer. He discreetly reached out for her hand and gently squeezed it. The bus stopped next to them. He let go and quietly said, "Good night, Sam, looking forward to seeing you again."

CHAPTER EIGHT

Work

M ike wanted to let out a long yawn, but he didn't want anyone to notice, so a little one came out instead. It had been another night of short sleep. One reason involved Sam. When he should have been sleeping, he kept thinking about the talking, laughing, and flirting they'd done last night. Another reason he hadn't slept much was a package that had been waiting for him when he'd walked into Mariner's last night. It contained some cookies from Mom and some old copies of *Popular Science* and *Popular Mechanics* from Dad.

His hands moved over the table in front of him and felt some familiar dents. They were the same dents he'd felt when he'd sat at this table for the first time, inside Stella's Café. He looked up when he heard Rocky's voice.

"Hey, Mike, good to see you. How you doing this morn'n?"

"Hey, good morning, good morning. I'm all right," Mike answered calmly, his voice sounding a little tired.

"You sound like you need a Coke. I'll bring one over, and a burger with fries after that?"

"That'd be great."

Mike watched her walk away, greet someone else, and then go into the kitchen. He thought about the first few times he'd eaten here. Back then, this had seemed like a big city café, less cozy than the ones back home. Now, it just seemed like his café. His thoughts shifted to the present after seeing Rocky walk toward him.

"Here you go," she said while pulling the tab off the can and setting the can and a glass of ice next to him. "What a week. I sure am glad it's Friday," she said and poured cola into the glass.

"Thanks. What's been going on around here?"

"Well, to be honest, people are just getting back to normal. The election a couple of weeks ago brought back some old problems, with Watergate, Nixon, and his pardon. I'm glad Thanksgiving is next week. Hopefully, people will get away from work for a while, spend some time with family, and just relax. What're your plans for Thanksgiving?"

"I'll go home for a few days, normal stuff with family like you said."

"I don't think I ever asked about your family. Is it very big?"

"A little bigger than most. I have three sisters and a brother. My mom and dad are going to pick me up next Wednesday, might even bring my brother with." Mike took a drink of the Coke and enjoyed the first caffeine of the morning.

"Well, that sounds good. You should have them stop by. I'd love to meet them."

"Maybe, but it's a long drive, so they might not stay long. They'll probably drive up here when Dad finishes work, pick me up, and drive back."

"Well, you tell them to stop by if they can, all right?"

"Sure."

"I better go check on another table. I'll be right back with your burger and fries."

Mike thanked her and started a new part of his breakfast routine. He felt around his parka until a hand went over a small box, which was inside a pocket. He reached into the pocket and pulled out a transistor radio with a cord wrapped around it. The cord was part of an earphone. He unwrapped the cord and put the earpiece in his left ear, which was closer to the wall than his right ear.

Using the ear that was closest to the wall reduced the chance of anyone seeing the earphone. People at Stella's, or any café, were used to seeing someone read a newspaper while eating breakfast, but they weren't used to someone wearing an earphone. He wanted to enjoy a peaceful breakfast listening to the news, instead of answering questions about what was in his ear. He flipped on the power switch, took a deep breath, exhaled slowly, and looked forward to the news.

Instead of the news, he heard an ad about the latest denim dresses and skirts on sale at Herberger's. Impulse told him to change the channel, like he would when watching TV, but Mike couldn't see the little dial well enough. When the commercial ended, the news started, and Mike rested back in his chair.

"Now, we'll return to the news that people have been talking about all week," an announcer said with enthusiasm. "Tomorrow's big game between our very own Minnesota Vikings and the Green Bay Packers. There's no team we like beating more, and my prediction is that we're going to clobber 'em just like we've clobbered everybody else this season. I'll go even further and say there's nobody, and I mean nobody, who will stop the Vikes this year. We're going all the way, and that's all there's to it. They don't call 'em the Purple People Eaters for nothin'."

Another announcer spoke with a more cautious tone. "Well, I can't disagree with you about beating Green Bay. They've had a lousy season, and we've had a great season. I'll even agree that the Vikes are on their way to a third Super Bowl."

The enthusiastic announcer spoke again, challenging and joking with his co-host. "But you're going to talk about the best and hope for the worst."

"No, no, that's not what I was going to say. All I'm saying is that the Vikes have made it to two of the last three Super Bowls, and we all got really excited. But then, they didn't exactly win."

The enthusiastic announcer laughed. "Well, I have a feeling this time is it. There's no way they can lose three Super Bowls in four years, just no way. We'd like to hear your thoughts on the Vikes, to-morrow's game, or how we're going all the way, just call us on our listener line, which is at 746 …"

Mike stopped listening and looked up when a familiar voice came into his right ear, the one without the earphone. "Here ya go Mike, a burger and fries."

Mike flipped the power off of his transistor radio and looked at Rocky. She set the plate down and joked, "With this kind of breakfast, I've been wondering what you eat for lunch."

He smiled, thanked her, and replied, "Corn Flakes, of course."

"Of course, and with a can of Coke, I imagine?"

"Of course," he answered. "Not mixed in with the Corn Flakes, though. That would just be weird."

"Of course," she said. "You wouldn't want to appear unusual. By the way, what's that thing in your ear?"

Mike had forgotten about the earphone, so he thought for a mo-ment, smiled, and answered, "It's the latest fashion from Radio Shack."

Rocky rubbed her forehead, smiled a little, and said, "Of course. Michael, you are one of a kind. I'll say that much. I have to go check on some friends. Let me know if you need anything else."

"I suppose."

Mike thanked her and glanced in the direction she walked. The table she went to wasn't far away, so he could hear some of their comments. It sounded like a few women were at the table. Some guys came in a moment later, talking by the door. Mike wished they would continue their conversation inside and shut the door, since he could feel a cold draft.

He looked at his warm breakfast and took a couple of fries from the edge of the plate. While munching on them, he reached for the bottle of ketchup and took off the cap. He ate a few more fries from the same spot on the plate and tipped the bottle toward the spot, wiggling it a little. Only tiny drops of ketchup came out. He instinctively pointed the bottle toward his eyes and looked down it. He couldn't see inside and wondered why people looked inside the bottle, even with sight. He pointed the bottle toward the spot again and wiggled it harder. That hand kept wiggling the bottle, and the other hand flipped the radio's power switch back on.

There was an ad for the latest film craze, about a boxer in Philadelphia. Mike thought how he preferred All Star Wrestling to boxing. That kind of wrestling had similar excitement and some jokes, without the pounding punches of boxing. A surge of ketchup came from the bottle, making a mess on the edge of the plate and table.

"Bummer."

He briefly thought about how the ketchup resembled the blood used in wrestling but focused on cleaning up the mess. He started by taking some fries from the plate and dipping them into the ketchup on the table. After that became less effective, he reached for some napkins from the chrome napkin holder that was next to the salt and pepper shakers. He wiped away as much as he could, listened to the radio again, and took a bite from the burger. The cautious announcer was giving his version of national news. Mike enjoyed the burger and listened.

"I'll start with some good news. Today's going to be a repeat of yesterday, with highs in the fifties. Currently, the temperature is just above freezing, at thirty-four. Better enjoy it while you can, though, because this weekend, things are going to get cold and messy. Highs will be in the mid-thirties with snow and sleet, just like last week."

Mike took another bite of his burger and thought about how this was just the morning he was hoping for, a good breakfast with the news.

"We'll move on to some national news. The latest numbers from Washington don't look the best. The economy isn't dropping off like it was a couple of years ago, but economic growth has flattened out. Inflation is increasing, and unemployment is holding firm at 5.9 percent. They're saying the main reason is that consumers are buying less than they used to. I admit this confuses me a little, since it's hard for people to buy more when things are more expensive and when the number of jobs is flat. I guess it doesn't help to complain about it, so I'll just move on to some other news from around here."

Mike flipped off the power, unconsciously. There was something in the news that needed careful thought. He took a couple of fries and started munching on them. It was the jobs report, something to do with the 5.9 percent unemployment rate. He liked to work and save money. After taking a drink of Coke, he thought about the unemployment rate for legally blind folks. It was fifty percent, if he remembered right. He stopped chewing and realized how that made 5.9 percent seem tiny.

He sighed and wondered how half the students at Bridgman's wouldn't work again. His thoughts continued while scanning the café. That half would no longer be part of this crowd, enjoying a meal or coffee before work. His appetite faded. Mike asked himself what it would be like if he were one of the unlucky ones. Being stuck at home all the time felt much more than wrong. If it were him, what would he do?

His forehead wrinkled as some answers came to mind. The wrinkles slowly faded, and a little grin appeared. He would probably find the best way to adjust his TV amplifier—for all seasons, temperatures, wind directions, dew points, or anything else that might matter. He could still see TV enough to enjoy it; might as well make the best of the sight he had. He'd probably get the basement organized, something he'd been meaning to do since building the house. Then, of course, there was his Atari. He'd been thinking about it more lately. If some blind folks could try skiing again, he could try Atari again, especially since it was much better than skiing anyway.

The pleasant thoughts faded with a sigh. He would still have to pay for all these things and more. He also liked a lot of things about a job—learning how machines worked, finding faster ways to operate the machine, and laughing with other people. That would be hard not to have anymore, all because of bad luck.

A simple phrase from Dad came to mind. "Sometimes, you have to make your own luck."

Mike thought about how to do that. He could spend a little time each day looking for work, even if it meant a little less time with the Atari. It might take a while, but something felt right about trying.

Something also felt right about trying soon, maybe even today at school. It couldn't hurt to ask some questions. There had to be some ways to increase his chances of being in the lucky half. That idea was intriguing, even exciting. His appetite came back, so he took another bite from the burger.

He went over his thoughts again, came to the same conclusion, and almost finished his fries. He scanned the café and heard a group of women laugh. It felt good to think he could still be part of this morning crowd. Mike decided to listen to the radio again, but after hearing a familiar voice, he paused while reaching for the power switch. It was from the group of women. He almost recognized the voice, but something wasn't right. It wasn't a voice he'd heard here before.

He stopped eating for a moment to hear better. Some unfamiliar voices were louder for a few seconds. Mike guessed they'd finished breakfast and were chatting over coffee. Hard to talk that much and eat at the same time. The familiar voice returned. It was a little more formal than the others and definitely more firm. That voice faded, so Mike ate the rest of his fries. When his plate was empty, he recognized the familiar voice. It was Margaret.

If her group had finished breakfast, he might be able to ask Margaret about work options as they walked out. That seemed easier than walking up to their table. He would need to be ready to walk out when they did, so he started his routine for finishing breakfast. He reached for the back pocket of his jeans to take out his wallet. Earlier this morning, he'd set aside the exact number of bills to pay for breakfast, folding and storing them at one end of the wallet. He took out the bills and dropped them onto the table. Then, he wrapped the cord around the radio and put both into the pocket of his parka.

He sat for a moment and drank his Coke while the women chatted. He became more certain that Margaret was at the table after hearing her speak up a couple of times. Some of the other voices became familiar, but he didn't know their names. He was relieved that Sam was not in the group, since that could complicate things.

Mike finished the Coke and thought about how the women sure could talk for a while. Maybe he shouldn't have put the radio away so fast. He pushed the can of Coke and dishes toward the edge of the table to pass some time and make it easier for Rocky to pick them up. The women were still chatting. He slouched in his chair, took a slow scan around the café, and moved the money away from the edge of the table so it was next to the chrome napkin holder. They were still chatting. His hands wandered over the bumps in the table. He started reaching for the radio and looked forward to hearing some news again, when one woman stood up, then a couple more, and finally all of them put their coats on—still chatting.

They didn't seem to be walking out very fast, so Mike slowly stood up and put on his coat at the same speed. They were still standing by the table, chatting. He moved the dishes away from the edge, so it didn't look like he was just standing there. One finally walked toward the door. Mike did the same. While walking, he pretended to look for something in the pockets of his parka, to take more time. He was still at the door before the woman who'd walked away first. After slowly opening the door, he wondered if it was simply impossible for him to move slow enough to match the speed of a group of women having breakfast.

"Oh, hi, Mike," Margaret said. "I thought I saw you."

Mike was relieved that Margaret was the woman who'd walked away from the group. "Oh, good morning. How're you doing this morning?"

"I'm good. Some friends and I were just having a quick breakfast." Mike smiled at the idea that their breakfast was quick.

Margaret continued. "We try a different restaurant each Friday."

"That sounds cool. Actually, I was just thinking of something I wanted to ask you about. Would it be okay to talk now, or did you have something else planned with your friends?"

"Actually, now's a good time. I had to leave a little early to stop by the grocery store next door. We need some things for another cooking class."

"Hey, buddy," a man's voice called out. "You mind closing the door? I like my breakfast warm." Mike wondered if it was one of the guys he'd noticed earlier, who'd also stood in the doorway.

"Sure, sorry," Mike answered, holding the door open and motioning for Margaret to go first.

Margaret talked about how great the warmer temperatures were going to feel, even though it still felt brisk. Her voice still had some teacher tones, even out of school. In a moment, the two were inside the grocery store next to Stella's Café.

Mike always felt comfortable walking into this grocery store. The smell of freshly baked bread was especially strong in the morning, and the old, yet clean, wooden floors still made him think of the small-town grocery stores back home. After taking a couple of steps inside, he instinctively picked up a basket.

"Do you need some things too?" Margaret asked.

"Oh, not really, I'm just used to picking up a basket since this is where I get my groceries."

"Well, since you have it, do you mind carrying the groceries for school while I pick them out?"

Mike said he would, and they walked into the produce section. Margaret looked over the vegetables, put a couple in the basket, and asked Mike, "You mentioned some questions for me. What's on your mind?"

"There was some news this morning about unemployment for the whole country. It got me thinking about jobs I could do after finishing at Bridgman's. I've heard that only half of blind people still work, so I thought it would be good to start asking about jobs soon. I know of a couple of jobs for the blind, but I was wondering if you could tell me a little more."

The two walked out of the produce section and next to shelves of fresh bread. The tone of Margaret's voice became less formal. "I absolutely love the smell of this bread. I don't need any, but I can't resist." She lifted a loaf. "Wow, it's still warm." She put the bread into the basket and continued in a tone that came closer to her teacher voice. "Actually, the fifty percent you mentioned can be accurate, but it's better to look at specific groups. More students like you find work, younger adults with some sight. Many of our students have lost their sight later in life. Their unemployment rate is closer to sixty-five percent, sometimes higher depending on which numbers you look at."

"Wow," Mike replied, feeling concerned for his older friends.

The two walked by some shelves full of cans without stopping. Margaret's tone became more reassuring when she said, "But, you're still right. It's better to start thinking about work sooner than later, regardless of age. Are you sure you don't want anything?"

They walked by the ice cream freezer, and Mike impulsively added, "Well, there is one thing." He set down the basket, opened the freezer, and quickly chose which one he'd have today, an Eskimo Pie. He pulled out the silver ice cream bar and put it into the basket.

"Michael," Margaret said in her full teacher voice. "You have all these wonderful breads, fresh fruits, and vegetables here, and you pick an ice cream bar for breakfast?"

Mike chuckled. "I had my healthy breakfast next door. This is dessert." He smiled while thinking of his breakfast at Stella's Café, which was always a burger and fries.

"I should ask how often you apply our lessons from the cooking class, but I'm not sure I want to." The two walked to the counter, chatted with the clerk, and paid the bill.

When they walked outside, Mike unwrapped the ice cream bar and asked, "So what can I start doing now about work?"

"You're going to eat that thing now?"

"Sure, they're a lot better when they're fresh."

Margaret rubbed her head and tried to sound firm, but Mike could tell she was either laughing a little, still puzzled about his dessert, or both.

"Well, whatever makes you happy, Michael. All right, I'll explain some common jobs."

They stopped at an intersection. Mike recognized the bells from Tank's gas station, and Margaret continued. "Your last job was working in a factory, making machine parts, right?"

Mike mumbled a yes and was impressed she remembered.

"You could continue making machine parts. There's a blind woman in Duluth who makes those parts every day, been doing it for years."

He was surprised that anyone could still run the machines he used to work on, without sight. "Wow, making those parts involves some precise measurements, down to a millimeter. How does she do it?"

Margaret started walking forward to cross the street. Mike didn't see any other people and wondered how she knew it was safe to cross. He didn't ask, though, since this conversation was more interesting.

"Actually, the measurements are less than a millimeter, but you're right. It is challenging. Fortunately, there are now machines with Braille and tactile settings. That part does make the training program longer than most. It's about two years, but your previous work could make it a good match."

Mike wondered how someone could work with their hands all day and still read Braille, since calluses were supposed to make it difficult to feel the little bumps. He also didn't like the idea of being in school for two more years. "Okay, I'll think about it. What are some others?" He took a bite out of his ice cream and waited for her answer.

"One common job for blind people is tuning pianos. Do you know music?"

"I can spell the word, sometimes. Does that count?"

"Probably not. Another common job is preparing and serving food in cafeterias, but you haven't shown much interest in cooking."

Suddenly, his jokes about the ice cream bar and healthy food seemed less funny. He spoke in a more serious tone. "Well, if I had to learn how to cook for work, I could do it. I just don't cook on my own a lot."

"In that case, maybe you should look into cafeteria work, but I still think the job running machines is the best fit."

"Yeah, maybe. Are there any others?" Mike asked and finished the ice cream bar.

"Well, there is one more, but I'm not sure I want to tell you about it."

"Really? Why not?"

"Because I worry about your health."

"Wow, I didn't know these jobs could hurt us." He thought about the safety gear he used to wear when making tractor parts. "Is it operating another kind of machine or something?"

"Actually, it is, but that's not the part I'm worried about. I'm worried about the effect it would have on your diet."

"My diet? What kind of job can change what I eat?"

Margaret sighed. "Filling vending machines."

Mike's voice picked up. "You mean like candy bars?" He started laughing a little. "And ice cream bars?"

"Unfortunately."

Mike smiled, bigger than he had in a long while. "Cool."

The two continued talking and walking together to Bridgman School for the Blind.

. . . .

Mike held back a long yawn. It had been a good day, but it had started before sunrise, and it was now well past sunset. He watched Shelly put one glass in front of him and another in front of George, sitting on the other side of their booth at The Slowstream Tavern.

"There you go, one pitcher of Red White and Blue."

"Thank you, my dear. Thank you very much," George said.

Shelly filled the glasses and asked, "Is it just beer for you guys tonight?"

George's voice became lively. "Oh no, tonight I'm having my favorite, a Cheddar Burger and, even better, a large order of Monster Rings. And even better still, you can give the bill for the burger, rings, and beer to my good friend, Mikey."

The comment made Mike hungry, especially the Monster Rings. Those massive onion rings went great with a cold beer.

Shelly looked at Mike. "How'd he rope you into paying for supper?" Mike couldn't answer because he was drinking his beer, so Shelly continued. "Please don't tell me you started betting with George during one of his drinking games. There's no faster way to lose."

Mike sat up a little from the slouched position he was in. "It's my good deed for the week. Every once in a while, George has a problem showing up on time to class."

"Yeah, every once in a while," Shelly interrupted. "And, every once in a while, he has a problem showing up."

Mike continued. "So, I told him that I'd buy his favorite supper if he was on time all week."

"And he made it?" Shelly added with a playful tone. "George, you better be careful. You have a reputation to protect."

"You two have all the fun you want. I can take a little joke. Besides, life is good. It's Friday night. I'm getting my favorite meal—for free, I might add. And I'm washing the meal down with plenty of cold beer." He raised his glass and took a long drink.

"Mike, I just want to make sure. You're only paying for the meal, not *all* the beer tonight? There's no telling what can happen when George has a night of free drinks, or how much it'll cost."

"Actually, George has slightly misunderstood that part of the deal. I told him I would pay for a meal and *one* pitcher, which is enough to wash down the burger and Monster Rings."

"Speak for yourself," George replied. "I've seen two or three pitchers go by, and there were still some rings left."

"I suppose. I'm sure you have, but a deal's a deal."

"Everybody gets so hung up on details these days, takes all the fun out of a drink or two."

"Good for you, Mike," Shelly said. "It's always good to see someone stand their ground against George's ongoing effort to get a free drink."

"All right, that's a Cheddar Burger and Monster Rings for George. What'll it be for you, Mike?"

"I'll have the same."

"Sounds good, two Cheddar Burgers and two Monster Rings. Anything else?"

"It'd probably be best to bring another pitcher," George answered. "The first one always goes fast."

"Com'n up," Shelly said, and then turned and walked toward the crowd.

George's voice changed to a tone that was more sincere than usual. "Seriously, though, I do want to thank you for helping me out with the whole on time stuff. I can answer most questions about most cars, and I can instantly tell you which bus to take to get to which bar, but I've never been able to get the whole timing thing down, especially with school. Of course, I'm not saying we should end our little bets since you still have a chance of winning one. It's an extremely small chance, but there you have it." He emphasized the point by raising his glass and taking a drink.

"No problem. School's always been easy for me, so it's easy to help."

"Yeah, I can imagine you as one of those guys who never had to study."

"Something like that," Mike said. "But I've always liked to learn, in and out of school."

"Makes sense. I guess you do have to enjoy it. That's probably why I got interested in engines. I started when I was a kid, helping my old man with his truck. I haven't really stopped."

"That reminds me of something I've been meaning to ask you," Mike said as he leaned forward in the booth. "Any news on the job at the parts store?"

"Actually, there is, but I admit it's not the best news."

"Really? What's going on?" Mike asked and rested his elbows on the table.

"It's kind of annoying, actually. Everything was going just hunky-dory at the store. I've been stopping by more often, answering some questions from customers, even did some math at the store with an abacus."

"That sounds great. What happened?"

"Actually, it comes back to school," George answered.

"Really? You mean Bridgman's?"

"Well, they do want me to finish at Bridgman's, but that's a different story. This involves another school."

"So what is it?" Mike asked.

"The owner has a nephew who just finished school, at a vo-tech. He finished a course in car repair or automotive maintenance or something like that. Anyway, the kid can't find a job."

"Damn," Mike replied as he put the pieces together. "So now, he's gone to his uncle at the parts store for the job you've been working on."

"Pretty much. We're still trying to figure something out, but the more hours I put in, the less hours the kid has for work if he's hired."

"That sucks, but aren't you more qualified?"

"Of course I am. I've been working on cars longer than the kid's been alive, but it's still harder for me to do some things, like math or finding a box in the backroom or finding the number of a new part."

"But those are all things you could figure out," Mike said, sounding annoyed.

"You're right, but there's something else that really gets on my nerves."

"What is it?"

George paused before answering. When he did, his voice had an unusual combination of frustration and compassion. "I actually like the kid. He's been stopping by the store for years." He turned his head toward the crowd in the bar and continued in a similar tone. "He's a little shy, which is probably why it's been hard for him to find work, but we hit it off right away."

Mike hadn't heard his friend this upset before and wondered which tension was stronger, the loyalty George felt to the kid or the disappointment of a rare job fading away. Both men took a drink.

After a moment, George looked toward Mike again and continued. "But, what the hell's a guy supposed to do? Scream at the owner? Scream at the kid? These guys are my friends, and that's not my style anyway." He took another drink and continued in a milder tone. "Screaming is almost worse than dwelling on sad shit. Both are addictive. I'd rather keep a clear head, solve problems, and enjoy life. I mean, of course, I'll gripe sometimes, but if I carry on too much, slap me or throw a beer at me or something."

Mike felt proud of his friend. The words dignity and courage came to mind. He'd heard them used sometimes, in the movies or the news, but this was a rare moment when they fit into an ordinary conversation, right in front of him. He held up his glass. "Here's a toast to you, George. That's tough news, but I like your style."

"Thanks, Mikey," George replied while moving his glass toward Mike's.

After the glasses touched, Mike continued. "But I have to tell you something."

"What's that?"

"If I throw a beer on you, it'll be yours, not mine. You're a great guy, but you're not getting my beer."

"Deal," George said with a laugh.

Both men finished their glasses. Mike refilled each and said, "I've been looking into some jobs as well. There's one that involves making machine parts, but that would require a couple years of school."

"But I thought you liked school."

"I like learning more than school, preferably topics I choose."

"All right, what other jobs are you thinking of?" George asked.

"There's one with vending machines that sounds interesting."

"I've heard of those jobs. They really can be interesting, at least that's what some buddies tell me. They've been fixing and filling vending machines for a couple of years. Most of the time, you end up working for the State, at rest stops, government buildings, or if you're lucky, at a university."

"They all sound like good places to work. What's special about a university?"

George chuckled. "Spring and summer. A couple of years ago, a buddy started working on the machines at St. Cloud State University. I've never been a big fan of studying at a university. My favorite way to describe it is the old saying, 'If you have a college degree, you can be sure of one thing. You have a college degree.' But he kept on telling me to stop by, so I finally did." George took a drink and said, "I had most of my sight back then, and I made damn good use of it."

Mike wondered what his friend meant, since he hadn't spent much time at a college campus. Mike knew they had some fancy buildings and landscaping, but that didn't seem to be what George was talking about. The answer came a moment later.

"I mean, in the spring and summer, the coeds are either soaking up some sun in those new string bikinis or walking around and barely wearing more. Those sights almost made me give up engines."

"I suppose." Mike took a drink and smiled at the story and how George seemed to be feeling better. He looked up when he heard Shelly's voice.

"I'm noticing a pattern here, guys." She slid a pitcher between the two men. "Whenever I stop by, you're talking about young women."

"Like I keep saying, we're just behaving like a couple of healthy twenty-somethings."

"And like I keep saying, you're not in your twenties," Shelly replied in a lighthearted yet serious tone.

"It's all a state of mind, my dear. It's all a state of mind."

Shelly set down the meals instead of replying to the comment. "Here are your burgers and rings." She filled each man's glass, and Mike thought about the Monster Rings.

They still amazed him. Mike still couldn't imagine an onion that was big enough to fill the battered rings. He almost asked about it but bit into one instead. The flavor matched the size, a large dose of fresh and soft onion with deep-fried batter. The only way to make it better was to add ketchup, so he pushed a few of the rings away from the side of the plate and reached for the bottle.

"Ah, there we go," George said. "Treats like this make all the effort worthwhile." He took a big bite of his burger.

Mike tapped the ketchup bottle, hoped it wouldn't dump out like this morning, and wondered about the effort George was describing. His friend was probably joking more than making a serious statement, but showing up for class on time didn't seem like a lot of effort. He almost said something but decided to try his burger instead.

"It looks like you guys are all set. I'll stop by in a little while to see how you're doing."

"Thanks, Shelly," George said with a mouthful.

Mike took a moment to enjoy the burger, drank from his beer, and said, "Your comment about effort made me think of something."

"What's going on?"

"Is there any news about a volunteer for the ski trip?" Mike asked.

"Oh yeah, I've been meaning to tell you about that. A buddy of mine from the store is going to help out. His name is Ben Davis."

"Cool, that sounds great. Just to be careful, I'm going to write down his name." Mike bit into another Monster Ring and took out a marker and some paper. "Any chance you have his phone number?"

"None," George answered while chewing a mouthful of burger.

"No problem, and thanks for finding somebody. I'll just have Fred call the ski resort to take care of the details."

George grunted in agreement, and Mike continued. "I've been meaning to ask you something else about the ski trip. What do you think of sharing a room? A room with two guys costs a few bucks more than a room with four, but I've always liked being in a room with less people." Mike was a little worried George would want a room with more people, since George enjoyed groups and looked for low prices almost as much as Mike.

"Yeah, that sounds good. The extra cost is a drag, but a room with less people works better for me too." His tone became playful but still serious. "Because sometimes, I may just come in a little bit late and be a little bit unsteady, if you know what I mean. In the past, that's caused a bit of tension with the three other guys in the room, especially the ones who go on a ski trip to ski. So, staying with one guy who can handle some inconvenience could work out very well for me."

"I suppose," Mike said.

"I'll take that as a yes, and the more I think about it, the more I like the idea. I have a feeling we're going to have a good time, a very good time indeed."

The rest of the night was also a very good time. Shelly brought more pitchers, and the two friends had many more laughs. Just before midnight, Mike thought about saying the current pitcher would be the last since tomorrow morning was already going to be tough. Just after midnight, he asked Shelly for another pitcher because he heard something for the first time. It was rough and loud, yet made Mike smile and laugh, more than he had in months. At that moment, he heard George sing.

CHAPTER NINE

Play

Minnesotans get used to cold weather, slowly. It starts in the autumn after the hot and humid summer gives way to the first frost. That change feels cold, but with some warmer clothes and a few weeks, they get used to it. But then, a few more weeks lead to lower temperatures. That makes it feel cold again, and they get used to it again. The wind is something that's hard to get used to. A gust can drop the temperature another ten degrees in seconds. It feels more than suddenly cold. It's the kind of cold that freezes exposed skin and stings nerves, physically and emotionally. The best way to avoid this situation is not to stand in the wind on a cold day. If that's not possible, sometimes, it helps to swear.

"Jesus Christ!" Mike grumbled as another gust blew by.

He was standing next to his gate on the ski slope at White Pine Ridge. It was the third of four total gates, as Mike had learned from a ski patrol. The man had given him a lift up here on a snowmobile. He'd also given Mike instructions. The first one was to listen for more instructions from loudspeakers along the ski run. A sports commentator would use those speakers during the race and to give occasional instructions.

The ski patrol then showed him where to stand to avoid the skiers. That was about an arm's length from the flag at Gate 3. The last thing Mike learned was when to shake the tambourine. He was supposed to start shaking it when a skier was about twenty yards up the hill from him. The ski patrol emphasized that it was important not to shake the tambourine too soon or too late. Shaking it too soon could make it difficult for the blind or blindfolded skiers to tell if the sound was coming from Mike or from the previous gate, about fifty yards up the hill. Shaking the tambourine too late could make it difficult for the skier to locate Mike's gate, or Mike.

He thought about that last part. Even though a few people told him that the chance of getting hit by a skier was small, he knew the impact of a hit could be large. After worrying about it for a while, he decided to take a deep breath a few seconds before shaking the tambourine. That would give him plenty of air to call out to a skier who came too close.

He was wearing every piece of warm clothing he'd brought to Portage Bay and a couple plaid shirts from George, but he still felt a small chill in his chest and a larger chill in his toes. He rocked left and right, which helped warm his toes. He also tried another trick to stay warm, which was to stop thinking about the cold.

He scanned the area around him. That was easier than usual because it was a bright day, sun coming from a clear sky above and light bouncing off the snow below. As Mike looked up the hill, he could see the blurry shape of a person that was another volunteer standing by Gate 2. Farther up, there was a grey blur that he guessed was the starting point for the race. Around it all, he saw some dark parts, which were the trees on White Pine Ridge.

He turned and looked down the hill. Another volunteer was below him at Gate 4. Further below, a fuzzy line crossed the ski slope, which was probably the finish line. Past that, the sight was mostly white with a dark spot in the middle. Mike guessed the spot was the ski lodge where all the white ski slopes converged. He thought about the lodge. George was in there laughing, telling stories, and enjoying a cold drink by a warm fire.

Mike thought about what he would do in the lodge, if he were there right now. The laughs, stories, and drinks could wait. If he were in the lodge right now, he'd put his cold feet up to the warm fire. He rocked back and forth again and looked around some more, and then a voice came from the loudspeakers.

"Good morning, everybody!" the announcer said in a tone that reminded Mike of the voices he heard during a Vikings game. "I want to welcome you to the 1976 Darkside Ski Race! You may have heard of people taking a walk on the wild side, but in this race, skiers race down the dark side. Many of you are probably new to blind racing, so I'll explain a little. In a short while, two teams of skiers will compete for the best time without the luxury of sight. One team is the Moonlight Skiers, who are all from the blind community in Portage Bay. The other team is the Risky Racers. They are sighted skiers who have volunteered to race while wearing a blindfold. There's one last thing. Since many of our blind skiers have some sight, all the skiers will wear a blindfold during the race. All this makes the Darkside Ski Race something where skill matters more than sight."

"Right now," Mike mumbled to himself, "my toes matter more to me than anybody's skill." He hoped the announcer would just tell the first racer to start, since watching a racer might take his mind off the cold. Unfortunately, the announcer continued with his introduction.

"We also want to keep things safe, so I'll explain a little about that. First of all, each racer has a guide. The guide skis close behind a racer and describes what's coming up. Another safety factor is that this race only has four gates, and they're spread out more than usual. All of our racers have been practicing for weeks or months, so they have a good idea of what to expect."

"All right, that's a great safety briefing," Mike mumbled again. "Now, my toes would really appreciate it if you'd tell the first skier to ski."

"There's just one more thing before we begin."

"Of course there is."

"This race wouldn't be possible without the help of some great volunteers standing by each gate. Each one shakes a tambourine to tell the racers where to turn. In case you're wondering, we don't use things like electric buzzers or whistles because they freeze out there. Everybody, please give a big round of applause for our volunteers!"

"I freeze out here too," Mike said while folding his arms close to his chest. He started making more of his own commentary when the applause surprised him. He hadn't noticed all the people who'd gathered to watch. He looked at them, waved, and listened to the announcer.

"The race will start in about a half hour. Anybody hearing this is very welcome to join us. We're on the ski run right in front of the chalet, so please stop by if you want to see a great race. It's free to watch, but if you feel like giving something to our Darkside racers, there are donation buckets along the route, at the finish line, and in the chalet. All proceeds go to the visually impaired in Portage Bay. Right now, I have some things to tell the volunteers shaking tambourines, so the next few announcements are just for them. The first thing I want to do is make sure all those volunteers can hear me. If you can, wave your hands way up high."

Mike was happy to comply, since it might warm him up a little.

"Good, good, it looks like we have everybody. You should do the same thing if any problems come up during the race. The next step is to give you some practice knowing when to shake your tambourine. We have some skiers at the top who'll help you practice. They'll take a couple slow runs and call out when you should start and stop shaking your tambourine. If anybody shakes their tambourine too early or late, I'll mention it from here."

Mike was relieved that something would be happening soon. It seemed like most group events moved too slowly. Normally, he just became quietly impatient, with an occasional joke to himself or anyone within mumbling range. At the moment, he was impatient, feeling colder in his chest, and feeling very little in his toes.

"All right, our first practice skier just started, so you'll be seeing her soon. When you hear her yell, 'Start shaking!' you should shake your tambourine. After she passes you, she'll tell you when to stop shaking."

Mike looked up toward the first gate, trying to see the skier. After a few seconds, he heard the sound of a muffled yell, due to the distance and snow absorbing some sound. A faint ringing followed, and then another muffled yell. The ringing stopped, and Mike could see a dot moving down the slope toward the second gate. The next sound he heard was clearer. He could barely understand the skier telling the volunteer above him to start shaking the tambourine. The ringing started, continued, and stopped with another yell from the skier. Mike's gate was next.

He'd become so focused on the skier and shakers that it took him a moment to shake his own tambourine when she told him to. He kept shaking it as she came closer to his gate, a bit closer than he'd hoped. He thought about taking a deep breath when he heard her call out, "Hi, Mike!"

He was pretty sure he recognized the voice and instinctively looked for long red hair. Sure enough, it was there, flowing in the wind behind her. When she called out again to stop shaking the tambourine, he realized he already had, probably when she said hi.

"Jesus Christ," he mumbled to himself. "She skis by, and you manage to show that you can't even shake a tambourine at the right time." He heard Sam call out to the last gate and hoped nobody noticed how his timing was off with the tambourine. When the last ringing sound stopped, he sighed and realized that his chest wasn't cold anymore. One small advantage of being annoyed at himself was that it might have warmed him up. He wiggled his toes. Mike sighed and mumbled to himself again, "Little feeling in my toes, not too much."

"All right, that went pretty good," the announcer said. "Everybody shook their tambourines at almost the right time, but I have to ask our volunteer at Gate 3 to start just a little sooner and keep shaking a little longer. Our next practice skier is ready to start, so we'll go through it one more time."

"Great," Mike mumbled to himself. "So much for people not noticing." He looked up the hill after hearing a muffled yell and ringing. When the next skier came by, Mike carefully started and stopped shaking his tambourine when he was told to.

"That was perfect," the announcer said. "Great job, everybody. I'd say we're now ready for the main event. Our first racer is in the starting gate, but I want to check with our volunteers one more time. Hold your hands high and shake your tambourines if you're ready!"

Mike held up his hands and shook the tambourine a little. When he heard how loud other volunteers were shaking their tambourines and cheering, he joined in, but his cheering was different. He knew his voice would be drowned out by all the noise, so he called out, "Yeah, I'm ready! I'm also freezing, so get going!" He laughed at his own joke, which had one more benefit. It made him feel warmer, possibly by taking his mind off the cold.

"That sounds great!" the announcer replied. He continued with enthusiasm, "Everyone watching, are you ready to watch some skiers race down the dark side?"

Mike heard the crowd cheer and saw people wave their hands.

"All right! That's the way to get our racers ready. The first racer is Sharon Carlson, and she's with the Moonlight Skiers, our blind skiing team. Sharon is sponsored by The Tacklebox in Portage Bay. They've been helping us with the Darkside Race since we started two years ago. They've had good luck with their racers, so we're hoping for a great opening run. I see the referee at the starting gate giving her a countdown. I think I see two, now one, and there she goes!"

Mike looked up the slope but couldn't see Sharon. He squinted, waited, and heard the faint sound of a tambourine from Gate 1. He looked at the source of the sound. A blurry dot appeared and moved through the white scene. A moment later, he could see another dot behind the first, which must have been Sharon's guide. The dots turned, and the faint ringing stopped. In a few seconds, a clearer ringing started. The moving dots were larger and faster. "Jesus Christ, she's going that fast and can't see? Wow." He could now make out the racer's shape, and how it shifted from tucked down to angled out when she shoved her skis into the turns.

A nagging feeling told him to stop watching and start thinking about when to shake his tambourine. The ringing from the gate above faded, so she would be coming to his gate soon. He watched carefully and waited for the moment to start shaking his tambourine.

He was surprised at how soon she reached that point and more surprised at how fast Sharon and her guide went past him. "Hey, great job!" Mike called out without even knowing he said it. He barely remembered to stop shaking his tambourine and never remembered to take a deep breath, to call out if the skier came too close.

"Wow, that was pretty cool," he said to himself while watching them ski to the next gate. He could briefly hear the edges of their skis cut into the snow, until that sound was replaced by the ringing from the next tambourine. He focused less on Sharon as she became a faint dot and as he noticed some cheers.

"That's going to be a tough time to beat!" the announcer said. "Sharon Carlson almost set a record, with a time of fifty-six point seven seconds! If she takes about two seconds off that time, she'll have the record. She could still get it, since all the skiers take two runs.

"Our next skier is now at the starting gate. His name is Johnny Anderson. He's the first sighted skier in today's race, and it looks like he's had some fun with his blindfold. It's certainly the most colorful one I've ever seen. Anyway, Johnny's with the Risky Racers and is sponsored by our friends at Northland Timber. He had the best time last year, so we're hoping for a great run. The referee at the top just started the countdown, two and one and Johnny's off! It looks like he's getting a fast start, so my guess is that he's trying pretty hard to stay on top."

The announcer continued, but Mike didn't pay attention. He was too focused on finding Johnny and didn't even think about his guide. The faint ringing from the first gate started. Once again, Mike used the ringing to find the racer, and once again, he instinctively added some comments. "Jesus Christ, did he forget that he's blindfolded?" He shook his head, amazed at how fast Johnny was skiing. Johnny was approaching the second gate when Mike added more of his own commentary. "All right, Johnny, do us all a favor and stay clear of the nice tambourine shaker, and please do the same for the next one—namely me." The ringing stopped, and he got ready to shake his own tambourine.

No comments came to mind as Mike watched Johnny come closer to his gate. The speed continued to impress him. As the racer and his guide turned by Mike, he was also impressed by the sound of their skis, as they cut into the snow around the gate. Mike instinctively cheered again and was even less certain that he stopped shaking the tambourine soon enough.

"Wow, that is pretty cool," he said while watching the skiers quickly change from the shape of people to shadows against the snow and finally to blurry dots. When the dots faded away, Mike noticed more cheers from the crowd.

"Another amazing run from the Darkside Ski Race!" the announcer called out. "Johnny Anderson has barely come out ahead of Sharon Carlson! He finished about a half-second faster, at fifty-six point one seconds. It looks like things will be neck and neck as we move to our next skier."

The next skier, and the ones after that, were slower than the first two, but they still impressed Mike. It was hard to believe anyone would ski so fast without sight, even with a sighted guide. Mike wondered if he should worry less while walking down a sidewalk. He also noticed that his toes didn't feel cold anymore. He fell into a routine of listening to the announcer, watching the skiers approach, shaking his tambourine, and hearing the sound of their skis around the gate. This routine changed when the last skier was called. That one caught his attention.

"The last skier in the first round is Samantha Smothers, skiing for the Moonlight Skiers. Samantha is sponsored by Bridgman School for the Blind in Portage Bay. It continues to be a close race, so a lot is riding on her run. Her countdown is on two, one, and she's off. She's approaching the first gate a little closer than other skiers. Wow, if she'd cut it any closer, she could've taken the tambourine from our volunteer."

"It's not a good idea to cut it close to the gate, Sam," Mike mumbled to himself and looked for her blurry dot.

The announcer continued. "It looks like she'll be doing the same at Gate 2. Yep, once again, she came very close to the flag at Gate 2. That's a risky way to ski when you can't see anything, but it does make for a fast run."

"Not good, Sam," Mike muttered. "You shouldn't cut it that close to the gate. The nice volunteers would really appreciate it if you'd not clobber them."

"She's now getting ready for Gate 3," the announcer said.

As she approached his gate, many thoughts went through Mike's mind—that he couldn't screw up with his tambourine, that he was impressed with her courage, and that her courage could lead to clobbering him if she misjudged the turn. The last thought was on his mind the most, so he stepped away from the flag and stretched an arm toward it when shaking the tambourine. That way, if she cut it too close, only his arm would get hit and not his body.

Now that he'd seen a few skiers approach, Mike could tell that Sam was faster than most but also more unstable. As she came even closer, he could see that she had to adjust a lot to stay in control. The speed may have become too much. She moved up from her crouched position to reduce speed and gain control. Skiing more upright stabilized her for a moment, but it was a problem at the gate. As she turned by Mike's gate, the additional height caused her body to swerve outward. She fought to stay above her skis and made some comments he'd heard before.

"Dammit! Goddammit! Goddammit!"

There may have been a growl at the end of her curses, like George had mentioned a while ago. Sam shoved her skis harder into the turn than any other skier, which Mike could tell from the sound alone. That kept her in control, but it also led to more of a sliding stop than a turn through the gate. She swore some more and quickly dug her poles into the snow to regain some speed.

"Damn, gutsy skier but lousy language," Mike said as she went by and continued down the hill.

"That was a tough run for Samantha," the announcer said. "But she'll have another chance in the second round. We'll start that round in a moment. For now, I'll give you the score. It's a close contest at today's Darkside Ski Race, with the Risky Racers just seconds in front of the Moonlight Skiers. The total time for the Risky Racers is seven minutes and twenty-five point eight seconds. The total time for the

Moonlight Skiers is only about ten seconds more, at seven minutes and thirty-five point two seconds. With a race this close, it all comes down to the second half. We'll start that half soon, but I see a few more people are watching the race now, so I'll tell you a little about it and invite anyone else to join us."

The announcer repeated the rules and asked people to make donations. Mike looked around and noticed some changes next to the ski run. Some dark areas he'd previously thought were small trees were now longer, shifting shapes created by groups of people. The crowd was larger than he expected. After enjoying the race, he could understand why they wanted to watch, but blind sports still reminded him of girls' basketball in high school. Even when his sisters had played, he and others hadn't shown up as often as they had for a boys' game. That thought made him appreciate the larger crowd.

His thoughts shifted to the racers. The first two stood out from the rest, with their combination of grace, power, and determination. Mike hadn't seen all that so close up before. Other racers clearly had less experience with blind skiing. They kept their speed lower by standing higher and took wide turns around Mike's gate. One of them had even called out a little joke to Mike, asking if he was headed in the right direction. Mike had just cheered him on and respected how less experienced skiers were also pushing their limits.

Then there was Sam. He shook his head as he thought about how her skiing matched her style when they'd had drinks a couple weeks ago, in a booth at Speakeasy. "She's a full-throttle woman," he said to himself with a little smile. Mike gazed down the slope toward the chalet and wondered what would happen later. A few people from Bridgman's had come along on this trip, which was good and not. He liked seeing people from school, but having them here meant that he'd have to be careful when talking with Sam. In the last few days and weeks, he'd heard more about how it was fine if students and teachers had fun together as long as they didn't flirt together.

The announcer was now talking about businesses that had sponsored some of the racers. Mike ignored him again and scanned the finish line, past Gate 4. He used to see the finish as a thin grey streak across the run. Now, it was a larger and darker line, since the crowd continued to grow.

A sudden thought concerned him. This was his first ski trip, so he wasn't sure what Sam would do after the race. Maybe she'd want to ski some more. Since he didn't ski, that would mean she'd enjoy herself without him or with other guys. Or maybe she would be talking with other skiers in the chalet, and who knows, maybe she was looking forward to spending time with one in particular, or more. Weeks ago, George had mentioned that Sam had a reputation for enjoying guys. That didn't happen by staying alone during weekend getaways, especially with a bunch of athletic men. "Bummer, never thought of that."

His toes were getting cold again, so Mike rocked back and forth. "In that case, I suppose I'll drown my sorrows with George and probably have a few laughs." He looked around again to take his mind off of the thought of Sam with another guy. He also wanted to enjoy the colors from White Pine Ridge, especially since this view was a lot better than the one from his room at Mariners.

"We're almost ready to start the second half of today's Darkside Ski Race. There is one more fact you might want to know about blind ski racing. This was the first year it was part of the Paralympics in Sweden. Who knows, if some of our skiers keep pushing their limits, they just may end up there someday. Right now, we're going to start from the top, so Sharon Carlson is in the starting gate skiing for the Moonlight Skiers. The referee is signaling, so the second half will start in two and one, and Sharon's off!"

Mike enjoyed watching Sharon fly by and Johnny after that. They were focused and controlled. When the ski run was straight, they stayed low to gain speed, and just before a turn, they skied more upright to lose speed and gain control. When they turned by Mike, the racers leaned in, dug their skis into the snow, and pushed their way past him. The sights were thrilling, but Mike enjoyed the sounds more, edges of hard skis scraping across packed snow. In the second round of the race, Sharon was slightly faster than Johnny, so the overall contest was close again.

Sharon and Johnny were a pleasure to watch, but in the second half, he also enjoyed the less skilled skiers. When the announcer called out their names, Mike almost recognized some, but he didn't try very hard to remember them since there was so much to see and hear during the race. In one case, the sights came a little too close. Mike had to step out of the way of a skier when she wiped out while lining up for Gate 3. That led to the first disqualification of this race, for the Risky Racers.

Another close call came from the skier who'd called out to Mike in the first round, asking if he was headed in the right direction. The skier asked the same question, but this time, Mike answered, "Just keep your skis pointed down." He regretted that answer when the skier laughed and wandered off track. Mike had to step out of the way again, quickly. The skier didn't wipe out, but he passed the gate on the wrong side. That led to another disqualification, for the Moonlight Skiers this time.

The announcer added some comments. "We're always sorry to see another skier get disqualified, but that means we have a razor-close race going down to our last skier. The entire contest now rides on Samantha Smothers. If she can get under one minute and two point nine seconds, she'll win it for the Moonlight Racers. That's just a few seconds faster than her first run, so she could pull it off, since Sam had some problems in Gate 3 last time. All she really needs is a smooth run through all the gates to give a win to the Moonlight Racers. She'll be off in three, two, and one. There she goes!"

"Come on, Sam, just keep it steady," Mike mumbled to himself as he tried to find her. He couldn't hear the faint ringing from Gate 1 this time because the crowd was too loud.

The announcer sounded more excited than before. "She's flying by Gate 1 again, fast and close to the gate. It looks like Samantha is trying to take off more than a few seconds."

"Don't be a hotshot, Sam," Mike mumbled and found her blurry dot. "And please, don't clobber the nice volunteers."

"Samantha is now lining up for Gate 2. She's fast but seems to have a tough time staying in control. Oh, that was tough! She had a little too much speed in Gate 2 and took a wide turn around the gate. Samantha lost some time on that one."

"Just ski, Sam," Mike said. "Don't push it so much. For God's sake, relax."

"She's really trying to make up for that last turn. I don't know if she could get any lower in her skis."

Mike watched Sam line up for his gate and focused on shaking the tambourine at the right time, knowing she would probably growl in anger if he shook it at the wrong time. He also repeated the technique he'd used during her first run, shaking the tambourine with an out-stretched arm in case she cut this gate too close.

Sam flew by Mike's gate with the same speed as Sharon and Johnny. The blur and sound of skis cutting around the turn made him cheer louder than he ever had. He quickly rotated and watched her line up for Gate 4.

"That was a beautiful turn through Gate 3, and she continues to pick up speed heading into Gate 4. It looks like she's standing up a little to lose some speed, and now standing even higher. Now for the turn, oh no!"

Mike couldn't see the problem but still cringed. "Dammit, Sam!" he said, feeling like the announcer's words were coming out in slow motion.

"Sam barely stayed above her skis in Gate 4, standing straight up on the outside ski just to keep control. It wasn't pretty, but she's now tucked back down, getting as much speed as she can for the finish. And that's it!

"Samantha Smothers gave us a great final run, but what matters most is her time, since the entire race depends on it. The judges seem to be talking it over more than before. I'm sure they just want to be careful. While they're double-checking, I'll say again that she needed a time of one minute and two point nine seconds to win it for the Moonlight Racers. All right, I've just been given her official time. Wow, you are not going to believe this." He spoke slower than before. "On the final run of the 1976 Darkside Ski Race, Samantha Smothers had a time of…"

After noticing how the announcer was pausing for effect, Mike called out, "Enough already!"

The announcer spoke slowly, emphasizing each word. "One minute and ..."

The entire ski slope was silent, for much longer than Mike wanted. "That's enough dramatic effect!"

"Two point ..." The announcer paused again.

"Jerk," Mike mumbled.

"One seconds! Samantha Smothers has won the race for the Moonlight Skiers, with a time of one minute and two point one seconds!"

The quiet ski slope burst into a roar of cheers. Mike and all the other volunteers joined in, jumped around, and shook their tambourines.

.   .   .   .

Mike cheered again, in the chalet this time. He and many others had been cheering for about an hour, after a meal and several toasts. After this cheer faded, he felt the friend next to him lean closer to ask a question.

"Hey, Mikey, mind filling me up again?"

"Already? Wow, George, I'm impressed."

"The first one always goes the fastest."

Mike slid George's glass closer on the long dining table where they were sitting. Then he picked up one of the pitchers of beer and filled George's glass. Before Mike could set the pitcher down, someone from across the table asked for it. Several people were sitting over there, so Mike didn't know who asked. He just handed it in the direction of the voice and added, "Here ya go," in case the person didn't have enough sight to easily see the pitcher. Mike felt someone take it and heard another comment from George.

"I have to give you credit, Mikey, standing out there in the freezing cold, dodging skiers. I heard you were at Gate 3, so I tried to keep up on how things went for ya."

The comment surprised Mike. "You mean you were outside watching the race?"

George laughed. "Oh no, I'd do a lot of things for you, but that falls short of standing in the freezing cold when I can stay nice and toasty in a chalet." George took a drink. "Especially when you're the one who volunteered to freeze out there." He laughed some more.

"Then how did you listen to the race?"

"The good people in the bar tried something new this year. They piped in the sound from the announcer, so we could listen to the whole thing. I gotta say, there were some tense moments." George chuckled again. "It's a good thing I had a cozy chair by the fireplace to relax, not to mention a cold beer. Otherwise, all those tense moments could have made me downright uncomfortable."

Mike laughed with his friend. "I suppose."

"Seriously, though, this was probably the best race yet."

"Really?"

"Yeah, the other two weren't that close. In the first race, our folks clobbered them, and last year, they clobbered us."

"I see."

"So, what kind of action did you see, all up close and personal? It sounded like Sam's close call may have been near you."

"Which one? She had a couple."

"Spoken like a man who was in the middle of the action." George laughed and took a drink. "It really is fantastic that you saw it all close up. I still think you're half-crazy for being out there, but it's still fantastic." Both men took a drink and George continued. "Now you got me wondering, which one of Sam's memorable moments stood out the most, from your up close and freezing perspective?"

The first answer Mike thought of was when Sam had called out his name during a practice run. He didn't want to give that answer, though, since it might tell George too much. Mike was still keeping things with Sam a secret. He took a drink and thought about the question.

"I admit that I was a little worried on her first run. She cut it close to most of the gates, and it looked like she was going faster than she could handle."

"That sounds like Sam," George replied.

"And you should have heard her when she messed up on my gate, swearing and even growling."

George laughed and said, "That sounds like Sam too."

"I was pretty impressed when she flew by my gate on her second run. Sam really did nail that turn, but the part I remember most is the tough time she had with Gate 4 on the last run."

"That's what I thought. Some guys in the chalet said she was standing straight up on one leg in that turn just to stay in control." George smiled. "I can almost see it, one more inch over that outside ski." He showed an inch with a thumb and pointer finger. The same hand moved down in an arch, and he continued. "And her body would have tumbled over in that turn, within sight of all the good folks by the finish line." He ended with a laugh. "She would have been so mad, I bet the snow would have melted around her."

Mike laughed with him and imagined Sam lying in the snow, cursing and probably growling. "Yep, that could've been ugly."

Both men laughed some more, and then George said, "But she hung on. That's what matters." They took a drink, and he made a suggestion. "Hey, what do you think of heading over to the fireplace? Normally, this crowd slowly makes its way over there. We can probably get a good seat if we leave soon."

Mike agreed, and George made another suggestion. "Why don't you liberate one of those pitchers and bring it with us? We really should do everyone a favor and have a pitcher over there. After all, they could easily forget to bring one when they finally walk to the fireplace."

Mike laughed, recognizing George's ongoing effort to get some free drinks. He stood up and took a pitcher of beer. The two men walked out of the dining room with their hands full. Mike had his glass in one hand and the pitcher in the other. George also had a glass in one hand and held Mike's elbow with the other. It was fairly easy for Mike to walk with his hands full, since the light was brighter than in most bars. The staff at the ski lodge had more lights on to accommodate the blind skiing group. As they walked closer to the fireplace, Mike saw the flames more clearly and noticed the scent of burning pine.

"Are there many tables open near the fire?" George asked.

"Most of them are full, but there might be one open." Mike walked to the table and put the pitcher on it. He then guided George to a large chair. His friend sunk into the overstuffed chair and sighed with delight. "This is my favorite part of a ski race. I could sit here for hours. As a matter of fact, I think I will." He took a drink from his glass, stretched out his legs, and crossed them.

"Glad to see you relax, George. You've had a tough day," Mike said with a chuckle.

"You're damn right. It's time for a nice long break."

"While you're recovering, I'm going to check out the fireplace. I put the pitcher on your side of the table."

"You're a good man, Mikey. Don't be too long, or else some gorgeous woman's likely to take your chair, and being a gentleman, I don't know if I could just tell her to go away."

"I suppose," Mike said while stepping toward the fireplace. He paused, examined it, and took a drink from the glass he was still holding. The fireplace was a large square in the center of the room. Each corner had a grey pillar, with open sides to make the fire visible from all around. A vague memory told him the fireplace was made of stone.

Mike touched one of the pillars and felt smooth stones in many sizes. He wandered around the fireplace, feeling more of the stones and examining the pillars. They changed to a stone arc over the fire, which came together in a wide chimney. He slowly stepped around it and enjoyed the glow, sounds, and smooth stones. The fireplace was between him and George when he stopped. A long, relaxed sigh came out, and no particular thoughts came to mind as he gazed at the fire.

He had no idea how much time had passed when a familiar laugh made him glance away from the fire. The relaxed feeling faded as he thought about the woman laughing. A group walked toward him, and he started feeling nervous. She was in the back, replying to people congratulating her.

Mike felt more nervous. He wanted to congratulate her too but wondered if this was her night of being a celebrity, which made him think his chances of talking with her were small. He realized she would be walking right by him and decided his chances were smaller if he said nothing. He hoped one of his clever comments would come out. They were getting closer. He guessed there were three or four people in the group and tried harder to find something to say. The first part of the group passed by. Nothing came to mind. Now, she was walking by. He had to say something. Mike took a step toward her and made the best comment he could.

"Hi, Sam."

"Oh, hi, Mike," she said while slowing down. "I was hoping I'd see you here. Are you having a good time?" She stopped walking.

"Yeah, a great time. I heard about the fireplace, so I wanted to check it out."

"It is a great fireplace," she replied.

Mike thought about asking her to enjoy it with him for a while, but she continued before he could say anything.

"We were just looking for a table, before they're all taken." She glanced in the direction of her group, which had kept moving.

Mike glanced toward it as well. The shadows of her friends were moving slower now and mixing in with the other, lower shadows of people sitting at tables. He looked at Sam again. "Good idea, the place is filling up fast."

"Yeah." She took a drink from her glass. Mike noticed it had a red-orange color and wondered if it was a Double Sloe Screw like the one she bought him a couple of weeks ago. He also took a drink from his beer. He thought again about asking her to join him by the fire, and again, she spoke before he could.

"I should go join them." An awkward pause passed. She looked at her friends again and back at Mike. "It looks like they found a table. Maybe you can stop by later. It'd be great to catch up."

Some thoughts quickly went through his mind about how the next few moments might unfold. The easy response was to say he'd join them later and stay by the fire. A problem with that response was that the place was filling up fast, so stopping by later could make it hard to even get a seat close to her, much less talk some more. After all, many people wanted to talk with the star of today's race. The other option was to take a chance and ask Sam if he could join her group right now. The answer seemed clear until someone else called out.

"Hey Sam, great race today! We'll try harder next year."

"Thanks!" she replied and turned toward the voice. "You *better* try harder next year. I'm only getting started." She laughed and turned back toward Mike.

He thought about how the young, attractive, and determined woman in front of him really was the star of today's race. She was also the most impressive athlete he'd ever known. The thoughts led to another moment of shyness and loss of words.

She spoke again. "Well, it was good seeing you, hope you stop by later." Sam looked toward her friends and took a step in their direction.

"Hey, Sam," Mike said.

She looked at him.

He still felt shy but forced out some words. "You really did a great job today. I couldn't believe how fast you went."

"Thanks. It was a lot of fun, and thanks again for helping." She seemed to wait for Mike to say something else. When he didn't, she did. "Well, I better get going." She took another step toward the group.

Mike quickly asked, "Would it be all right if I stopped by now? I mean, if that's okay. I've been standing here for a while, so it'd be great to sit down and relax."

She smiled. "Of course it's okay. We're just over here." She took a couple of steps away from the fire and glanced back at Mike one more time.

After a few steps, Sam set her drink on a table with two other people sitting at it.

"Mike, you probably remember Fred. He was at the planning meeting you joined about a month ago."

Mike told Fred that it was good to see him again, and Fred said the same.

"And this is Johnny," Sam said, introducing the other man at the table.

The man held out a hand and said, "Hey, Mike, how ya do'n?"

After shaking his hand, Mike put his beer on the table and sat down. He felt like he should know why Johnny's name was familiar, but Mike was so focused on Sam he couldn't remember.

Sam answered the question. "You've actually been close to Johnny a couple of times when he went by your gate today. He's the star skier from the Risky Racers."

"Oh yeah," Mike said. "I couldn't believe how fast you were going with a blindfold on."

"Thanks," Johnny replied. "I used to ski in college, so it's a lot of fun competing again."

"He did a little more than compete in college," Sam added. "He went to the State Finals twice."

"Wow, that's pretty cool," Mike said.

Johnny took a drink and replied, "Yeah, it was fun, but I was firmly in the middle of the pack both times. These days, I ski for the fun and a challenge, which is how I started wearing a blindfold."

"Johnny's a little modest," Sam added. "He still gets the best time."

"And Sam can be a little flattering," Johnny said. "Sharon beat me this year."

Mike also wondered why Sam was being flattering toward Johnny.

Fred joined the conversation. "I went by you too, but I'm not quite as fast as Sam or Johnny."

Mike stopped wondering about Sam's comment to Johnny and focused on Fred.

"Being slower does allow me to enjoy the race in different ways, like joking with people shaking tambourines. I think you said something back to me once, something about keeping my skis pointed down."

"That was you?" Mike asked, feeling embarrassed. "Sorry for not recognizing you."

"Yeah, that was me, and no problem. It's hard to keep track of everybody out there. I got a kick out of your joke, and besides, you gave me an excuse for missing your gate. Now, I can say it was your fault I was disqualified again." Fred laughed and continued. "Everybody has a reputation to keep. Johnny wins. Sam pushes the limit, and I usually get disqualified."

The group laughed and took a drink.

"It looks like we could use another round," Johnny said. "I'll go pick it up."

"That'd be nice," Sam said, while touching his wrist.

"Hey, Johnny," Fred added, "would you mind guiding me to the fireplace? I haven't been there yet."

Johnny said he would, and the two men stood up. Fred took Johnny's elbow, and they walked toward the fire. Mike was surprised to suddenly find himself alone with Sam. He also wondered if she was more attracted to him or Johnny. Maybe she was interested in both. He took a drink and thought of a way to find out more.

"Johnny seems like a great guy," he said, wondering how she'd reply.

Sam took a drink and answered, "Yeah, he really is, and a great skier too."

"How long have you known him?"

"Ever since I started racing. He was part of the group that gave lessons in racing without sight. Sharon Carlson set the whole thing up and did most of the teaching, like telling us to think of the tambourine sound as a place to turn instead of just a sound. At first, we just walked by some ringing tambourines, but then we jogged by them. After we practiced that for a while, we did some real ski runs. Johnny and other experienced skiers shook tambourines at the gates." She looked down and remembered more about the lessons. "They used to yell out how many yards before each turn. I can still hear them calling out, 'Thirty yards! Twenty! Get ready to turn! Ten Yards! Turn!' It was a lot of fun learning with everybody else." Sam took a drink and looked back at Mike. "I'm sorry for carrying on. I've been meaning to ask, how was it out there for you? And be honest, I know shaking a tambourine on a cold hill isn't exactly glamorous."

Mike liked being asked the question. "It was actually a lot better than I expected. I admit that, at first, I was a little worried about the cold."

"That makes sense. The wind can be pretty bad out there."

"Actually, it was all right."

"Good."

"Except for my toes."

"Oh no. I hope they were okay."

"And my fingers."

"Oh dear."

"And just about everything in between."

"This doesn't sound good," Sam said while laughing and smiling.

"And some other things I won't mention without more drinks."

Sam laughed some more.

"Little humor, not too much."

Both of them laughed, and Mike added, "Actually, I was fine. It was cold at first, but once the race got started, just watching the skiers took the chill out. I still can't believe how fast some of them go, including you. What's it like going that fast?"

"The speed is great, but I gotta tell you something."

"What's that?" Mike asked.

"I love how you do that."

"Huh?"

"The whole little humor thing you do. I love that."

He hadn't heard that before, so he simply thanked her.

Then, he felt her foot rub the inside of a leg. He wanted to enjoy the way she was touching him, but he also felt cautious, which led to his next question. "I thought you liked Johnny." He felt the rubbing fade.

"I do like Johnny. He's a good guy and a great skier." She took a long drink. "But I'll tell you a little secret. I've been flirting with Johnny more than usual for an unusual reason. It involves Donny."

"You mean the school president?"

"Yes. He had a long talk with me last week, saying that I've bent the rules a little too much. The problem is that I really want to bend them just one more time."

Mike thought of a few questions he'd like to ask but settled on a simple response, "Okay."

"So, I wanted people here to think I was interested in Johnny. That way, they may not notice if I spend time with someone else, someone a teacher working for Donny probably shouldn't spend a lot of time with."

He smiled at the hints Sam offered, the flirting tone she used, and the clever question he thought of. "Anybody I know?"

She smiled back and gave a clever answer. "From what I hear, it's someone you talk to a lot."

He didn't understand the comment at first, until he felt her foot rubbing up against a leg again. Then he realized that he must have been caught talking to himself, maybe a few times. "Well, since I know him pretty well, I'll share a little secret with you too. That particular guy is all right with bending the rules once in a while."

Mike slowly reached for Sam's hand. When he felt her fingers, she gently rubbed his for a moment.

"I hate to say this, but I still want to be careful, at least in public."

He pulled his hand away. "That makes sense."

They gazed across the table, and just like before, Mike enjoyed the unique color of her eyes, at least at first. That changed when he saw the feelings in them. They held the gaze until a voice called out behind them.

"All right, this is our table."

Sam and Mike looked toward Johnny and saw a group of people following him. He set two pitchers on their table, and someone else set down one more.

"I asked a few friends to join us, so we're probably going to need another table, maybe two. I see a couple we could bring over."

Mike watched them move around him when he heard Sam again. "Hey, great! We can put a couple of tables together. Mike, why don't you help bring some chairs over."

He was a little surprised at the comment but agreed, stood up, and heard Sam say something to Johnny.

"I'll be back in a minute. It's time for me to pee."

Mike stepped away to get some chairs and heard Johnny reply that he'd see her soon. Mike picked up the chairs and heard a whisper from behind him.

"When you're done with those chairs, it'd be great if you would buy us a couple of drinks at the bar. I'll meet you there."

He lifted the chairs, watched Sam walk away, and wondered if it would look too strange if he sprinted to the bar. "Probably shouldn't, the place is too crowded now. I'd probably trip over someone." He carried the chairs to the place where the group was sitting and set them down, trying not to attract attention. The last thing he wanted was to be invited into a conversation. Fortunately, he was able to quietly wander away.

As he stepped toward the fireplace, he noticed the room was darker. Maybe the staff turned the lights down as part of the normal lighting for a Saturday night, or maybe some new staff started working after the ski race and dinner were over.

Several people were now standing around the fireplace, enjoying it as Mike had earlier. Getting through the crowd was too much trouble, so he tried going around it. Fortunately, both hands were free, since he'd left his beer at the table. He held out one hand low to feel for chairs. He used the other to gently nudge people, while repeating "Sorry" and "Excuse me."

Mike thought about unfolding his white cane, which was in his back pocket as usual, but he didn't want to make that small effort. He just wanted to walk past the fireplace, find an easier path, and see Sam. Unfortunately, the gap he was walking through filled up with another group walking toward him. He started to imagine Sam waiting at the bar, which made him feel impatient. He took a step forward and felt a little better after hearing some familiar singing.

That gave Mike an idea. If he could hear the singing, maybe this crowd could hear him if he spoke louder. His polite efforts hadn't worked very well, so it couldn't hurt to experiment.

He raised his voice, while still trying to sound polite. That led to standing still, next to a crowd enjoying a laugh. He tried again in the same voice. Someone pushed her way past Mike, making him move back a step. He spoke louder. Some heads turned toward him with bodies that stood still.

He had a memory of the bartender in Speakeasy when she delivered drinks. That bartender spoke loud and pushed forward. Mike tried more of both. Someone complained. He said, "Sorry," much louder and pushed harder. He started enjoying the process of calling out and moving forward, even felt a little disappointed when it was over.

The crowd was thinner when he pushed past the fireplace. He walked right by George and thought about making a joke to his friend, but that could wait for another time. Right now, Mike wanted to get to the bar and order a couple of drinks.

The bar was emptier than he expected. He wondered if the fireplace had drawn people away from the bar. A bartender walked toward Mike, and he ordered two Double Sloe Screws.

"Say again," the bartender replied.

"I'd like two Double Sloe Screwdrivers."

"That's a new one on me, hell of a name though. What's in 'em?"

Mike's head turned when he heard a familiar voice. "Two shots of sloe gin in a tall glass, fill the rest with orange juice, and add some ice."

"Coming up," the bartender said, as he turned and walked away.

Mike smiled, stepped toward Sam, and looked at her. "Sorry it took me a while." They both heard George try another tune, so he joked, "I couldn't resist the urge to enjoy some singing on the way over."

Sam laughed. "No problem, I heard you coming through the crowd. I do like a man who can make things happen." She stepped closer to him.

"Sometimes, I like to make things happen. Sometimes, I like to go with the flow, and other times, I like to surprise people."

She stepped even closer, stopped less than an arm's length away, and spoke in a low voice. "What do you feel like doing now?"

He smiled. "I feel like getting these drinks and getting away from the crowd for a while on a little walk. Care to join me?"

"Maybe. Are you leading me or surprising me?"

He laughed. "I'm giving you the chance to find out."

"I do like taking chances."

The two gazed at each other, and Mike thought about taking a chance right now. He wanted to slowly lean over, kiss her, stop caring if someone from school might see.

"Here you go, two Double Sloe Screwdrivers. That'll be four bucks."

It took Mike a moment to look away from Sam and at the bartender.

"Hey, buddy, things are getting a little busy over here, mind taking care of this?"

"Oh, sure." He took out his wallet, moved it a few inches from his face, and took out a bill. "Here you go."

The bartender looked at it and said. "This is only a buck. I need four."

Usually, Mike felt awkward about the mistake and said he was sorry. This time, he just gave the bartender another bill. The bartender took it, set down the one-dollar bill and quickly walked away.

Mike gave Sam one of the glasses, took the other, and raised it. "To your winning run."

She touched her glass to his, and replied, "To a little risk." They both smiled and took long drinks.

The bartender returned, thanked Mike, set some bills on the bar, and walked to another customer. Mike took them and asked, "How about that walk?"

"I'd love it."

He led her through the bar, wondered about where to go, and took a few more drinks, hoping they'd give some inspiration about where to walk. The dining room might be a good idea, since most of their group had moved out of there and into the room with the fireplace. Mike decided against it. Other groups might be in the dining room having a late meal, like families or other groups of skiers. He kept walking.

They came close to the front door of the chalet. He briefly considered taking her outside, hoping they'd find a place to enjoy some moonlight. That idea also had too many risks. There was some momentum going with Sam that would probably fade if they had to put on their coats and go into the cold. He wanted to decide soon, so he turned a corner and walked into a darker room.

"You wanted to take me on a walk into the coatroom?"

"You said you liked surprises." Mike put an arm around her waist, slowly pulled her close, and gave her a gentle kiss. She responded with a kiss that was less gentle, and he did the same. He dropped his glass and suspected she dropped hers. They wrapped their arms around each other, and the passion became anything but gentle. Eventually, other things dropped next to them—coats, hats, and gloves. Their embrace ended when Sam almost fell over, after stumbling on some boots.

"I think we need to go somewhere else," she said.

"How about your room?" Mike quickly asked.

"That won't work. Two of the women in my room are teachers who turn in early. How about your room?"

"It might be okay, but George might be surprised."

"George might also think it was something he dreamt after too many drinks," she said in her low voice.

"That's true, and we could probably hear him coming; he's not exactly quiet."

"I'm less sure of that, but we could give it a try."

The two anxiously walked to Mike's room.

Hours later, they didn't hear George stumble to the room and through the door, but there was no missing his singing after walking in. Mike quickly started singing with his friend. Both men laughed loud. Mike kept on singing to give Sam a chance to get dressed and sneak out. He felt a little guilty, taking advantage of the fact that George couldn't see her, but this was one time when he felt comfortable bending the rules.

CHAPTER TEN

Luck

At a minute past nine in the morning, Mike decided that he better walk to Room 5 after waiting for George in the dayroom. Since George had been doing so well with being on time, Mike was a little disappointed in his friend. Maybe he'd slipped into his old ways, hopefully for just a day. When Mike stepped into Room 5, he expected a comment from Margaret. She wouldn't scold him, but she usually made it clear to students that she noticed when they were late.

After taking a few steps into the room, he was surprised not to hear or see her in the place she always stood at the start of class.

The room felt strange without George or Margaret in it. Mike mumbled "Good morning" to the three people who were at the table and heard similar comments back, followed by a question from a deep voice.

"You seen Margaret?"

Mike replied that he hadn't.

"I can see why George is late. His luck had to run out eventually, but Margaret's always here."

Another comment came from Mary's soft voice. "I hope she's okay."

"It's probably just a late bus or something," Albert said. "I heard the roads are really slippery after the sleet we've been having."

"You got a point there," Norman added. "Driving worries me more and more. The roads are hazardous enough in good weather. Maybe they were in the wrong place at the wrong time."

"That's a scary thought," Mary said.

"I don't think we should overreact," Mike replied. "Besides, the chance of both of the being in an accident is small. There's probably a perfectly good explanation."

"Maybe," Norman added, "but we've all heard about the risks in the Orientation and Mobility class. And speaking just for myself, I've had a few close calls with cars."

"I agree with you," Albert said. "But I think Mike has a good point. I don't like worrying too much when there could be a good explanation."

"I'm just being a realist," Norman replied with more force in his voice. "I think we should at least tell somebody that they're both late."

"That might be a good idea," Mary said.

Since Mike had the best sight, he decided to volunteer. "It probably is a good idea. I'll go tell the receptionist. Anybody want to come with?"

"I'll go," Norman said. "I've never been very good at waiting."

Albert added an idea. "If they show up, I'll go to the front desk and let you know."

Mike and Norman stood up and walked to the door. They were almost there when Mike heard a jolly voice. "Good morning, everybody! Sorry I'm a bit late, but I decided to bring in some treats."

Mike saw George carrying a tray of colorful doughnuts, but Norman didn't. George bumped into him and a couple of doughnuts rolled down Norman's shirt.

"Dammit, George!" Norman grumbled. "You should watch where you're walking!"

"Sorry, Coach, but today, even a grouch like you ain't gonna bother me. Hey, Mikey, why don't you take this and put it on the table for me?"

Mike mumbled that he would.

"You got any napkins on that tray?" Norman asked. "I want to wipe off all this frosting."

Mike handed a few napkins to Norman and walked back to the table with the tray.

"What's the special occasion this time?" Albert asked.

"Yeah," Mike added. "We just had these things a couple of days ago, after the ski race."

"You guys aren't asking the important question," Norman said. "Have you seen Margaret?"

"If you can stop asking so many questions, I'll answer them," George replied while taking a doughnut. "All your questions have the same answer, but I should wait until Margaret shows up before telling you."

"She's okay, then?" Mary asked.

"Of course, she's all right," George answered. "Margaret just needs to talk with Donny for a little while longer, that's all."

"Ah-ha," Norman said. "So you and Margaret had to talk with Donny. You must have really messed up this time, which doesn't surprise me."

"Say what you want, Coach," George said while biting into a doughnut. He chewed for a moment and spoke, while still chewing. "You're going to be the one who'll be surprised."

By now, everyone was sitting at the table having a doughnut. As usual, George was on Mike's left, and Norman was on his right. This was a familiar scene, although it was unusual not having Margaret in the room.

"C'mon, George, give us a hint," Mike said. "What's going on?"

"I'd be happy to, normally, but this time, I really should wait for Margaret."

"That's a new one," Norman replied in one of his happier tones. "You're waiting for her, instead of the other way around."

"That's a good point, Norman," Margaret said as she walked into the room and set another tray on the table with a pot of coffee and cups. "It's actually kind of satisfying, now that I think about it."

Mike hadn't heard Margaret sound so upbeat in a while.

"I do want to apologize for making everyone wait. We have some news to share, but first, can I pour coffee for anyone?"

Everyone said they'd like some, except Mike. He asked for a glass of water.

"Could somebody please tell us what's going on?" Norman asked, while Margaret filled the cups.

"Of course, I'll start and ask George to finish." She started pouring a cup for herself and continued. "As you know, we like to have a little going-away party when people leave our school, and as you have probably noticed by now, people leave at different times. That's an intentional part of our curriculum. It's flexible, to allow students to choose exactly when they finish. Most finish in three months, but some will stay longer to focus on skills they want to improve. Others will leave sooner, to return to family or if a job comes up." She sipped her coffee again, looked at George, and added, "With that, I'll ask George to share his big news."

Mike felt excited for George but suspected he would be around less, which wasn't exciting.

"I'd be happy to. As I've mentioned before, I've worked on cars for years, actually many years. A few months ago, I stopped by a parts store that a buddy owns. One thing led to another, and I was helping a customer. I ended up stopping by more often and helping more customers, mostly for the fun of it. After a while, I figured it couldn't hurt to ask if this could be some kind of job, part-time or maybe fill in for somebody."

Mike recognized this story and remembered it wasn't that simple, something to do with the owner having a nephew who wanted the same job.

"Really?" Norman asked. "I hate to say it, but I'm impressed."

Mike was surprised at Norman's compliment, but Mike had learned that Norman was the kind of person who respected a full day's work. He'd also learned that Norman and George had reached a strange truce over the last few weeks. They still enjoyed annoying each other, but it had become more of a rivalry than a battle.

George continued. "Thanks, Coach. I admit that some parts became a little complicated, but I have to tell ya, my counselor really came through. Just when I thought this job was going to fall apart, I mentioned it to her. She told me there was some funding from the State to encourage businesses to hire blind folks. It's some trial effort to help us get back to work."

"I don't like the idea of getting special treatment," Norman grumbled.

"That's fine," George said. "I'm just saying that it helped bring this job back when I thought it was gone."

"I still don't like it," Norman replied.

"That's fine, Norman," Margaret said. "We can debate this issue later. For now, we only have a little while before George has to leave."

"You're leaving already?" Mary asked.

"That's right, unfortunately," George answered. "Another reason I got the job is that they need somebody soon, like today. They're opening a new store across town, and one of the guys helping with that store just took a better job in St. Cloud. I still wanted to finish things here, so this morning Margaret and I talked with Donny about some ways I could finish all my classes."

"I think you mean Donald," Margaret said. "After all he's done for you, the least you could do is use his proper name."

The comment intrigued Mike as he thought about the school president. Margaret had to know his reputation, but maybe part of her old-school style meant that you still showed respect to any authority.

"Yeah, maybe," George replied. "Anyway, I'm going to work with a couple of teachers on nights and weekends to finish."

Mike felt excited about George's good news, sad that he would see him less, and curious about what had happened to the owner's nephew at the parts store.

"Wow," Albert said. "All that happened fast. How much longer are you going to be in school today?"

"Actually, I should leave soon. I don't want to be late on my first day," George said with a smile.

"In that case," Norman added, "I hope it's all right if I ask about something that I've wondered about for a while. Now, if you don't want to answer, that's your business, no problem."

"Go ahead, Coach, what's on your mind?"

Norman leaned forward and looked directly at George. "Well, we're all good friends here, and I'm sure we've all wondered about your *unique* experience with the school. I'll get to the point. How was it that you started last year and finished this year? Like I said, you don't have to answer if you don't want, but since we may not see you again, I wanted to ask."

Mike was surprised at the question, but Norman had a way of saying what he felt, even if it made others uncomfortable.

George took a long drink from his coffee, in a way that reminded Mike of the long drinks his friend sometimes took from a beer.

"That's a fair question, Coach." He sipped his coffee again. "And I'd be happy to answer."

"Are you sure?" Margaret asked.

"Yeah, why not. I do like being a *modern man of the seventies* who's in touch with his emotions and all that." He sipped his coffee again. "The truth is ..." George paused. "The truth is that this whole blindness thing was harder than I thought. I showed up here a year ago, went to classes, and was even on time once in a while." George held his coffee cup on the table and looked toward it. "But eventually, all this classroom stuff bored me, and I've never done real well with boredom. I wanted to get back to engines, back to my buddies, back to work." He looked across the room and shrugged. "So, I got ahold of a couple of guys from the garage, bought 'em some drinks, and convinced them that I could still work on cars as good as any teenager or college grad."

For the first time, Norman sounded humble. "You don't have to say any more."

"Once I start a story, I like to finish it." George took another sip of his coffee. "So I showed up at the shop, just like I used to. Somebody came in with one of my favorites, a 1968 Dodge Charger. It has that classic muscle car look, before they were turned into economy cars or family cars. Anyway, the Charger sounded pretty bad, but I knew exactly what the problem was. It needed a valve job. That can take a while, but it was a job I did a lot. I was looking forward to putting the roar back into that beautiful V8. Unfortunately, things didn't go so well. I needed more help than I expected just to get to the valves, and when we finally did, I had to leave work early to get a finger stitched up in the emergency room. That made my manager worry about what his insurance company would say about a blind guy working on engines."

"I'm so sorry that happened, George," Mary said. Her voice sounded rough at the end, like she might start crying.

"Thanks, but we still tried to work something out. My manager told me that finishing my classes here would make it easier to deal with his insurance company, and he's looking at equipment that could help me work on cars again."

"And now," Albert said, "you have another job. That's extraordinary, George."

"Thanks, I'm looking forward to working again, but I actually think it's pretty ordinary. I just like talking to people, often over a beer. I don't think the stuff I do is extraordinary."

"I'll second that," Norman replied with a chuckle. "Seriously though, I didn't know you spent so much time looking for work. You do surprise me sometimes, George."

"Life is full of surprises, Coach, but really, I've never spent that much time looking for work. I just talk to people, and work is something we talk about. Then, nothing shows up for months, and all of a sudden, a couple of jobs show up in a week. This time, only one job showed up, but the week isn't over yet." George took the last bite from a doughnut, chewed, and continued. "Well, speaking of work, I better get going."

"All right," Margaret said. "We'll take a break now and start with our normal class in fifteen minutes. If you want another doughnut or some coffee, please take some. I'll clean up the table during the break."

George grabbed a couple of doughnuts and stood up. Albert and Mary walked over and wished him luck. George instinctively raised his hand a little for a goodbye handshake. Albert shook George's hand and congratulated him again. Mary gave him a hug while saying, "You take care of yourself and be sure to let me know if you want a good meal. I could make you something in the kitchen, when you're at school again."

George said he would and thanked her.

Norman walked up next. "Well George, we've had our differences …"

"And probably always will," George quickly added with a laugh. He held up his right hand again, and Norman shook it.

Norman chuckled and replied, "At least we're ending with something we agree on. Seriously, it's great that you found work so fast. Best of luck to you."

"Thanks, Coach."

After a moment, only Margaret, George, and Mike were left in the room. An impulsive question occurred to Mike. "Hey, Margaret, would it be all right if I walked with George to work? Somebody should make sure he gets there on time." He hoped Margaret would get his real meaning.

"That sounds like a good idea. Just talk with me tomorrow to get the key points of today's class."

Mike mumbled he would.

She spoke to George. "Well, congratulations again. I'm looking forward to working with you next Saturday at ten sharp."

"Thanks Margaret, especially for your help this morning and for working with me on a weekend. I may even show up early."

Margaret smiled and said, "I hope you have a good first day at work." She turned toward the table and started cleaning up the doughnuts and coffee.

Mike guided George out of Room 5 and toward the dayroom. They had to stop a few times, as teachers and other students walked up to George to offer their congratulations, a handshake, or a hug.

When they finally walked out of Bridgman's, Mike said, "Damn, George, if you were any more popular, we wouldn't get to your new job until tomorrow."

"That's the price I pay for my fame." He paused for a moment. "I admit that I'm going to miss the place. Funny how things work that way. Last year, I tried so hard to leave, and now, it stings a bit."

"I know what you mean," Mike said. "A smart guy told me once that life is full of surprises."

"Maybe he was right," George replied in one of his rare serious tones.

"Really though, this did come up pretty fast," Mike said. "I remember you mentioning it a few weeks ago, even before Thanksgiving, but I hadn't heard anything since then."

"It did come up fast," George replied. "Mostly last night when I stopped by the store again. That's when I learned about the other guy who took the job in St. Cloud. I called my counselor, and we found some good options. I went to The Slowstream to celebrate, but you weren't around. Actually, you haven't been at the bars much at all this week."

Mike was hoping his friend hadn't noticed. He'd been away from the bars because of the time he was spending with Sam. Earlier in the week, George had asked Mike to go out for a drink, and Mike gave a vague answer, saying he might see George at a bar later. Mike still wanted to keep things with Sam a secret, although maybe that could change since George would be at school less. For the moment, Mike gave a safe answer. "I just took a little break after the ski trip, but if you want to buy me drinks all night, the least I can do is stop by."

"Sure, I get a job worth celebrating, and now you want me to buy your drinks."

"Makes sense to me, now that you're making the big bucks." Both men chuckled, and Mike continued. "So what exactly are you going to do? Are they starting you off as the boss, or did you ask for something higher?"

George smiled. "They offered it to me, but I decided to work my way up through the ranks, starting as the guy who opens the door."

Mike laughed, and George replied, "Don't laugh, there's great tips in that. You'd be surprised how generous some of those grease monkeys can be."

Mike laughed again, and George spoke again.

"What's the phrase you use? 'Little humor, not too much.'"

Mike smiled wide and looked at his friend. "I suppose."

They slowed down to join a group of shadows, at a place where Mike heard a few cars idling.

"Really though, what are you going to do in the store?" Mike asked.

"It's pretty much what I told you before. I'll be helping customers and organizing the stockroom. I've spent a lot of time in that room lately, to memorize where everything belongs. By the way, the help you gave me with the abacus really paid off. Part of working in the stockroom is counting how much stuff we got and what we gotta get."

"I'm glad it helped, but what about the owner's nephew?" Mike asked. "I thought he wanted the same job."

"He's still part of the picture. We're splitting the job for six months. That's when the extra money from the State runs out."

The shadows moved forward. Mike sighed and followed them, while still guiding George. "What happens then?" Mike asked.

"Then, we talk things over and hopefully extend the job some more."

"Wow, I hope it works out."

"Something always works out," George said. "Since this is a part-time job, maybe the kid will look for better-paying work in his spare time. Maybe I will too, or maybe the boss will hire both of us after six months."

Mike appreciated George's hope but still felt disappointed for his friend. "Or maybe, he'll only keep his nephew around part-time."

"Maybe," George said. "But that wanders into worrying about sad stuff. I never liked doing that for long, because it gets addictive. Besides, there's something else I've been meaning to ask you about."

"What's that?" Mike asked.

"When I left The Slowstream last night, I was on the bus and thinking how good things have been going with the job, the ski trip, and other stuff. Then, a few things came together that made me wonder about something. The first thing was how you've been at the bars less often. That's all right, but it made me think of how you also disappeared a little early in the chalet, during the ski trip. The third thing was also from the ski trip." George's voice became playful. "It's something very small, very small indeed—just a little giggle. Of course, I had a few drinks that night, so I could be imagining that little giggle. Still, the memory is really clear, but I only have the wildest guess about who she was."

Mike smiled and saw George do the same.

George was really having fun when he said, "Michael, my very good friend, could you tell me more about that giggle? After all, you were there when I heard it."

Mike laughed. "Well, it's hard to say. After all, there were a lot of people laughing around the fireplace."

"You're right. People were having a great time by the fireplace, but this memory isn't from there. Besides, we didn't spend much time together at the fireplace."

"A lot of people were laughing at the bar too."

"You're right again, but it's not from there either, and we didn't spend any time together at the bar." George laughed while he spoke. "I heard it after I walked away from the fireplace, after I walked out of the bar, and after I opened the door to *our room.*"

Mike was laughing too. He still wasn't going to give in easily. "I'm taking the Fifth."

George continued laughing. "Your Fifth Amendment right to silence applies to cops, not me."

"I'm still taking the Fifth," Mike said with a guilty smile.

"You go right ahead, but I'm going to continue my cross-examination. At first, I wanted to ask which teacher it might be, since that's the only reason you'd sneak someone out of our room. But then I remembered some other things. She was always more friendly when you were around and never had one of her temper tantrums. And then I thought of a question that really made me wonder. Why would you volunteer to shiver on a ski slope with blind skiers headed right at you?"

Mike continued to smile and said, "I have a right to stay silent, since anything I say can and will be used in a bar to get more free drinks."

George laughed. "Damn, Michael! You're really seeing Sam? I mean, it's obvious now, but I still had to hear it to believe it, since she can be a bit edgy. I thought that might turn you off, but she is a hell of a lot of fun."

Mike replied in a confident yet playful tone. "You're right. She is."

"Wow, you are my hero. How long has this been going on?"

"A couple of weeks."

"I should have noticed earlier, since I do pride myself on my perception," George said.

"We've been trying to keep it a secret."

"Well, I'd say it worked. I won't say anything, promise. I don't want to mess things up for my hero."

"Thanks, George."

The two men walked a few steps without saying anything, until George spoke again in a more serious tone. "There was something else I was thinking about on the bus last night. I know how most folks ended up at the school, but I don't think I've ever heard your story, or is that something else you like to keep secret? It's no problem if it is."

"No, it's not a secret. I'm surprised I didn't tell you. Maybe we just found other things to talk about."

"Yeah, probably," George replied.

"The main reason I lost my sight was bad luck."

"Yeah, you've said that before. Most of the people here lost their sight to that kind of luck. What kind of bad luck brought you here?"

The two friends took a few steps before Mike answered. "A weekend. My bad luck was a weekend."

"I don't get it. Weekends are good, even in my new job. How were they bad for you?"

Mike started telling the whole story. "I need to go back a ways. I was born premature. That left me with a bad eye and a good eye. I could still drive and everything, but I started seeing rainbows around lights when I worked for the tractor parts factory. I left work early one day to see an eye doctor in St. Cloud. He's a good doctor. My mom still goes to him, but when he looked at me, he missed a test. He didn't dilate the pupil in my good eye."

"Crap," George said. "I think I know where this is going."

"He told me to take it easy for a while, so I took a couple of days off. When I went back to work, my vision was better, but something still felt wrong."

"Your head was probably adjusting to the change in your good eye."

"Probably." Mike sighed. "Then on that Friday, I was driving home from work and things got worse just before getting to my house. It was like somebody slowly turned the lights down. I managed to turn into my driveway but couldn't drive all the way down it. I got out of my car and walked to my sister's place next door. She took me to a hospital in St. Cloud. It didn't take them long to figure out that there was nothing they could do, so they put me in an ambulance to a hospital at the University of Minnesota. I stayed there on Friday night. On Saturday, they realized the retina was coming off in my good eye. There was a new laser surgery to fix it, and they had an expert with the procedure; one of a few in the country. He was the same guy who would have worked on JFK, if he'd lived."

"Wow, that sounds like very good luck."

"Unfortunately, he doesn't work on weekends."

"Crap," George said. "I'm sorry, man. So, you laid in the hospital over the weekend, while your good eye got worse."

"Yeah, it couldn't get much oxygen, since it was detached from the rest of my eye."

"That is bad luck." George sighed and added, "a lot of bad luck."

"I guess, but a smart guy told me not to think about sad stuff too much, because it gets addictive. The same guy said life is full of surprises, about half are good ones. That works for me."

The last few words came out without much thought, but Mike thought about them now. Telling the story of his bad luck was easy enough, but it was still hard to believe, or maybe accept. He looked up and saw the two neon signs, which reminded him of the night when Sam had bought him a drink. He wondered if that night was good luck, just part of making new friends, or part of making a new life. His thoughts were interrupted when George replied.

"I suppose."

Mike smiled at the response, and the two men kept walking, silently. Mike knew George would find something else to say soon, since he always did. Intuition told Mike to think more about luck, work, and all the good people he'd met here. At the moment, he couldn't think through all these issues, so he focused on what he could do. He could get George to work. He could keep trying to find his own job, and he would keep laughing. All this wouldn't take away the sadness or frustration of bad luck and blindness, but it would probably help, and probably lead to making some of his own luck.

A Message from Steven

Thank you for reading this book. I'd like to share some thoughts about why I wrote it and make a personal request. As you'd expect, the main reason I wrote this book is the respect I have for my brother, Mike. In this story, I tried to show his particular style of courage, determination, and humor. I've always been proud of the way he slowly works through large problems, so writing those details was uniquely fulfilling.

Similarly, I thoroughly enjoyed writing about the more playful challenges Mike has experienced, like not finding the right words when talking with Samantha and when he was shivering on the ski slope. Many brothers have some kind of rivalry. With Mike and me, it's more of an exchange of misadventures and laughs. I hope this story made you laugh and think more about your own courage and determination.

I also hope others experience the same feelings from this story, which leads to the request I mentioned. I would personally appreciate it if you would write a review of this book. Reviews don't need to be long. They just need to be honest. If you can write two or three sentences about this story, the chances quickly increase that others will consider it, maybe read a few pages, and learn more about their own particular style of courage and determination. Information about submitting a review is in the Reviews section of the website for this book. The URL is http://walkingoutofthedark.com/. Thank you for considering this request.

www.ingramcontent.com/pod-product-compliance
Lightning Source LLC
Chambersburg PA
CBHW071259170626
46809CB00001B/278